The
Darkest
Unicorn

Published in the UK by Scholastic Children's Books, 2020
Euston House, 24 Eversholt Street, London, NW1 1DB, UK
A division of Scholastic Limited.

London – New York – Toronto – Sydney – Auckland
Mexico City – New Delhi – Hong Kong

SCHOLASTIC and associated logos are trademarks and/or
registered trademarks of Scholastic Inc.

ISBN 978 0702 30063 9

A CIP catalogue record for this book is available from the British Library.

Printed by CPI Group (UK) Ltd, Croydon, CR0 4YY
Papers used by Scholastic Children's Books are made
from wood grown in sustainable forests.

1 3 5 7 9 10 8 6 4 2

www.scholastic.co.uk

The
Darkest
Unicorn

ALICE HEMMING

SCHOLASTIC

For Paul and Cheryl

Every song and every story starts somewhere. Fairy tales and nursery rhymes whispered to babies in their cribs all once began as ideas and musical notes in someone's mind. How do they become so well known? How do words and rhymes spread across entire kingdoms and beyond? The answer is simple: there must always be a reason to sing a song and a reason to pass on a tale.

This is one such tale…

IN THE REIGN OF

QUEEN AUDREY

CHAPTER ONE

LULLABIES FOR THE COWS

Linnell took the wooden pail from the hook by the door and stepped out on to her porch, into the brand new morning. It was early, and the sky was the colour of orange hawkweed. She tended to her little bird, scattering some seed in his cage, then she turned and breathed deeply, treating her lungs to the cool, crisp air and her eyes to the spectacular mountain view. The great giant, Mount Opacus, stood strong and tall, its peak shrouded in thick cloud whatever the weather, and guarded on either side by smaller mountains known as the Sentries.

Her own home was opposite these giants, on the lower slopes of the Grey Mountain, but on a day like today, its name was hard to comprehend. The bright sky contrasted with the dark green of the pine trees and the lush green of the meadow. Green mountain would have been a more appropriate name.

Maybe those who named the mountain long ago lived on the other side – the Essendor side – where it was said to be grey and rocky. Essendor was the capital city after all. But Linnell had never been to the other side of the mountain. There was no real reason to go. Besides, there was no tunnel through, the journey around would take days, and Linnell's father said that only a brave man or a fool would travel upwards, crossing the mountain peaks.

The nearest village of Arvale was just a few miles downhill, but Linnell couldn't really claim to live in the village at all: where she lived was more of a hamlet. Just a few dilapidated farmhouses clustered together. But despite the low population and the early hour, she passed no fewer than three people on her way to the cow barn.

Piet, the old farmhand, stopped shovelling hay and nodded his head in polite greeting. "Good morning to you, Linnell. I like the way you are wearing your hair today."

Linnell touched her hair, which she had braided and twisted around her head. "Good morning, Pict. Thank you."

Across the way, Madam Lavande was rocking on a chair on the porch, a crocheted blanket on her lap. "I bid you good morning, Mistress Linnell. I do like your hair plaited in that way."

"Thank you, Madam Lavande."

And, just as she reached the barn, little Johan jumped out at her from behind the hay cart, making her start. "Boo!"

"Be off with you, you imp!" said Linnell, chasing him away.

She made her way into the cow barn, where she could finally hide away. Here it was dark and warm, and it smelled of manure, hay and the cows themselves. The strong smell might have bothered some, but not Linnell, who had grown up with it. She found Nettie, her favourite cow, and led her to the milking stall. Nettie clomped along happily enough and began munching the grain in the manger. Linnell pulled the milking stool up close, wiped Nettie down and began milking.

Her hands worked automatically and the milk squirted into the pail. She sighed heavily. She would like to be able to part her hair whichever side she chose and braid it in whatever style she fancied without it being a talking point for everyone.

Linnell had lived in this out-of-the-way place all her life

and nothing had ever changed. Every day, her father farmed the meadows, tended to the animals and prepared food for the markets. Every afternoon, Linnell helped with the farm and every morning she studied her schoolbooks.

Nettie must have sensed Linnell's mood and shuffled her feet. The waiting cows mooed unhappily. Disgruntled cows made her job much more difficult, so Linnell began to sing. The cows liked her singing and her voice echoed pleasantly in the barn. She sang her favourite song – the one her father had written for her mother and her mother had sung to Linnell in her cradle:

"To me you are a diamond,
To me you are a pearl,
To me you are an emerald,
To me you are the world,

"I'd give you a diamond to shine the whole day long,
But I have no diamond, so I give to you this song."

Linnell sighed again. She had never seen a diamond before, or an emerald, but she would surely like to. She would like to wear a dress of silver brocade, encrusted with tiny pearls. She would like maids to wait on her and style her hair however she chose. She continued singing and the cows stood by peacefully.

"To me you are the mountain,
To me you are the sea,
To me you are the forest,
You're everything to me."

Linnell loved the pictures that the song brought into her mind, of snowy mountain peaks and the billowing sails of great ships on the ocean. She would love to be free to explore, to travel and see the world, but she knew that she would not. In just a few short years, Linnell would leave childhood behind and start working on the farm permanently. Her father was old and he couldn't bear the weight of their existence alone. With no siblings to share the responsibility, Linnell knew that her route in life had a fixed course.

As if conjured up by her thoughts, Linnell's father came into the barn. He leaned just inside the doorway, listening to her song. Then he joined in, his voice deep and powerful.

"I'd give you a diamond to shine the whole day long,
But I have no diamond, so I give to you this song."

When they had finished, Linnell thought she saw tears in his eyes and guessed he was thinking of her mother, who had died when she was a small child.

"You sing so well – better than she did, even. Your voice is a true gift."

Linnell smiled wistfully. Her father told her this often. Which was nice, but what good was a sweet singing voice when she was stuck in a cow barn near a village that no one had heard of?

"She was my diamond and you are my pearl, Linnell. The most precious things in the world."

Linnell embraced her father. He was so sentimental. Foolish, really. But it was a good moment to ask for a favour. "After I have finished my chores for the day, may I go to the meadow or the forest?"

"What about your schoolwork?"

"I shall take my schoolbooks with me. It's going to be such a lovely day that it seems a shame to stay cooped up inside."

"Then, yes, you may, Linnell. You're a good girl and you do so much for me. I don't know what I'd do without you. Just make sure you don't stray too far, be back by lunchtime and don't talk to anyone you don't know."

At this, Linnell laughed. The chance of meeting anyone she did not know was so remote that if she did, she would probably be struck mute from the surprise.

THE SINGING FOREST

Today, Linnell chose the shade of the forest over the openness of the meadow. It was going to be a hot day and she had more chance of concentrating on her schoolwork without the sunshine reflecting off the bright white paper of her books. There was also something about the forest that stirred Linnell's curiosity. She had heard people talk of sightings of the Midnight Unicorn, which was rumoured to roam these parts and protect the citizens of Essendor. Linnell doubted that the unicorn would come to Arvale, let alone venture up into the foothills of the mountain, but if it did, she was more likely to encounter it here in the depths of the forest, rather than out in the open meadow.

She sat on a treestump, took a small stack of books from her satchel, and opened the first one. History. Not her favourite subject, but then none of them were. Apart from music, of course. She could see the use in learning to read and write music, whereas the other subjects seemed like a waste of time. She failed to see how history or arithmetic would help her milk the cows. She flicked through the pages. It was all about kings and queens. She ignored the long chunks of text and gazed at the illustrations instead. The royals wore such fine clothes, in fabrics that she'd never seen: velvet, mulberry silk and linen.

She would probably never meet a queen, even though she was just a few miles away from the royal city of Essendor where Queen Audrey ruled. She was a popular ruler, unlike her uncle, King Zelos, had been. It was rumoured that he had killed his sister, her husband and the twin babies in order to take the throne as his own. But the twins had survived and returned to claim their birthright. Sometimes she imagined that she was a lost princess. How fine that would be, to discover that she was born into royalty. She could have anything she wanted. A great castle and gardens in which to play, delicious food and elegant clothes. She could wear her hair braided, or curled, or swept up with sparkling hair combs.

She traced a finger over the floral pattern on one of the dresses. Just beautiful. She glanced briefly at the words, which listed the many achievements of these great royals who had lived so many years ago. Row after row of dates and battles. Linnell couldn't concentrate. She rested the book on her knees.

She gazed at the flowers dotted around: celandine, dandelions and merrybells. Weeds to some, but Linnell thought them rather beautiful, their bright colour enhancing the beauty of the shadowy forest like jewellery worn against bare skin. If she would never see real jewels, then these would have to do. She let her book fall to the ground and began to pick a bunch of sturdy leaves: the ones with long flexible stems. She wound three stems together and then gradually added more and more to the row, poking yellow and white flowers into the gaps. The melody from earlier was stuck in her head and she sung it again.

"To me you are a diamond,
To me you are a pearl…"

Her voice sounded different in the forest compared to the echoing stillness of the barn. Out here, the notes drifted away from her to mingle with the other sounds of the forest: the chorus of the birds, the light breeze in the trees and the buzz of nearby insects.

She wound the strip of leaves and flowers into a circular crown.

"…To me you are an emerald,
To me you are the world…"

She placed the flower crown on top of her head. Now she really did feel like royalty. The white and yellow flowers would bring out the golden highlights in her hair. She began to dance slowly, with her hands raised high above her head, imagining herself performing in a real theatre, in front of the queen.

"I'd give you a diamond to shine the whole day long…"

Linnell sang, but then stopped suddenly when she heard music. She had the most curious sensation that the forest was singing back to her.

THE COLOURFUL STRANGER

Linnell slowly turned her head to listen. The notes were quiet, but she could definitely hear them, drifting out from the trees. Was someone singing along with her? It sounded magical. Maybe it was a unicorn. Did unicorns sing? But no, it was the sound of a pipe. Someone was playing along to her music. She sang the next line:

"But I have no diamond, so I give to you this song."

The sound of the pipe matched her singing, note for note. How could that be? This was her own special song that her father had written. She followed the music, taking small footsteps and singing as she went. She recognized the instrument: the music was coming from a wooden fipple pipe. It was beautiful. Then she peeped through the bushes, watching and listening.

The pipe player was also beautiful. He was young and slight, with slim limbs and skin the colour of a walnut shell. She could tell from the brightness and cut of his clothes that he was not from around here. Dark blonde curls peeped out from under a red alpine hat and he wore a long jacket of striped patchwork.

As he played, he danced, skipping lightly from one foot to the other. This, combined with his sharp features, gave Linnell a fleeting feeling that he was not entirely human; he must have some fairy in him. But then he turned and she saw he was a boy.

Just a boy.

She stepped from her hiding place and he caught her gaze, but carried on playing to the end of the song. She sang along; it seemed like the only thing to do. Then he stopped playing, lowered his pipe and smiled, showing even, white teeth. "You sing well."

Linnell smiled too. "You play well. How did you know the tune?"

"I can play any song I hear." He picked up the pipe and played another, merry tune that she didn't know.

She tapped her foot along to the rhythm and then clapped when he'd finished. They gazed at each other until Linnell felt the need to break the silence.

"My name is Linnell. I live over there," she said shyly, pointing towards the village.

The boy took off his cap and bowed low. "Sander. Pleased to make your acquaintance." He looked in the direction she pointed and shook his head slowly as if puzzled. "I can't imagine living out here."

The heat rose in Linnell's cheeks. "There is a village a few miles away. We are not as remote as it might appear."

"Still, it is a sleepy place."

Linnell wished she could defend her home, but it was true. It was beyond sleepy; it was dead to the world. "Why, where are you from?"

"I am from nowhere and everywhere. Today I am from this very forest. Yesterday, I was from the mountains. I go wherever I want and do whatever I please. I live only for adventure."

Linnell let this sink in for a moment. *Adventure.* Just the word sent a thrill right through her. "What sort of adventure?"

"Any sort of adventure. For a time, I slept on a home-made raft, floating down the river. When it drifted ashore, I would get out and explore. When it did not, then I just stayed afloat for days."

Just drifting. For days. So different from Linnell's own life, with its unvarying sequence of chores and activities. "Don't your parents mind?"

"I wouldn't know, I've never asked them." Sander stopped and picked up a large, shiny beetle from the forest floor. It scurried up his arm and he laughed, transferring it to his other hand and then back on to the ground, where it disappeared under some leaves. "It would be easier to tame that beetle than to stop my wanderings. I cannot imagine another way to live."

Linnell could not imagine how such a carefree lifestyle

would be possible. "But how *do* you live? How do you eat ... clothe yourself?"

"Sometimes, I play my pipe for people in taverns or at festivals. A few coins in my hat go a long way. Sometimes, I tell stories. People pay to hear my tales of the mountains and the things I have seen: fairies, dragons, flying wolves…"

Just imagine. Sander had experienced more excitement on his journey than Linnell had in her entire life. He spoke only of doing what *he* wanted, with no care for anyone else's wishes. How she would love to be that free.

"Are the stories true?"

"All my stories are true. You wouldn't believe the things that I've seen just moments from here. The Midnight Unicorn of Essendor roams freely if you know where to look—"

Linnell gasped. "You have seen the Midnight Unicorn?"

"Yes, I've had the pleasure of seeing it dancing in the moonlight on many occasions; but the Midnight Unicorn of Essendor is not the greatest sight you will see. What does that horned horse even *do*? Rescue people from rivers? Save sheep from wolf attacks? The Midnight Unicorn does nothing that you or I couldn't do; its powers pale in comparison to those of the Greatest Unicorn."

"The Greatest Unicorn?"

"Yes. A more powerful and majestic beast. Of all the sights I have witnessed on my travels, it is he who takes my breath away."

"Then why do ordinary folk not speak of him? I have not heard a single tale of his great feats."

"He is hidden away in a castle in the clouds. Only a true adventurer would ever find him."

"What does this unicorn – the Greatest Unicorn – look like?" whispered Linnell.

Sander lowered his voice to match Linnell's. "He is white. No, not white. Clear. He is translucent – like ice."

"Like a diamond?"

Sander smiled. "Yes, like a diamond. But not hard like a diamond. Strong and sinewy but still soft. And his mane shimmers with gold. He has real power."

"Power?"

"Oh, yes." Sander picked up his pipe and played another pretty tune. Linnell wished he wouldn't. She wanted to hear more about the unicorn. The *Greatest* Unicorn. She waited patiently until the end of the song and then, before he could play any more, she asked, "What power?"

Sander smiled. "If he chooses, the Greatest Unicorn can

grant wishes. He can make any wish come true."

Any wish. Linnell thought of all her hopes and dreams of getting far from here. Of beautiful jewels, fine clothes. And freedom.

"What would you wish for, Linnell?" asked Sander.

Linnell shrugged. She felt foolish saying her dreams aloud.

Sander played a few notes on his pipe. Her song.

To me you are a diamond,
To me you are a pearl.

He put down his pipe and gazed directly into her eyes. "Diamonds around your neck? A dress decorated in exquisite seed pearls? Just imagine. If you looked like that, you could do anything you wanted. You could travel to great kingdoms and sing for royalty. They would pay you handsomely and then you could buy more fine clothes."

Linnell nodded, slightly unnerved by how easily he seemed to read her dreams. "I would love to live a life like that."

"Then live it. There is nothing to stop you. If there is something that you want, just do it."

"How? How could I just do it?"

"Well if you wanted it to happen right away, you could ask the unicorn."

"I *could*? But how?"

Sander ran a hand along some long grass. "I could show you where to find him. He can grant any wish, as long as something is given in exchange."

Something in exchange. That was the problem. Linnell had nothing. No money or even belongings that she could sell.

"What does the unicorn take in return?" Linnell asked.

Sander sighed. "Oh dear. Are you one of *those* people?"

Linnell didn't know what she'd said wrong. "One of which people?"

"One of those sorts of people who like to ask questions. 'Why?' 'How?' And 'Why' again. If you ask too many questions then you end of talking yourself out of what you really want. If you want something then you must grasp it and not let go. Forget the questions."

Just imagine the freedom if Linnell just thought about herself and what *she* wanted for a change. What sort of life would she lead if only she could experience that? Her father would find help with the farm, or maybe he wouldn't need the farm any more: she would keep him in luxury too.

Linnell could go and see the unicorn – ask him to grant her wish. The idea was so liberating that she laughed out loud before she asked, "May I come with you?"

"Well you *may*, but I will be surprised if you *do*. I meet many people on my travels but few have the inclination to venture very far past their own doorsteps. As far as I know, I am the only person who has ever set eyes on the Greatest Unicorn."

"I am different from the others," said Linnell earnestly. "I really want to come and meet him. Please may I accompany you?"

Sander looked pleased. "Of course, it's not too far." He picked up his pipe and bag, brushed himself down and turned towards the trees. "This way."

Linnell's heart beat faster. Surely he wasn't going straight away? "I must let my father know where I am going."

"That's a shame." Sander began walking further into the forest.

Was he really leaving this very minute? He couldn't expect her to just walk after him without telling anyone, could he? "It will only take me a few minutes. You could come too." It would be worth it to see Madam Lavande's face as Linnell walked past her cottage with this colourful stranger.

Sander stopped, turned and sighed. "A few minutes will

easily turn into a few hours. Your father will no doubt refuse to allow you to go, you will protest and barricade yourself in your bedroom. He will start up with the Whys and the Hows, then in all likelihood you will never go anywhere at all. I understand. Some of us are not made for adventure. But as for me, I am leaving now. So I bid you farewell."

Sander walked off towards the trees and Linnell watched him leave, startled by his impatience. She could not – should not – follow a stranger into the forest on a whim. After all, what would her father think if she didn't return home that afternoon? Sander began playing his pipe once again: a sad, wistful tune. As he drew away and the notes grew quieter, panic rose in Linnell's chest. What if she was letting her one chance for real adventure slip away? She would regret it forever. If the unicorn did grant her wish of freedom then her father would not be cross – he would never have to work again. And if the unicorn did not grant her wish, or she wanted to return, then she would just return home straightaway. Sander said it wasn't far, after all.

"Wait for me!" she cried and sprinted after him, her flower crown tumbling to the ground.

CHAPTER TWO

AN OMEN

Linnell was on her way to meet a unicorn and her life was finally going to change. She was so excited that she practically skipped as she followed Sander on the meandering forest path. He walked quickly but Linnell kept up without difficulty, firing questions at him as they went.

"Will the unicorn mind me turning up uninvited?"

"You *are* invited. I have invited you. That will be enough."

"Does he talk?"

"In his own way."

"What will he ask me—?"

Linnell's question was interrupted by a harsh screeching sound, loud enough to make her jump back. "What was that?"

"Just a bird," said Sander, pointing into the tree above them. A large black bird with a flash of white at its throat perched on one of the lower branches, shifting its weight from foot to foot.

"A raven," said Linnell. "I've never seen a raven in these woods before. Don't people say that they are bad luck?"

Sander laughed loudly. "Those rural superstitions are just stories that people tell one another to stop themselves from doing anything fun! They are nonsense."

Linnell felt foolish. Sander already thought that she was a cautious type from a humdrum hamlet. Now he would think she believed in local superstitions too.

The bird watched them for a few moments and then dived from the tree in front of Sander's face, flapping its wings and making the same screeching sound as before. Linnell shrieked and Sander batted his arms around his head. His hat fell to the forest floor.

The bird flew up to the tree for a few seconds and then dived again, aiming straight at Sander. "Be gone, bird!" yelled Sander, continuing to hit at it. Then he removed his pipe from a holder at his belt and blew into it, hard, making a screeching sound at a volume far louder than the bird. Linnell put her hands over her ears. The bird flapped away into another tree further away. Sander waited and then blew again. The bird flew away. Sander stopped the awful noise, picked up his hat and patted it back into shape. Linnell lowered her hands. She heard the bird calling in the distance. It was too far off to tell, but to Linnell's ears, it sounded like *Go back, go back…*

UP AND UP

Linnell followed Sander further into the forest and out the other side. They reached a stream. He led her to its narrowest point, jumped across and reached out a hand to help her.

Then they progressed in the direction of the mountains. She didn't skip along quite like she had before but still she walked swiftly, thinking of the unicorn and of how her life would change.

"Is it far? Which way are we heading?" asked Linnell. She never normally walked this distance from home and she found herself looking back in the direction of her cottage, calculating how long it would take her to return.

"Questions, again! Always so many questions," said Sander. "Just relax and enjoy the sights and sounds of the journey. There is so much to see everywhere. Why don't you look over at those mountains in the distance? Tell me what you see."

Linnell looked where Sander was pointing. In the distance, a waterfall flowed down the side of one of the mountains – the smallest Sentry. She could not see where it began or ended, only the streak of white, which must be the cascade of churning water, and the fainter line it drew through the trees.

"It is many miles from here, of course, but it is said that great treasures lie in a cave behind the falls. Sapphires the size of my palm." Sander held up his hand to illustrate his point.

Linnell stopped walking for a moment. How had she never heard this tale before? Without Sander, she would know nothing about the magic and hidden riches that lay so close to her doorstep. "Why does nobody claim the treasure? Why don't you?"

"The sound of the waterfall is thunderous, like an avalanche, or a stampede of cattle. It is so loud that nobody can get within a few miles of the waterfall, for fear of losing their hearing," explained Sander. "It is not the cascade of water alone that makes that sound, of course. The waterfall is enchanted with a sorcerer's curse. When he trapped the treasure he also trapped spectres, that scream and shout to be free. To claim the treasure, one would have to get close enough to the waterfall and undo the sorcerer's spell."

"It would be impossible."

Sander smiled knowingly. "Nothing is impossible. If I were to embark upon that particular quest, I should lull the spectres into a slumber with my pipe playing. It would be relatively simple. But I have no particular need for material wealth. Besides, other adventures beckon. I prefer to gaze at this particular waterfall from afar. It is a treasure in its own right."

Linnell looked and sighed, wistfully. Sander was right. It was beautiful. All this magic, right on her doorstep, that she had never noticed before. She was on the biggest adventure of her life. Sander played a tune on his pipe. Linnell listened, with her eyes closed. The music certainly was magical enough to undo a curse.

Sander stopped and Linnell opened her eyes. He looked kindly at her. "I don't mean to be cruel about the questions. It is natural to wonder but sometimes it can ruin the experience. Try to relax and enjoy each step we take."

Linnell nodded, trying to ignore the blisters that were forming on her heels.

"Sometimes you know the answers to these questions, anyway, without having to ask me. You ask which way. We are seeking a unicorn in a castle in the clouds. So, you tell me, which way will we travel to find this unicorn?"

Linnell thought for a moment. "I suppose … up?"

"Up! Exactly!"

And up they went.

They walked up a wide dusty path that grew steeper as they went along. Linnell could see the white clouds not far above them, but no castle. She had lived in these mountains her whole life and had never, not even on the clearest day, seen a castle above the peaks. She wondered how far they would have to walk before they saw it.

After a while they reached a wall of rough grey rocks. The foothills were behind them now; this was proper mountain territory. The path took a sharp, steep turn to the left, zigzagging up the mountainside. It was made up of small stones, bigger than pebbles, but smaller than rocks. Linnell wondered if they had been laid by hand, or formed naturally. She was tempted to ask Sander but was trying hard to limit her questions.

Sander broke two long branches from a nearby tree and handed one to Linnell. Then he embarked on the steep path, using the branch as a walking stick. Linnell followed his strides, keeping up reasonably easily. Her legs were strong and she was accustomed to walking up and down slopes. Some might think that her daily walk between the cow barn and her home was more of a climb than a stroll.

The higher they climbed, the more out of breath she grew, but she tried to speak normally. She would show Sander that she was capable of this adventure. "My father says that only an adventurer or a fool would climb this far up a mountain."

Sander laughed at her comment and did not reply. Which was she? she wondered. An adventurer or a fool? She wished she could be sure.

As they climbed higher, the path grew narrower until there was no path at all. A small rock fell from somewhere up above, tumbling and bouncing down the near vertical slope to her right. If she fell now, would she be able to halt her fall with a handhold or would she keep sliding and bouncing down the mountainside as the rock had done?

Sander turned to Linnell. "A tumbling rock can sound distant, but you should never turn your face in its direction. If you hear a rock fall, then cover your head with your hands and make yourself small."

Linnell lifted her chin. "I have lived my whole life on the foothills of a mountain. I don't need advice on what to do in an avalanche."

She wished she felt as confident as she tried to appear. Sander laughed in response.

Higher and higher they climbed, and as the sun moved westwards, Linnell tried not to think about her cosy home and how worried her father would be getting. They had reached the clouds that she had been staring up at earlier. It was a strange thought. They swirled, thick and white, around her – a bit like fog but active and unpredictable. At least they blocked the dizzying drop from her sight. She felt wobbly – lightheaded – but wasn't sure if it was fear or the change in air as they travelled higher. Maybe it was even hunger – she hadn't eaten since breakfast – although she didn't feel as though she wanted food. It was hard work and her feet didn't want to move as they had before. She gripped the slender trunk of a tree on her left and moved into it, the bark rough against the inside of her elbow and her cheek. She took a couple of deep breaths, in through her nose, but this deep breathing didn't settle her the way that it usually did. She felt as though the thick mist might suffocate her.

"Just keep going," said Sander. "One foot in front of the other."

Linnell took his advice. She tried not to look down the mountainside again and just focused on her feet, taking tiny steps and moving slowly forwards.

Finally, they rested. Sander sat on a rock a few paces further up. He gazed down at her without speaking, reached into his bag and handed her an apple. She bit into it gratefully, enjoying the sweetness. She ate the whole thing and dropped the core. This time, as she watched it fall and bounce, she didn't feel scared, just interested. She wondered where it would land, and if an apple tree would grow. Wouldn't that be a strange sight, here amongst the pine trees?

The apple gave her a little more energy.

"That's better," she said, and smiled with an enthusiasm she didn't feel. They must be nearly there. Linnell wanted to ask how far, and exactly how they would reach the castle, but she was still trying not to ask too many questions. It didn't stop them whirling around in her head. She would have to train herself out of it.

They set off again. Now, even the narrow, stony path had disappeared, and they had to forge their own path across the rocks and through the spindly trees. Sander managed it easily, skipping along lightly. Linnell, despite being fit and used to the mountains, found it a struggle. The uneven rocky surface pressed through the thin leather soles of her shoes and in time, the slope grew so steep that Linnell abandoned the walking stick and used her hands as well as her feet to scramble up the mountainside.

A memory came to her. When she had been five or six, a local goatherd, a friend of her father's, had fallen down the Grey Mountain. He had survived the fall but died soon afterwards of his injuries. She peered over her shoulder. If she fell up here, then she would roll quickly downhill. If she were lucky then a bush or tree would break the fall and save her. If not, then it would be the end for her. What would her father say when they found her body broken at the bottom of the mountainside?

She stopped, breathing rapidly, unsure if she could go on. Sander must have sensed her fear and took a long rope from his bag. He looped one end through his leather belt and tied the other around her waist with a figure of eight knot. "This knot won't tighten if you fall," he said. "I'll go a little way ahead, and you follow."

Linnell nodded. She felt safer with the rope around her but still, she wasn't sure if she could physically move any higher. She watched Sander travel up the steep slope, hands and feet naturally seeking out holds within the rough surface of the rock. He made it look so easy.

Sander perched on a rocky protrusion above her, the rope snaking between them. "You can do this, Linnell," he said, and he took his pipe from his belt. He played an uplifting tune that made her think of birds and clouds and unicorns. Her eyes were drawn skywards and she felt a pressing urge to go up, to join Sander on the rocky ledge. She placed her hands and feet exactly where he had done and climbed. She no longer thought about falling; she just thought of her destination. And it was easy.

They continued on like that, without speaking, Sander climbing ahead and playing his pipe, and Linnell following him and his music.

She managed the journey all the way to a wider ledge, where Sander untied the rope that joined them. "We've reached the summit," he announced. But, in the thick cloud and fading light, she couldn't see the peak or the view below; she could only just make out his features.

Linnell felt as though she was just waking up from a dream. She forgot about limiting her questions. "Are we there? Where is the castle?"

Sander nodded. "We have reached the top of *this* mountain, but the castle lies above Mount Opacus, to the west." He pointed out into the clouds, into the nothingness. "We cannot get there by foot."

Linnell felt hot tears behind her eyes. She didn't understand how they could possibly travel to another mountain peak. Sander took a couple of paces and disappeared into the mist. Panicking, Linnell followed him.

"Just a few more steps up on this side and we'll get you across," he said. She saw then that they were near a wooden structure. Eight or nine steps led up to an open platform like the lakeside jetties that the fishermen used in Arvale. Linnell had no idea what it was for, although she was fairly certain that nobody would be fishing all the way up here.

She followed Sander up the steps and stood as close to the middle of the platform as she could, away from the open edge. To her left, a metal wheel was fixed to a tall wooden post, with a thick rope wound around it: some kind of pulley system. Sander reached up to the rope by the wheel and pulled at it. The wheel squeaked and turned and a deep square woven basket swung into view: the sort that held firewood, but deeper, almost up to her shoulders. He pulled it up so that it was resting on the platform edge.

"Here is how you get across."

THE OTHER SIDE

Sander unclipped the side of the basket, which swung open like a door, and she saw that he meant for her to get inside. Linnell peered at the pulley rope, which stretched out into the clouds. She couldn't see how far it went, or to where. Would it take her weight? Her heart beat faster. Climbing up mountains was one thing, but baskets pulled on ropes were quite another.

"I can't do this," she said.

"It is the only way. Trust me. I will get you across to the other side," encouraged Sander.

"Are you not coming too?"

"It isn't big enough for two."

Linnell saw this was true, but her whole body protested at the idea of getting inside. "I've got the basket," said Sander. "You just need to take one step inside. The whole journey will be over in mere minutes."

Just one step. After the journey they had undertaken, Linnell could surely manage one more step. She leaned forward and held on to the upper edges of the basket, and then as Sander held the basket firmly on the platform, she stepped inside. It didn't move; it was secure.

Then Sander clipped the side firmly shut with one hand. She gripped the edges tightly as he let go and began pulling at the rope. "Don't look down," he said. She squeezed her eyes shut.

The basket shifted towards the edge. "Hold on tight," called Sander, and the basket fell a few inches off the platform, jolting her alarmingly. Linnell shrieked. She opened her eyes; it was better with them open. The basket swayed and swung in the thick white mist. Sander was disappearing from view. Linnell could only just make out his ghost-like figure, pulling at the pulley rope. She had no idea how far up she was or if she was crossing air or water. Despite the depth of the basket, she had the unnerving feeling that she might topple over the edge, so she crouched down inside, reaching up to grip the edges.

The base of the basket creaked and squeaked beneath her. She felt sick. She wanted to sing to herself, to pray, to do anything to make herself feel better, but she couldn't even breathe. All that lay between her and a neck-breaking fall was the simple pulley mechanism. What if the rope broke? What if it jammed and she was left suspended halfway across?

But she told herself over and over that she could do it. It was all going to be worth it. And the journey was quick. The second mountain must have been close by, because after just a couple of minutes, the swaying stopped, as the basket hit something solid, and Linnell felt the base dragging on flat ground. The mist was still thick but she could see that she had reached the other mountain. With another sudden jolt, the basket tipped and emptied Linnell on to the hard ground. She lay there on her side for a moment, palms down on the flat cool rock, grateful to be in one piece. Then she sat up. The basket had deposited her on a small, level section on the mountainside. The thick, white cloud still swirled around her gave her the feeling of sitting on a cloud in the sky. She looked up but she still couldn't see a castle.

"I made it! Sander, I'm here on the other side!" Her voice sounded strange as she spoke into the thick cloud, as if she was the only one in the world. For a heartstopping moment, she imagined that he might not reply. What if she was left here all alone?

But Sander did reply. She couldn't see his face, but his voice was clear. She couldn't have travelled far from him.

"Send the basket back," he called.

Linnell stood, slowly and carefully, and straightened the basket so that it was upright on the rocky ground. To her right was a wooden post with a pulley system attached, just as there had been on the other side. She reached out and pulled the upper rope towards her. The rope moved easily and the empty basket moved, back in the direction from which she'd come, lurching off the mountainside.

"It's coming!" she cried, but this time there was no response.

Very soon, the basket was lost in the mist.

She kept pulling on the rough rope, until she could suddenly no longer pull. It must have reached the other side.

"Have you got it?" she cried.

"Yes," floated back the answer, much to her relief.

There was a long pause, during which Linnell guessed Sander must be climbing into the basket. She hoped she would have the strength to pull him across.

"Are you ready?" she called, after a while.

There was a long pause. Then Sander's voice. "Linnell, listen to me carefully. You have to keep going on your own, now. Follow the steps up."

Even at this distance, his voice sounded wobbly. Was Linnell imagining it, or did he seem as scared as she was? "Sander, aren't you coming too?"

"You won't be able to pull the basket with me in it."

He was leaving her here! "Let me try! Or take me back again. Don't let me go on alone, please!"

Linnell didn't want to go anywhere, especially not further up. She wanted to go home. She pulled on the lower rope, to bring the basket back to her. She would pull herself back across if necessary. But it was fixed in place. Then she pulled on the other rope. That wouldn't budge, either. The realization washed over her: she had sent the basket back to Sander and only he could free it. She was stuck here and she had to do what he said.

"You can't turn back now," he called. "I must leave you to complete this last part of the journey on your own. I'm sorry, Linnell."

He did sound as though he was really sorry. But for leaving her, or for something else? She couldn't tell.

"What?" She practically screamed the word across the gulf. "You're abandoning me?"

His voice drifted over to her again. "Just listen to me. Keep going up. Find the steps."

Linnell began to feel desperate. She looked frantically around for some steps but there was nothing. "I can't!"

"I will play my pipe so that you will know I am still here. Trust me."

Trust him? She hated him! And she hated herself. Why had she left the woods with him? He was a stranger after all, however charming and carefree. Right now, she should be sitting at the kitchen table with her father, sharing some bread and wondering whether the day would be wet tomorrow. How did she get here? She tried to steady her breathing, breathing in through her nose and out through her mouth. But still the panic rose up in her. She tasted acid in her throat. She might actually be sick.

Sander's voice floated across to her once again. "Be careful what you give to the unicorn. He can't take anything without your permission. Do you understand?"

He really was sending her off on her own.

"No! I won't go! You can't just leave me here," she cried.

But there was no reply. Just the sound of Sander's pipe. The hateful, traitorous pipe that had brought her here. "Enough," she cried. "I never want to hear that sound again!"

Still, she couldn't help but listen. The tune was high and sweet. It made her think of birds. There were birds, not far below her. She had climbed higher than the birds.

Linnell took a deep breath. She *could* just stand here and shout, but there was nobody to rescue her. Sander had abandoned her. She must go on. Steps. She must find the steps. She gazed around and found the steps easily. They were carved into the rock and looked narrow and steep but sturdy enough.

The pipe continued to play and she put her foot on to the first step. There was no rail, but the rock jutted out a little at waist level, providing something for her to grip. She clung on, concentrating hard in her effort not to fall. She stepped up on to the next step. And then the next. Slowly, steadily, as the pipe music played on.

CHAPTER THREE

THE CASTLE IN THE CLOUDS

Linnell didn't count the steps but there must have been hundreds, snaking up into the sky. She continued steadily, in time to the sound of the pipe, which grew fainter and fainter. The colour of the steps changed from dark grey to pure white as she climbed. She didn't think about the increasingly tired muscles in her legs or her breathing. She couldn't go back, only forward.

After a time, the pipe playing stopped. Linnell did not know if she had climbed too far for the sound to reach her or if Sander had given up on her and gone home. What would she do if

Sander was no longer there when she came out? The thought of being stuck up here in the clouds forever was more than she could bear, so she pressed on.

From up here, the clouds looked like padded cushions on to which she could jump. But every here and there, this illusion was broken by gaps in the clouds showing glimpses of the green and grey mountain landscape below. This changed as she climbed higher and higher. She stopped seeing any mountain at all through the gaps. Only the last layer of cloud. Layers and layers of cloud. It was cool, too. She shivered in her lightweight frock.

The steps took a sharp turn to the right and Linnell finally broke through. The change came suddenly, like rising from a lake after swimming underwater. Her head poked through into a brand new world. The light was no longer dim. It was so bright that Linnell closed her eyes and stopped climbing. She gradually opened them, still squinting, and tried to take in the scene before her.

The castle. She had reached the castle. She had never seen a castle before and she was open-mouthed at the sight before her. Towering into the sky, it must have been at least four storeys high, each floor smaller than the last. At the very top was a pointed turret, spiking upwards, reaching higher even than the giant mountains below.

Behind it, there were no trees or buildings to obstruct her view and the bright, yellow-white sky was vast – bigger than she'd ever seen before. The blue grey clouds that she had broken through still swirled around her legs and up to her waist.

She climbed the final steps slower than all the rest. Then the white rocky ground flattened out and she approached the castle as if in a dream. A sob rose up in her chest. It may have been relief that she was finally here, that the castle actually existed. It did seem like the kind of place where wishes would be granted. She released the sob, making a gulping sound, which sounded strange up here in the silence.

As Linnell walked right up to the wide castle steps, she couldn't see her feet moving: a curious sensation. From the steps, she was unable to see the top of the castle – just smooth white walls stretching up. There was no moat, no drawbridge, no guards even. This was not a building that was made for defence. But then why would it be, when nobody knew of its existence? Had any human being ever been here before her? Sander of course. But from what he had said earlier, maybe nobody else. Perhaps she was the very first female to set foot on this mountain. A proper adventurer – not a fool after all.

Why did Sander stay away? He told her that he was unable to work the basket pulley on his own but that couldn't be true. He had come here before on his own, hadn't he? She would have thought that this gleaming white castle would be impossible for someone with his thirst for adventure to resist, yet he seemed happy to wait at a distance.

There was not a sound. No birds, no voices, no wind. The clouds and the whiteness seemed to soften everything. She approached the gigantic, arched doors that were over twice her height and made of coloured glass, in subtle hues of pink, yellow and blue, interspersed with diamond-patterned leading. It was bright and beautiful, as though a rainbow had been captured there. To her right, was a long bell pull made from knotted rope. There were three wide steps leading up to the door. She walked up them, then took a deep breath and pulled on the rope. The clanging of a bell echoed from deep within the castle, and she waited.

ICE AND MARBLE

Who would hear the bell? Would the unicorn come to greet her at the doorway? Or did he have staff to perform such tasks? Linnell wished that she had asked more questions, despite Sander's complaining, so that she knew what to expect. The tall doors swung inwards, but nobody was behind them. There was no one to greet her and no one to turn her away. Linnell stepped over the threshold of the castle in the clouds.

The entrance hall was vast, white and luminous, and Linnell had to shield her eyes from the brightness. The floor was laid with marble tiles, in a circular pattern, in different shades of white and cream. Light flooded in from arched windows high above Linnell. They had the same leadwork pattern as the doors and scattered colourful little diamonds of sunlight throughout the hall. A corridor stretched straight ahead, leading into the depths of the castle. It grew dark and she could only see a few yards of marble floor. Two symmetrical marble staircases on either side of the corridor led up to a mezzanine level, at the centre of which were some more arched double doors. These doors instantly drew Linnell's eye because they were black and all the white made them appear blacker, like a tunnel. She somehow knew that what she sought would be behind those doors.

So, once again, Linnell began to climb. This time her legs moved automatically, as if she was being pulled towards a stronger force. She gazed around at the emptiness. Perhaps the castle had been abandoned.

When she finally reached the two heavy double doors she could examine them more closely. They were made from a black, shining stone – quartz perhaps – and studded all over with tiny sparkling gemstones. Linnell wondered if she had just seen her first diamonds. She felt a thrill run through her. That was why she was here. What was it Sander had said? *Diamonds around your neck? A dress decorated in exquisite seed pearls?*

There was no bell pull at this door. No knocker or handle. Linnell laid both her palms flat against the right-hand door, which felt cold and smooth. She pushed experimentally to see if they would shift, and to her surprise, they swung open as if they weighed nothing.

Linnell stepped through into the room and the door swung shut behind her. Like the rest of the castle, there was nobody here and the silence was almost too much to bear. Still, there was no doubt that she had come to the right place. The sight before her was so spectacular that she didn't have a chance to gather her thoughts; she just gazed around her.

She had reached the throne room. Once again, everything was white, but here everything was icy and glittered with a blue tinge. She shivered and warmed herself with her arms. There didn't appear to be any windows, but candles flickered in arched alcoves high up in pillars by the walls. Perfumed smoke, perhaps from the candles, wafted in the air. It smelled of warm fires and gingerbread, quite at odds with the frosty air. Ice sculptures stared out at Linnell from around the room. Mainly animals: eagles, deer, lions and wolves.

Near the back wall was a great marble throne, with steps leading up to it. In the centre of the room was a round pool, frozen solid. From there to the throne was a walkway, with fountains flowing into long rectangular pools of water on either side. Pretty pinks and blues sparkled in the water. More candles lit the way, and two flaming torches in iron sconces blazed on either side of the throne.

Linnell walked towards the pool. As she did so, she saw that the ice was crystal clear, not white, as a frozen lake might be, and she could see clouds in motion far below. She passed around it, walked along the walkway and stood before the steps to the throne. She didn't dare climb them.

On a plinth to the left of the throne was an astonishing sculpture of a unicorn, the size of a real-life pony, looking down on Linnell. The Greatest Unicorn, she supposed. It was white and almost translucent, without joins or lines, as though it had been carved from a single block of ice. It was incredibly realistic. Although it stood in a relaxed pose, the unicorn looked proud and somewhat stern. Its horn glinted gold and the rest of its body was a blue-tinged white.

Linnell took in every detail. Its mane, which flowed in a sheet like a girl's long hair. The muscly legs and the rounded muzzle. She wanted badly to touch it, and although she knew she probably shouldn't, there was nobody there to see her. She tentatively reached up a hand and touched the sculpture lightly on its fetlock.

It was warm. This sculpture was not made of ice, she realized with a gasp. Linnell spread out her fingers and felt its softness. Sander's words from earlier came back to her. The unicorn was … *like a diamond. But not hard like a diamond. Strong and sinewy but still soft.*

Just as she realized that this was not in fact a sculpture at all, the unicorn reared up on to its back legs, its hooves close to Linnell's face, and neighed as it leaped from the plinth.

THE GREATEST UNICORN

The unicorn's deep neighing call was loud and unexpected, and the sudden strangeness of it sent her staggering backwards. She tripped and fell, banging her hipbone on the hard floor. She was not badly hurt – it would just be a bruise – but she stayed curled up where she was, gazing up at the majestic creature. Even the floor itself was frozen – although strangely not wet – and she shivered.

The unicorn tilted his head slightly, looking at her with his dark blue eyes. "You may rise."

It was a woman's voice, low and rasping. It was not the sound that Linnell had expected him to make. Still, Linnell rose as she had been instructed to do, and saw a woman standing behind the unicorn. She must have been the one who spoke. She was old, leaning on a staff, and she wore a floor length white gauze dress. Her wrinkled skin and long plaited hair were both pale, which gave her a ghostly appearance, yet she looked more solid than the unicorn. Who was she and how did she get into the room? Linnell hadn't seen anyone enter after her.

The woman spoke again. "I work for the Greatest Unicorn. My master doesn't share your language, so I will interpret for him."

Linnell nodded and stared at the unicorn again. She felt she should say something. She dropped a clumsy curtsey and said, "Your Majesty."

The unicorn perked his ears slightly forwards. Wispy white steam emerged from his nostrils as he breathed gently.

"He says you look cold."

Linnell nodded.

"This will pass."

And strangely, it *did* pass. Warmth spread through her. Was it his magic?

"You have come here for a reason?"

Linnell nodded. She knew what she wanted to ask for but was too scared to speak. "Fine things. Freedom," she managed eventually. Her voice sounded small and silly.

But the unicorn seemed to understand. He walked towards her and she took a few steps backwards, until she realized that she was standing in the middle of the frozen pool in the centre of the room. Her feet didn't feel cold, and although she saw the clouds beneath her, she didn't feel afraid as she had done on the mountainside.

The unicorn circled the pool, his long tail swinging slowly and the muscles working in his hips and shoulders. "You want expensive jewels?" said the woman's voice.

Linnell nodded and a light white mist sprang up around her. The unicorn paced faster. "You have expensive jewels."

It was true. Linnell could feel the weight of a necklace at her throat. She stretched out her hands. There were rings on her fingers and bracelets around her wrists. Golden bracelets studded with gemstones. Diamonds and other coloured stones that she couldn't name. She gasped. Her wish! Sander had spoken the truth. This unicorn really was able to work powerful magic. Something began to fall from the ceiling. At first, Linnell thought it was a hailstorm, although she knew that made no sense. Little hard white spheres rained down upon her, bouncing and rolling across the icy floor. One caught in Linnell's hair and she plucked it out and examined it. It was a pearl. They were all pearls.

"You want exquisite dresses?"

Linnell nodded again. She could hardly believe that this was happening. The unicorn continued to walk around her and she felt her loose, farm girl's frock and apron change into fine clothes. The bodice squeezed her midriff and the sweeping blue gown reached to the floor. Linnell gazed down at the skirt, every inch of which was covered with delicate gold embroidery. This was just what she had always wanted. She turned in a slow circle, feeling like a dancer on top of a music box. She stretched out her skirts with her hands and pointed a toe. Her shoes, also golden, had a jewelled buckle and a heel. She touched her hand to her head. The pearls were there, attached to a comb. She stood taller and straighter. Now she felt like the *real* Linnell, like the girl she was supposed to be. She could walk into a royal court and no one would question her. She could be whomever she wanted. Linnell lifted her chin and laughed.

Then the unicorn stopped in front of her. His dark blue eyes stared into her own. "Now, it is your turn to give something to me."

Linnell's heart beat faster. What could she give in exchange for all this? Nothing. Maybe now the wish would not be granted. The unicorn would be angry that she'd wasted his time. He would take all the fine things away from her and throw her out on the cold mountainside once again.

Linnell lowered her gaze. "I have nothing to give you … sir."

She braced herself for the unicorn's wrath but it didn't come. Instead, he started circling again, but faster than he had done before, at a trot and then a canter.

Linnell could no longer see the interpreter but she could hear her voice. "Everyone has something to give, Linnell. Think very hard. What do you have that you can give? What is your greatest gift?"

Her greatest gift. When they put it like that, of course Linnell knew what it was – her father told her all the time. Her voice.

She began to sing:

"To me you are a diamond,
To me you are a pearl,
To me you are an emerald,
To me you are the world."

As she sang, she thought of her father playing the fiddle. His kind eyes and his hand resting gently on her shoulder that morning. She thought further back, to the hazy memories of her mother.

"Thank you, Linnell. This is exactly what my master was hoping for. Are you willing to give your gift to him?"

Sander's voice came back to her: *Be careful what you give to the unicorn. He can't take anything without your permission.* Her singing voice was her mother's gift to Linnell. Would she be willing to give it up for the sake of material things? As she sang, she knew that she would. Linnell nodded and spoke directly to the unicorn.

"Yes. My gift is yours."

The unicorn lowered his head in response. There was a pause, where Linnell wasn't sure what she was supposed to do next. Should she continue singing? As she began the second verse the interpreter spoke again.

"Thank you, Linnell. The unicorn is most grateful for the gift of your memories. He will take them from you now."

MEMORIES

Her memories? No – that wasn't right. She was supposed to be giving him her singing voice. Linnell tried to speak, but she could not find the words.

The unicorn's hooves moved more quickly, although they didn't seem to make a sound. Soon he was galloping around her and the white mist surrounding darkened to a greeny blue, rising from his hooves like dust clouds. She tried to watch but felt dizzy, confused. Surely he couldn't really take her memories? She wouldn't give those up to anyone.

Yet, as the unicorn galloped, she felt the images in her mind slipping away. There was a fairy in the woods, dancing to the sound of the pipes. Someone rocking in a wooden chair with a crocheted shawl on her lap. Herself, at the age of three, chasing chickens. The smell of sweet hay and cows. Her father, his hair white, his face weathered. The feel of the cows' udders as she milked and the sound of the milk hitting the wooden pail. A little yellow bird, trilling sweetly. The orange hawkweed on the mountainside and the matching sunrise that morning. Had it been that morning? Maybe it had been last week, or last year. She couldn't remember. She wanted so badly to remember.

There was a song. What were the words? If she could remember the words then it would all come back to her. An old man used to sing the song to her; or was it a woman? She couldn't be sure. Something about diamonds and mountains. She could still sing the notes perfectly. She sang to the unicorn. He was beautiful. She could not remember quite what she was doing here but she knew he was beautiful. She wanted to stroke his mane.

The unicorn slowed and steadily came to a stop in front of Linnell. He breathed hard through his nose and the old woman came and stood by him. He moved his head up and down in a slow nod.

"My master thanks you. Now, you each have what you desire."

Linnell looked down at her fine clothes, felt the embroidery under her fingers. She was so lucky. But she was sure there was something more. "I wanted freedom…"

"Yes, your freedom is granted. You may leave whenever you choose."

Linnell gazed around at the icy white room, the clouds beneath her feet, the sparkling light on the water and the ornate throne. She tried to think of a place where she might go but her mind was blank. She could not think how she had come to be here or from where she had come. Where could she possibly go that was more beautiful than this place?

"Come with us now, child," said the interpreter.

Linnell smiled and followed her and the unicorn through a second set of doors. As she went, she hummed to herself. Such a sweet melody. She just wished she could remember the words.

TWO YEARS LATER

ESSENDOR

$\mathcal{C}$HAPTER FOUR

FOOLISH RULES FROM
RULING FOOLS

Thandie

The four of them sat high up on the slope just inside Essendor's city walls. The summer sun was setting in the sky behind them and Thandie swatted at an occasional biting insect. She was teaching Tib the game of Merels. He was only five summers old, but he had picked it up quickly and would soon be better than she was. Finch sat cross-legged nearby and Hetty was on her own, a little further off, stitching something – probably embroidering a cushion cover or one of those other pursuits that Thandie couldn't stand.

Although Thandie didn't love Essendor at the moment, she did love this spot, where she could see the goings on in the city, but also the river, the houses, the fields and the mountains all stretching out beyond. When others thought of Essendor, they might picture the castle, or the Midnight Unicorn. But to Thandie, the whole view was Essendor. The vast majority of the city's population lived outside the city walls, just as she did.

Hetty stood up, tucking her fabric under her arm as she walked over to where they were playing. She watched the game for a few moments before she spoke. "It's getting dark."

"And?" asked Thandie. Hetty was always worrying about one thing or another.

"We have to be back by nightfall. The curfew – remember?"

Thandie didn't look up from the game board. She currently had three of Tib's men blocked and if she didn't concentrate and moved the wrong piece, he would take the lead. "It's ridiculous to have a curfew. It's still warm. On summer's evenings we should be able to stay out for as long as we want. I'm at least going to finish this game."

Tib looked at Hetty and then back at Thandie. He played his next move, grinning. If Thandie was staying then he wasn't going anywhere either. Thandie gave him a quick smile. She could always count on Tib.

Hetty put her hands on her hips. "It's not like it's just Madam Tilbury we have to answer to – the curfew was ordered by a royal decree!"

Thandie rolled her eyes. "It can't be a royal decree when none of the royal family are here."

Their young queen, Queen Audrey, had been struck by a mysterious sleeping sickness and her twin sister Alette was leading a party to find the cure. "Anyway, what are the watchmen going to do – cart us off to the dungeons if we're not in bed on time?"

Finch stood up. "Come on you two. Hetty's right. The guards will be doing their rounds soon and we need to be on the other side of the city wall. We don't want to get locked in, do we?"

Thandie sighed. "He's beaten me anyway," she said as Tib lined up three counters in a row, making a mill and stealing Thandie's last piece.

She shook Tib's hand and together they poured the wooden pegs back into their little drawstring bag and picked up the board. They all headed towards the gates.

On the way, Hetty carried on talking. "You do know the curfew is to keep us safe? The streets are dangerous at the moment. People are going missing and nobody knows why."

She directed her words at Tib, although Thandie knew they were meant for her. Just days after Alette left Essendor, people – older children and not-quite-adults – started going missing. It had been happening in smaller villages and towns for months, even years, but since Queen Audrey had taken the throne and the Midnight Unicorn had returned, Essendor had once again felt like a safe place to be. The thirteen-year reign of King Zelos seemed like a bad dream. But now their unicorn protector had forsaken them once again and the people of Essendor feared for their future.

Thandie refused to believe that the Midnight Unicorn had abandoned them – at least, not forever. The unicorn was probably off fighting a battle on Essendor's behalf. But in the meantime, the city's inhabitants had to protect themselves. The royal council had decided that this meant a curfew: everyone should be home by nightfall. After that, the city gates were locked and watchmen were posted at the city walls. Anyone entering had to prove their identity or be locked out until morning. Those within the city walls, the royal family and their courtiers, were safe. People outside the city walls, the normal folk, were advised to lock their doors and not to leave children asleep on their own in bedrooms. This was no problem, since not many children on the outskirts of Essendor had the luxury of their own bedroom.

Thandie thought the whole idea was a joke and she told Hetty so.

"The curfew is ridiculous. A foolish rule from ruling fools."

"Our rulers are not foolish! They are a respected ruling council, chosen by the queen. They are doing the best that they can," Hetty said.

"I have to admit, the curfew sounds quite sensible to me," said Finch.

"The rules are foolish for three reasons." Thandie held up her forefinger to indicate the first. "Firstly, they are made only for rich people. All the people locked in behind the guards are the rich and the important ones. On the other side, where the normal people like us live, we do not have sacks of gold or proper weapons or even locks on our doors. If a dragon or anyone wanted to carry us off, they just would, curfew or no curfew."

"So it's a dragon taking people, is it?" said Hetty incredulously.

Thandie ignored her and held up her second finger.

"Secondly, not all the people who went missing disappeared in the darkness. The first Essendor child to go missing was the youngest of the stolen ones: little Clover Malling. She was taking some pears down to her mother's market stall first thing in the morning. And Lilith Grain was coming home from school on a sunny afternoon."

"What about that boy from the Elithian circus? He was snatched in the dark." Hetty shuddered at the thought.

"Yes, it was dark, but we don't actually know that he was snatched," said Thandie. None of them knew any of these people or exactly what happened to them, but they knew their names and the stories of their sudden disappearances. They remembered the growing panic in the city and the search parties going out and coming back with nothing. "Night-time isn't a more dangerous time. It just feels more dangerous and the curfew makes the royal council feel as though they are doing something. They want to be seen to be acting whereas they are probably panicking."

Hetty tutted at this rant, which she'd heard before, but Thandie continued anyway.

"The most sensible thing to do would be to enforce an all-day curfew but then the fields wouldn't be ploughed, the crops would be ruined and it would be all their fault. Much better to put a useless night curfew in place. Then the people won't riot through fear and the city will just lose the odd child here and there."

Tib might not understand everything she was saying but he

listened to every word. When she paused for breath, he grinned up at her, his white teeth gleaming in the near-darkness. "What's the third reason that the rules are foolish?"

Thandie grinned back. "The third reason is that if you make rules, there will always be someone who wants to break them."

They had nearly reached the city gates by now and the two watchmen turned at the sound of their footsteps.

Thandie pulled her cloak up over her head and pressed herself into the shadows. "You three go ahead," she whispered. "I'm going to stay here. I'll show you just how easy it is to sneak past a couple of idle guards."

Hetty sighed. "This is really quite ridiculous. Can't we just go home?"

"You go! I will see you back at Madam Tilbury's in a few minutes, or if I fail, you can visit me in the castle dungeon in the morning."

"This isn't funny, Thandie. And why do you always say Madam Tilbury's? Why can't you just say 'I'll see you back home' like the rest of us?"

"Because it's not my home," whispered Thandie furiously.

The two girls stared at each other for a good few seconds until Finch guided Hetty away by the elbow. "Come on, it's not worth trying to persuade Thandie when she has her mind made up."

Thandie watched the three of them walk towards the gate. One of the soldiers spoke. "You're cutting it fine tonight, young 'uns. Get yourselves back to bed and keep yourselves safe." Finch muttered something in return and they shuffled through the gates, turning east towards Madam Tilbury's.

Three minutes and forty seconds later, Thandie was on the other side of the wall, running west. It was just as easy as she had said. A handful of pebbles thrown at a wooden door distracted the watchmen long enough for her to slip through unnoticed.

Now, if she ran quickly enough and used her favourite shortcut, she would be back at Madam Tilbury's before the others. Hetty would be furious!

Thandie only stopped running as she swung the cottage door open. She slammed it shut behind her, and leaned back against it, laughing to herself.

Madam Tilbury was sitting at the kitchen table, hands clasped around an earthenware mug. She had the look of someone who had just sat down for the first time that day, which was perfectly possible. She raised her eyebrows slightly. "You look exhausted! What have you been doing, child? Is everything all right? Where are the others? I was beginning to wonder where you'd all disappeared to."

Thandie just giggled a little and shook her head. "They'll be here soon."

Madam Tilbury stood and reached into the pantry for a jug of milk. She poured it into four cups and sat back down again. By the time Hetty, Finch and Tib burst in, Thandie's red cheeks had returned to their usual colour and she was sitting across from Madam Tilbury, looking like she'd been there for hours. Hetty glared at Thandie. She couldn't say anything in front of Madam Tilbury, of course, but Thandie could tell she was cross. She would probably have been happier if Thandie had been caught by the guards.

Madam Tilbury pushed a cup of milk across the table towards each of them and they all sat down. Thandie was fond of Madam Tilbury. She knew a little of what Thandie had been through. Like Thandie's mother, Madam Tilbury's husband, Berwick had disappeared for months when Zelos was on the throne. She didn't know for a long time whether he was alive or dead, but then he had turned up out of the blue along with the royal princesses. That was one of the reasons why she had taken the four children in. She understood. The only difference was that Thandie's mother had not returned. Yet.

When Queen Audrey came to the throne four years ago, one of the first things she did was to put measures in place to care for the city's orphans. A lot of children had been left without parents, either through the disease and hunger that was rife in Zelos's reign, or from the recruitment drive for his special army. Queen Audrey herself was an orphan. She was only nineteen – just a few years older than Thandie. Thandie felt sorry for her. Becoming queen at such a young age was a lot of responsibility. But she did a good job and made a difference. To help the orphans she appealed to ordinary families – families who'd never had any children of their own, or families like the Tilburys whose children had grown up and left home. Madam Tilbury didn't have to think about it for very long. Now her husband, Berwick, was on the royal council, he was away a lot and she wasn't keen on an empty house.

Madam Tilbury insisted her house was not an orphanage. She said the word made her think of rows of beds and children scrubbing floors. Hers was a home – her own home – and she had just made room for a few more. There were only four children and they each had to share a room with just one other: Thandie with Hetty, and Finch with Tib. They had three meals a day, which is more than some children ate in poorer families.

The others all called her "Ma Tilbury" but Thandie stuck to "Madam" however fond she grew of her. She had her own mother, after all, even if her mother happened to be missing right now. That was the big difference between Thandie and the others. Finch, Hetty and Tib all knew the sad stories of what had happened to their parents, but Thandie did not. As far as Thandie, or anyone else, knew, her mother was still out there somewhere.

They drank their milk quickly, glancing at one another over their cups. She could tell that the others wondered how she'd got home so quickly, but no one could ask in front of Madam Tilbury. Thandie would tell them all about it later, but as far as Madam Tilbury was concerned, for now they were all ready for bed.

Thandie's bedroom was small and simple with a dark wooden floor, a rag rug and a double bed, which she shared with Hetty. She threw on her nightdress as quickly as possible, leaving her clothes in a tangled bundle on the floor, and jumped into bed. She and Hetty had made the bed this morning as always, but Madam Tilbury must have changed the sheets that day because they were stretched tightly across the bed in the way that only she could manage. The sheets smelled the way all Madam Tilbury's washing smelled, like a cross between lemon and lavender.

Hetty came into the room and got into her nightclothes in silence, carefully folding any clothes that she would wear again the next day and putting them into her trunk. Hetty was giving out the sort of signals that showed she wasn't interested in speaking to Thandie. Thandie knew what Hetty could be like; she was annoyed with Thandie for leaving the city after them and probably would ignore her for a week now.

No matter, she would use the peace and quiet to write in her diary. Thandie reached over and took her worn book from the pocket of the tunic she'd been wearing that day. She kept it on her at all times, as she would hate to lose it. Today's account was half a scribbled page about tricking the guards.

"What are you writing?" asked Hetty, looking over at the book as she slid between the sheets next to Thandie.

Now Hetty wanted to talk. Some people seemingly found nothing more interesting than someone quietly jotting sentences into a small book. Thandie angled the pages away from her. "Nothing much."

"Are you writing about me?" asked Hetty.

"No." Thandie finished writing her sentence and snapped the book shut.

"Why not?"

"What do you mean?"

"I mean … you see me every day, we share a room, a bed and a breakfast table. I am virtually your sister, so why don't I make it into your diary?"

Thandie sighed and put the diary on her nightstand. "You're not my sister."

"I know that," said Hetty, rolling over on to her side to face Thandie. "That's why I said virtually." She sighed. "When I was growing up, I always wanted a sister. I thought I might have a younger sister with curly hair and gaps in her teeth. I certainly never imagined someone like you. But sometimes life turns out differently to the way we imagined, doesn't it?"

Thandie put out the light and lay on her back, staring into the darkness. "I don't mean to be impolite but I am not looking for a sister. I have my own family. My mother. For all I know, she's still out there somewhere. Until she returns, I'm on my own and I don't answer to anyone else."

Hetty sighed again, ostentatiously. Thandie couldn't see her expression but she could hear that she was trying to keep her voice calm. "Look, I'm not trying to start another fight. And I wasn't earlier, either. I was just worried that something might happen to you – I wasn't trying to tell you what to do."

"I should hope you're not trying to tell me what to do, seeing as you are approximately six weeks older than me!" Thandie knew she shouldn't react but sometimes Hetty rubbed her up the wrong way.

Hetty sighed again. "I'm just saying that they are the rules and we don't want to get into trouble. Or into danger."

Thandie's eyes began to grow accustomed to the darkness and she watched the shadows from the trees outside flicker on the ceiling. Shadows that could be anything: dragons or damsels or dancers. She grinned to herself. "And all I am saying is that we could have some real fun with this curfew."

DARES IN THE DARK
Thandie

Just half an hour later, when Madam Tilbury had gone to bed, the girls snuck into the boys' room as they often did. Finch and Tib's room had a low window that opened up on to the shallow-sloping roof over the back of the house. The ground behind the house ran uphill to meet the forest so that on the roof, they were level with the bottom trees and didn't feel that high up. It was quiet and private as well as picturesque.

Finch had been the one to discover the spot. He was a keen birdwatcher (he had no choice with a name like that), and found it a useful place for watching for birds and other wildlife. Tib had soon followed him out there and eventually the girls had joined them too. The location had the advantage of being at the back of the house, far away from Madam Tilbury's room. She couldn't hear them out here as long as they kept their voices low. As a result, the roof became the place where they had shared their hopes and dreams and sometimes their secrets.

Tonight was a perfect roof night. The air was stifling inside and none of them would be able to get to sleep until it cooled down. But it was too hot to go exploring anywhere else. Finch sat sideways under their bedroom window and Tib sat next to him on the windowsill, his legs resting on Finch's knees. He didn't like going too near the edge, even though it was a comparatively low roof. Hetty and Thandie didn't mind and sat with their legs dangling off the edge. The sun was down but the moon was out and the night sky looked more orange and grey than black, sprinkled with tiny white stars. The longer they sat, the more Thandie could see. The trees and houses in the distance were black silhouettes and the occasional bat emerged from the trees and performed its unique fluttering display before disappearing again. Thandie turned to the others. They seemed to be watching the night sky too and were much quieter than usual.

Tib was particularly quiet. He had a secret, she could tell: he was sitting in an unnatural way, with one arm crooked at the elbow, hand resting lightly in his pocket. Every so often he took his hand away and had a quick peek inside the pocket.

It was Thandie's guess that he had something living in there – a snail or a mouse. "What have you got there, Tib?"

"Nothing."

She smiled and didn't probe further, but after a few moments he brought his hand out of his pocket and showed them all anyway, smiling proudly: an egg. A large white egg, but bigger than a hen's.

"Yum! Is that for my breakfast?" asked Finch, making to take it from him.

"No!" said Tib, huddling over it protectively. "I found it by the river. It was still warm. It must have rolled from the nest and the mother duck didn't come back. I'm going to hatch it. I'll keep it by my body in the day and in a box of straw at night time."

Hetty peered at the egg. "I really wouldn't keep it in your pocket if I were you. You don't want to break it. And I'm afraid it's not at all likely to hatch without its mother."

The hopeful look on Tib's face fell a little. Thandie felt for him. Hetty was right and the egg probably wouldn't survive. She'd brought eggs home herself when she was small and they'd never hatched, even if they were warm when she found them. Still, there was no need to be so negative. There was always hope, and maybe Tib's egg would hatch. "You'll make a wonderful duck father, Tib," she said kindly. "You had better practise your swimming!"

Finch had been teaching them all to swim in the river and Tib was learning fast.

"And learn to speak duck," added Finch.

Tib quacked loudly, and Hetty shushed him. "Let's not wake Ma Tilbury," she said.

"He wasn't that loud," said Thandie.

Hetty sighed. "Why do you always have to do that? If I say something to Tib, you always stick up for him and argue with me."

"It's because you sound like this," said Thandie, making a quacking sound back at Hetty and moving her hand like a beak.

Tib giggled and Finch interrupted, obviously keen to avoid another argument between the girls. "Maybe a giant duck has been stealing people for her ducklings. Quack, quack!"

It seemed that whatever subject they chose, the conversation would always come back to the stolen ones and the curfew.

"It's not a duck that's taking the people. Thandie seems to think it's a dragon," said Hetty. Thandie could tell that Hetty was still cross with her.

Finch turned towards Tib, his face animated. He was still trying to lighten the mood. "I think so too! I heard that a fire-breathing dragon has demanded a fresh human sacrifice each month, and if he doesn't get it … he will burn the whole city down" He winked at Tib, whose eyes had gone very wide.

"Is it really a dragon?" he asked.

Thandie smiled at him and shook her head. She didn't want the poor boy to have nightmares. "Maybe a fire-breathing duck," she said, and he laughed.

Hetty shuffled closer. "I heard people are disappearing because of a new dancing plague, like the one that happened in the Western Isles. People hear imaginary music and their feet won't stop moving. They dance themselves off cliffs, into the ocean and even dance themselves dead from exhaustion."

Hetty was trying to impress Tib, which niggled at Thandie. She shook her head. "It's not that."

"You sound very sure," said Hetty.

"I am."

Thandie couldn't understand why people assumed the stolen ones had even been stolen, unwilling. To Thandie, the scariest option was the one that the others hadn't considered: maybe all these people had wanted to go. Perhaps they longed to get away. Perhaps there was just no one around here that they cared enough about to stay. Perhaps that is what had happened to her mother – she had received an offer of a better life.

But Thandie kept these thoughts to herself – she didn't think they'd understand. Instead, she said, "I don't know why everyone's so frightened. I'm sure there's no dragon or dancing plague out there. People are just trying to spoil our fun and make us keep to the curfew. And, as I explained earlier, the curfew means nothing to me, whether it comes from the royal council or not."

"You might say that but you actually kept to the curfew just like the rest of us," said Hetty. "We were all back in by nightfall."

"Yes, but I stayed inside the city walls after the guards told us to go."

"That was quite easy, though Thandie. Any of us could have done that," said Hetty.

Finch looked at the two of them wearily. Hetty was beginning to get under Thandie's skin as she always did. "You couldn't have done it, Hetty," sneered Thandie. "You're always whinging and playing by the rules. If it was up to you we'd probably stay inside and work on our tapestries all day."

Tib laughed. Hetty's face flashed a dark red. "Everything's so easy for you, isn't it, Thandie? But you're just as scared as the rest of us. You wouldn't want to be wandering around after curfew if there are monsters out there."

"It really wouldn't bother me."

"Do it then."

"I shall." Thandie stared at Hetty defiantly.

"When?"

"Now, if you like."

Finch leaped to his feet. "Let's not do this. Why don't we play a game of something? Merels? I've been meaning to learn that for an eternity." But they all ignored him.

"What's the monster game called?" Tib asked.

"Dares in the dark," said Thandie, standing up. "Where would you like me to go?"

Hetty pursed her lips. "Breaking out of the city is easy. Like you said, all the protected people live inside the city walls. They are more concerned about somebody breaking in. Why don't you try to get inside the city walls?"

Finch looked concerned. "Not in the dark, Hetty. Let's leave it until tomorrow."

But there was no stopping Hetty now. "She says the dark doesn't scare her and it's just as safe as the daytime. So in that case, Thandie, I dare you to break into the castle tonight. Go through the forest and up to the city walls and past the guards. What's stopping you?"

"Absolutely nothing," said Thandie. She brushed herself down, ready to go. "I'll do it now."

"Please don't pay any attention to Hetty," said Finch, putting his hand on Thandie's shoulder. "You could be walking into real danger."

"You don't really believe that, do you?" Thandie shuffled to the edge of the roof and dangled her feet over the side. She wasn't remotely scared, mainly because she doubted she would run into anyone on such a mission. Nasty things always took you by surprise, didn't they? You didn't just run into danger when you went looking for it.

She held on to the roof with arms bent behind her and lowered herself even more. Her feet were still a little way from the ground but she had done this enough times to trust that she could make the jump. She dropped down to the ground, knees bent, managing to stay upright.

The others all rushed to the edge to watch her go. Hetty began fussing, as usual. "You don't have to go tonight. You could go tomorrow. Or, do something different. We could all go—" Thandie could tell that she was wishing she'd never suggested it. But Thandie wasn't going to go back on her word just to make Hetty feel better.

"No, I accept your original challenge"

Tib just grinned. "Thandie is brave. She can do anything." He reached into the pocket of his trousers and pulled out a catapult that Finch had helped him make from a Y-shaped stick. He passed it to Finch, who handed it down to her. "Take this weapon in case you need to fight any monsters."

"Thank you, Tib," said Thandie solemnly, taking the catapult and a couple of walnuts that he had saved for ammunition. She doubted that she would be likely to slay any monsters with these. Still, it was a kind thought. "I shall give it back when I return."

Finch and Hetty carried on arguing up on the roof.

"Come on, tell her you didn't mean it, Hetty," said Finch.

Hetty lay on her stomach and looked down at Thandie. "I was only joking. Thandie, I didn't mean it! Come back!"

But Thandie was already striding out into the moonlit darkness, Tib's catapult in her pocket and a smile on her face.

Luckily, Thandie didn't have to sneak past any other houses on the way to the forest, as it was so close. She strolled towards the trees with her head held high. Finch, Hetty and Tib would be watching her for as long as they could, and she refused to scurry off like a frightened mouse. She couldn't have Hetty thinking that she was just talking about being brave. That wasn't Thandie at all. If she wanted to do something, then she did it. She had nothing to lose. Besides, adventures were few and far between around here and she meant to enjoy this one.

It was dark and quiet outside – the sort of darkness that was hard to ignore and the sort of quiet that drew attention to ordinary sounds. Thandie was strangely aware of her own breathing and footsteps on the ground. But darkness itself was not a frightening thing. People were only really scared of what the darkness could conceal, and Thandie was sure that there was nothing lurking tonight. Still, she felt in her pocket for Tib's catapult just in case.

She walked through the woods, using the well-trodden pathway that folk took from the cottages to the city walls. She had walked this way with the others on a near-daily basis and knew every twist and turn, so it hardly mattered that it was night-time.

She kept up her confident gait, as she knew that if there was someone hiding in the darkness this evening they would be less likely to approach someone who looked brave and self-assured. And she felt brave. Or to be more accurate, she felt as though she had nothing to lose.

She left the darkness of the woods and emerged once again into the moonlight, where she joined the main dirt road. She planned how she would get past the watchmen at the gates. She could use a distraction like last time, but as Hetty had correctly explained, the guards would be much more alert to people trying to get inside the city walls than those trying to get out. She would be better off talking to the guards and trying to trick them. She could tell them that she was a member of the royal household who had been delayed on a journey that day, or that she was a messenger with an important piece of news.

She had reached the city walls now. This would be easy. Once she'd had a quick chat with the guards, she would turn around and walk back to Madam Tilbury's. Then Hetty would be proven wrong.

Just as she neared the gates, her heart nearly jumped out of her chest. There was someone: a lone figure lurking by the city walls, under the trees.

CHAPTER FIVE

THE FIGURE IN THE SHADOWS

Thandie

Luckily, Thandie's instincts were sharp and instead of crying out, she only gasped quietly and flattened herself against the wall. It was a boy. Had he seen her? It appeared not. His face was turned away.

He was definitely hiding, in a perfect place to see but not be seen. Yet, right now, Thandie could see him and he could not see her. The thought made her want to burst out laughing and she clapped her hands over her mouth. Why was he out roaming in the dark when the rest of the city was shut away through fear?

He was either, like her, rebelling against the rules, or he was new to these parts. He turned, still not looking in her direction, and she got a better look at him, although she was not close enough to see his features in detail. He was youngish and wore a pointed hat and a raggedy coat. She couldn't see much more, but she was fairly sure she didn't recognize him. He could not be from around Essendor.

He took an object from his belt and lifted it to his mouth. At first Thandie thought he was taking a swig of something from a flask but then she realized it was an instrument – a pipe. He began to play. She had thought of a pipe as a child's instrument and, to begin with, it sounded as though this boy was practising his scales, just as she had done as a young girl. Then the notes changed and turned into a repetitive but sweet tune which gradually grew more complicated. After a while, Thandie wasn't listening to the notes at all; she was transported somewhere else entirely. She had the strange and sudden urge to feel her mother's arms around her, and tears sprang unexpectedly to her eyes. After a while she realized she had been standing there stock-still, in a kind of trance. She shook herself out of it. Still, he played on.

He was a better player than many of the pipe players that entertained the crowds in the streets of Essendor. But he had no audience. Why would someone come all the way out here in the dark to practise his pipe playing? It didn't make sense. Even if he had no home, it would seem an odd thing to do at this hour, and she was surprised it hadn't caught the attention of the guards. But maybe that was how he got so good: practising at all hours of the night and day.

Thandie knew that she should probably turn around and go straight back to the others. She had gone far enough to prove that she had no fear of the abandoned streets, and they would love to hear her story of the pipe player in the darkness. But Thandie didn't want to go back. She wanted to find out who this person was and what was he doing there.

Whether it was excitement or nerves, some silliness bubbled up inside her and, on an impulse, she grabbed a handful of earth and small pebbles from the ground and threw it towards the boy. He glanced up briefly but didn't stop his pipe playing. If Thandie wanted to attract his attention then she was just going to have to walk right up to him.

She left her hiding place in the safety of the shadows and began walking across the flat grass towards him. She took long strides and held her chin up in the air as she had done in the woods. Essendor was her town and he was the visitor – she had everything to be confident about.

When she was just a dozen or so long strides from him, he glanced up again but carried on playing his tune. She could see him much more clearly now. A stranger, yes, and strangely dressed, but was he the kidnapping monster that had prompted panic throughout the kingdom and a curfew in the capital city? Surely not. They had imagined a monstrous creature or burly kidnappers, not a slim young boy. She watched him for a little longer. He looked only slightly older than her. A few locks or hair curled out under his hat as though he had arranged them there purposefully. His features were sharp and even – quite handsome – but there was something unsettling about him. Thandie couldn't identify what it was but, although he was certainly no monster, she did wonder if he was someone she could trust.

As she drew nearer, their eyes met. He continued to play and did not at any point look shocked to see her, which left her wondering, at what point had he realized that she was watching him? Perhaps he was playing to an audience all along.

She spoke first – showing him again that she was confident.

"Who are you, and why are you sitting out here playing your pipe in the dark?"

QUESTIONS
Sander

Sander had found that in the smaller villages, where word was beginning to get around about the missing children, people were suspicious and, as a stranger, he stood out. In the bigger towns and cities it was easier to go unnoticed. And so he had come to Essendor, the biggest city of them all. But within minutes of arriving, he had been confronted by shut doors, closed taverns and guards at the gates. He was locked out of the city for the night and was unlikely to meet anyone by chance in these dark hours. He would need to make a new plan.

Yet just as he sat, planning and piping, an athletic-looking girl with black hair in short plaits walked out of the shadows and right up to him. Surely not many people would approach a stranger after dark in that way. His first thought was she was with a bigger group, who were lurking around the corner waiting to pounce. But he looked over her shoulder and couldn't see anyone at all. His next thought was that she suspected him of something and had come to accuse him. She certainly looked accusatory, standing there with her hands on her hips and her eyes narrowed.

And then she spoke. "Who are you, and why are you sitting out here playing your pipe in the dark?"

Something about her small round nose and self-assured nature instantly appealed to him.

"I'm Sander. And I'm playing my pipe in the dark because it's what I felt like doing. Who are you and why are you accosting innocent pipe players in the dark?"

There was a pause and then she smiled widely. "I'm Thandie and what I am doing here is not your concern."

She turned and for a second, he thought she was going to walk away in the direction from which she had come, but she didn't. She plonked herself down on to a rock a few yards away and swivelled around to face him as if she were expecting him to read her a story.

He tried not to think ahead, how her smile would later fade. He had a job to do. "Why are you sitting there? Do you want me to play you another melody?"

"I'm sitting here because it is exactly what I feel like doing," said the girl, Thandie. "But you may play if you like. Is that what you do?"

Sander threw back his head and laughed. "I don't really do anything. I am a traveller – a wanderer – an adventurer."

"Really? And how exactly does an adventurer spend his days and weeks?"

Sander took a deep breath.

"I could never lead an ordinary life so when I was still quite young, I decided to set out to see the world. For a time, I slept on a home-made raft, floating on the river. When it drifted ashore, I got out to explore. If it did not, then I just stayed afloat for days."

Thandie screwed up her nose. "I think I would feel quite queasy if I were to stay on a raft for days. You are rather exposed to the elements are you not? And biting insects have a tendency to cluster near open water. I think I would be afraid to sleep for fear that I might roll off right into the water. No, I would not like that at all."

Sander stared at Thandie. This story had never failed to entrance, but he could see that she was different. He would have to try harder. "Do you not seek adventure? Do you not wonder what is out in the wide world or are you happy to stay here for the rest of your days?"

Thandie lifted her chin. "Yes, I seek adventure! And yes I want to get away from this place!"

Sander could see that his words were working their magic. She was getting angry with him. He knew the type. She would want to prove her courage to him. In less than an hour they would be walking away from here together.

Thandie pulled out two battered books from the front pocket of her dress. One was a reading book, the other a worn leather diary. "I want to get away, but I have a plan. My plan involves these, and a lot of hard work. Bobbing about on a raft is not the way I would choose to learn about the world."

Sander did not reply. He played another tune on his pipe to give him thinking time. But Thandie continued to talk loudly over his music.

"My way is to read. And to write. It will take time but eventually I will have my own adventures. And in the meantime, there are lots of adventures in here to keep my brain happy." She tapped her reading book.

Sander stopped playing again. He was starting to realize that this girl was not quite like anyone he had ever met, but that wasn't going to stop him. He had faith in his powers of persuasion.

"Ah, but you can't learn everything from within the pages of a book. There are some things that you can only learn by experiencing, and others that you have to see to believe."

"Like what?"

"Like many things. Too many even to think of. Enchanted

waterfalls, laughing lakes, even a unicorn in the clouds…"

Sander paused for a moment and looked sideways at Thandie. She might be trying to hide it but he could tell she was interested.

"A unicorn in the *clouds?*" she asked.

Sander nodded. "I have seen so many strange sights that they become almost commonplace after a time."

"But why would there be a unicorn in the *clouds?* Unicorns don't fly, do they? We have a unicorn here at Essendor – not that the Midnight Unicorn has been seen for some time – but nobody has ever mentioned it flying."

"This unicorn is far greater that the Midnight Unicorn. He is the Greatest Unicorn. Greater in strength and power. And no, he does not fly. He lives up there. In a spectacular castle in the clouds."

"If he doesn't fly, then how did he get up there? Are there steps? I can't imagine a unicorn would be very good at climbing steps. Or was he born up there? If he was born up there then there must have been a mother and father unicorn at some point—"

"—some things defy explanation," interrupted Sander, who was growing weary from the questioning. "All I know is that the Greatest Unicorn commands such magic that he has the ability to grant anyone's wishes.

Thandie wrinkled her brow. "You are telling me that an all-powerful unicorn trots around in a castle up in the clouds granting people's wishes all day long? If he did that, wouldn't he have queues of people at his doors? And wouldn't he want something in return?"

Sander sighed. "Oh dear. Are you one of *those* people?"

Thandie looked confused. "One of which people?"

"One of those sorts of people who like to ask questions. 'Why?' 'How?' And 'Why?' again. If you ask too many questions then you end up talking yourself out of what you really want. If you want something then you must grasp it and not let go. Forget the questions."

Thandie stared at him. Then she laughed loudly. "That is the most *foolish* thing I have ever heard in my life! Forget the questions? If I stopped asking questions then how would I know anything? I would still think the same way as Tib: that I could hibernate through the winter like a woodland animal, or that when the moon disappears, it's because it is sleeping. Questions and answers are essential for life: they are how we learn."

Sander felt less confident now. He took off his hat and ran his hand through his hair. Then he picked up his pipe and began playing once again – a jaunty little tune – as if she wasn't even there.

CONFRONTATION
Thandie

The tune irritated Thandie, as did this boy's strange manner. There was something about him that didn't seem quite right. He was clearly used to his daring and witty personality having an engaging effect, but she was not drawn in.

"Will you please stop playing your pipe for a second? It is so rude to play while someone is speaking to you," she said, but he continued playing, looking into the middle distance as if his thoughts were somewhere else entirely. She raised her voice over the sound of the pipe. "I have some more questions for you... Who are you? Why are you creeping about in the dark? Does it have something to do with the people going missing?"

Sander stopped and shushed her but that just made her angry. Who was he to tell her what to do?

"No, I won't shush! What have you been doing? Who are you working for? Is it the unicorn? What is he doing to people?" Thandie raised her voice louder, knowing she might draw attention from the guards. She didn't care. She may have been breaking curfew but he, as a stranger to Essendor, would definitely arouse more suspicion.

"Be quiet! Someone will come!" Sander threw down his pipe and stood up, fists clenched.

"No, I will not be quiet," said Thandie, shouting now. Without warning, he grabbed her shoulder with one hand and put his other hand over her mouth.

Her first reaction was fear. She was all alone out here and no one was coming to her rescue. But very quickly, anger took over. "Get off me!" she tried to shout but her voice was muffled by his hand. How dare he! Thandie twisted in his grasp and jabbed her elbows back repeatedly into his ribs. Although Sander had used the element of surprise, Thandie was stronger and much angrier than he was. She ran the heel of her heavy boot down his shin and stamped hard – very hard – on his foot. As he reached for his foot, she got away and turned to face him, clutching her side as she got her breath back.

She reached in the pocket of her dress for Tib's catapult and quickly drew back the shot. He looked up briefly and she released the projectile straight into his eye.

WALNUT
Sander

The shock of the sudden pain in his eye stopped him – brought him to his senses. What was he doing? He was not the sort of person to grab hold of someone like that – he was used to relying on his charms. He was ashamed of himself. He cried out and sank to the floor, hugging his knees to his chest, face buried in his knees. He rocked gently back and forth. "I'm sorry... I'm so, so, sorry," he kept muttering.

A TERRIBLE THING
Thandie

It was just a walnut – it couldn't have hurt him that much, surely? Sander sobbed for a long time, his face in his hands. Thandie could run away, flee back to Madam Tilbury's, but she didn't. She watched his back heave up and down, until his sobbing subsided. She was slightly concerned that she had badly injured him. She couldn't see his eye at all and hoped she'd only bruised him – given him a shock. But he didn't seem to be particularly bothered by his eye any more. He wiped his face and kept muttering how sorry he was. She did feel a little bad for him, and nearly told him that it was all right and that he hadn't hurt her. But she didn't. It wasn't all right and he shouldn't have grabbed her. She sat, still holding the catapult, and waited until he'd finished crying. Then he looked up.

"I've done a terrible thing," he said.

Something about his expression told Thandie that he wasn't talking about what had just happened. This was a *really* terrible thing he was talking about. She could guess what. "The stolen ones?"

Sander nodded. Thandie passed him a handkerchief from her pocket. She kept a good grip on the catapult, just in case.

"What have you done?"

Sander hung his head.

"You can either tell me now, or I'm going straight to the watchmen to report you. I'll tell them what you said and they'll have you arrested."

"No – don't do that!"

"Then tell me."

Sander took a deep, juddering breath. "I know something. I … saw something."

Thandie nodded slightly, encouraging him to go on. She wanted badly to hear what he had to say. Her fingers and toes were fizzing with adrenaline. "What did you see?"

"A girl. About your age. She was held captive. Her name was Linnell. Linnell Redfern."

Linnell. From near Arvale. Thandie had heard her name, passed around in the usual city gossip. She had been the very first of the stolen ones.

"Where did you see her? It was with that unicorn, wasn't it? The one you told me about?"

"Yes. In the castle in the clouds…"

And Sander told her. He told her of another great adventure, how he had climbed further than he'd ever been before, and he had found the unicorn. He had seen that Linnell was there but done nothing.

"I should have rescued her. I should have done something, but I just left her there. I never told a soul. He threatened me with death if I breathed a word." Sander looked away, as if telling the story was painful to him. "The unicorn had not harmed her physically, but he took something from her: her memories. Her face was blank, her smile empty. She didn't know, doesn't remember her own name. Just hums and sings melodies with no words. The others must be there with her now and it is all my fault – I could have stopped it."

Thandie shook her head slowly, taking it all in. "That is so sad. The poor girl. Her poor family. Why did the unicorn do it?"

"I don't know," said Sander, "but I suspect he uses the memories for his own purposes."

"What about the other people? Did you see anyone else?"

Sander shook his head. "The others only began to disappear afterwards."

"So there was no one else there? No one older?"

"I do not think so. After I saw Linnell I was filled with guilt. I vowed that one day I would return to rescue her and all those other people who went missing afterwards. So I have been roaming the kingdom, sleeping in the daytime and coming out at night, but always looking over my shoulder in case the Greatest Unicorn is after me, wanting to keep me quiet."

"So who is leading the stolen ones away?"

Sander shrugged. "Perhaps the unicorn himself. Or perhaps he has someone in his employment. I cannot tell you any more."

Thandie thought for a moment. She still wasn't sure about this boy. But there was no doubt he had valuable information. She knew what she *should* do. She should report Sander to the guards and see what they made of his stories. But she had found this strange piper. She would be the one to use his information. "If you have done a terrible thing, then you must do everything in your power to put it right," said Thandie.

UNIQUE
Sander

Thandie stared at him intently. "You could find the castle again, couldn't you? You might not know who's taking the people but you would know where to find them?"

Sander nodded.

Thandie's eyes were bright. "Would you take me there?"

"Take you to the castle?" Sander had seen many things on his travels but Thandie was possibly the strangest person he had ever met. He had explained the unicorn's dangerous power and yet rather than turning and running, she wanted to go and meet him. There was something … some reason that she was not telling him. When he had told her about Linnell, the first question Thandie had asked was if anyone else there in the castle: anyone older. She had lost someone – he was sure of it.

Thandie drew back her shoulders and put the catapult into in her pocket. "Take me there and together we will free the stolen ones."

Sander stared at Thandie. This was not the way it usually worked. He had been willing to leave Essendor for a while in case she talked about him. He had certainly not expected to walk away from here with her.

"I'm not sure... I don't know if I can face the unicorn again."

"This is your one chance to redeem yourself," said Thandie, pushing back her shoulders."You can reunite these broken families. Wouldn't that be worth something? You are supposed to be a brave adventurer – would that great reward to our society not be worth some small risk to your personal safety?"

She was unique. He was almost convinced himself. But would he be able to put up with her constant questioning, arguing and spirited nature?

"You put forward a good argument. And I may live to regret this, but yes, I will show you the way to the castle. We will face the unicorn together."

CHAPTER SIX

DON'T GO

Thandie

They agreed that Sander should wait where he was while Thandie went back to gather some belongings. She needed good boots on her feet and supplies of food for the long journey. She ran all the way back to Madam Tilbury's through the woods. She arrived back breathless and full of excitement. Finch scrambled to meet her, putting out a hand to help haul her back up on to the roof.

Hetty greeted her with a frown. "Where in the name of the Midnight Unicorn have you been?"

Thandie shrugged. "I went to the city walls, just as I promised.

You didn't have to wait up. Where's Tib?"

"Tib fell asleep waiting for you. We put him to bed," said Finch.

"If you were trying to scare us then it's not funny," said Hetty. "We thought you weren't coming back – that something terrible had happened."

Thandie shook her head frantically. She felt she had so much to tell them but no time in which to do it. "No, nothing terrible has happened and I am quite well, as you can see. But I have discovered something. I can't tell you what, but I think I know where the stolen ones are. And I think I can be the one to save them."

"What are you talking about?" cried Hetty.

"Come on, let's go to bed," said Finch. "We can talk about this tomorrow."

"You don't understand. I am leaving tonight. I need to get some things, and I shall fill you in as much as I can, but I have to go. Wait here."

"What do you mean? Where are you going?" asked Hetty.

Thandie didn't reply, and Hetty and Finch shook their heads in bewilderment as she climbed through the window of the boys' bedroom.

Thandie tiptoed past Tib's bed where he lay sleeping, out through the corridor and into her bedroom, leaving the creaking doors open so as not to disturb Madam Tilbury. She grabbed the big bag that she had used when she moved in three years ago, and stuffed it as full as she could with clothes and other personal possessions: a washcloth, a hairbrush. She patted her apron to check that she still had her diary and reading book, then she crept downstairs. She took as much food as she could from the pantry without feeling as though she were depriving the others. It was only what she would eat if she were here after all.

Then she went back upstairs to face Hetty and Finch. They had climbed back inside and were waiting for her in the boys' bedroom, Finch sitting on his bed and Hetty on the floor by the window. They both looked as if they were about to nod off.

Hetty stared at her bag and shook her head. "Where exactly are you going?"

"I can't tell you. Just that I saw something out there by the city walls that gave me a clue to what has happened to the stolen ones," Thandie whispered. She specifically didn't tell them about Sander, or lead them to believe she had talked to anyone at all. If they thought she was going off with a stranger then they were sure to tell Madam Tilbury.

Hetty shook her head in disbelief. "What? What did you see?"

"I can't tell you that either. Just that it has something to do with a unicorn."

"The Midnight Unicorn?" asked Finch.

"No, another unicorn. A bad one. I can't tell you any more but I have to go."

Finch didn't say another thing but got up from the bed and walked towards her.

Hetty pursed her lips. "What about Tib? Are you going without saying goodbye to him? He'll be heartbroken."

"No, of course not," said Thandie, who hadn't exactly been thinking about Tib at that minute, but would never forget about him all together. She put down the bag and went to Tib's bedside. He was sleeping on his side with one loosely curled fist resting under his chin. He hadn't bothered with bedsheets as the night was still so hot. His little body was curled carefully around a wooden straw-filled box. Thandie didn't need to investigate it to know that it contained his precious duck's egg.

She kneeled down next to the bed and put a hand gently on his back. He stirred and his dark eyelashes fluttered open.

"Thank you for the catapult," said Thandie. "It came in very handy. I have to go away for a little while. May I take it with me?"

Tib frowned and put his arms around her neck. She didn't know if he was properly awake but he spoke clearly, clinging on to her. "Don't go, Thandie!"

His voice – his little voice and its pleading tone – stirred a memory.

"Don't go!" That's what she had said to her mother. And her mother had laughed. "Just go to sleep. Dream sweet dreams. I'll be back before the cockerel crows."

Maybe she shouldn't go. She was Tib's closest friend. He trusted her. She knew how it felt to be abandoned by the person you trusted the most. But this was different. She would return: she would make sure of that. And she would find the missing people. All of them.

She unwound Tib's arms from her neck, settled him back on his pillow and looked him straight in the eyes.

"I will come back, I promise."

He closed his eyes, smiling, and she made sure that his egg box was safely nestled next to him. Then he was asleep. He might not even remember their conversation in the morning.

She turned to face Hetty and Finch. This goodbye would

not be as easy.

"What did you mean about the catapult coming in handy? Did you use it?" asked Finch.

"Let me guess … you can't tell us?" said Hetty.

Thandie shrugged.

"So you really are going?"

"Yes." Thandie narrowed her eyes. "Promise me you won't tell. You won't wake Madam Tilbury?"

Hetty shook her head slowly from side to side as if she couldn't quite believe what was happening. "No, Thandie. If this is what you mean to do, then I won't turn you in. It is obviously something that, for whatever reason, you feel the need to do. I will say to Ma Tilbury that your bed was empty in the morning. But, in case my opinion is of any interest to you, I think you are being incredibly selfish."

"Thank you." Thandie ignored the last part. "Finch?"

Finch shrugged. "The same as Hetty said."

They both stared at Thandie as if the world had come to an end.

"I wish we had never played this ridiculous game," said Finch.

Thandie smiled. "It might be the most important game we ever played. I promise I'll be back soon."

Hetty was still shaking her head. "People will all think that you have been taken, you know. They will be so worried. What do we tell them?"

Thandie pulled out her diary, scrawled a message on one of the back pages, then ripped it out and handed it to Hetty. "It says that I've gone to find the missing people."

"You're breaking curfew. You'll be in big trouble."

"No one will care about that when I've found the stolen ones."

"You won't find the stolen ones. I don't believe you're even looking for them. You're looking for someone else, but you won't find her," said Hetty, eyes flashing.

"Who?"

"Your mother. If she was going to come back, she would have returned with the others when Zclos died, five years ago."

Anger burned in Thandie's core but she refused to show Hetty. She kept her voice calm. "This has nothing to do with my mother."

Hetty began to raise her voice. " You may be lying to us – lying to yourself even – but it's obvious it has *everything* to do with your mother. You won't find her, though, Thandie. When will you realize that other people care about you? We are your real family now – you just have to let us in."

"Shhh," whispered Finch, touching Hetty's arm and pointing downstairs. "You'll get us all into trouble. Speaking of which, what are we supposed to tell Ma Tilbury when she asks? Or the guards?"

She climbed out of the window and leaned back in. "Give them the note. Tell them you don't know any more. Tell them that I just walked out of here and that was the last you ever saw of me. Tell them anything you want. But I'm going."

And Thandie launched herself off the roof and down into the darkness.

ONE IN A HUNDRED
Sander

Sander waited, making a bet with himself as to whether or not she would return. Ninety-nine out of a hundred people would not return. They would reach the comfort of their home and try to forget the encounter with the stranger in the dark. But Sander strongly suspected that Thandie was that one in a hundred. That is why he'd taken the risk and let her go. His bet was that she would return.

He played a complicated, haunting tune on his pipe, to

distract himself from the waiting.

And then there she was, walking through the moonlit clearing as if she were strolling along the side of the river after a picnic luncheon. Here was someone who was not frightened of the dark. Here was someone who was not frightened of being alone. Here was someone who was fiercely independent with a thirst for adventure and who kept their true emotions deeply buried.

Here was someone just like him.

CHAPTER SEVEN

THE JOURNEY BEGINS

Thandie

The first few miles that night were the strangest. Despite all their talking outside the city walls, they made their way in silence. Thandie had decided to save her energy for the long journey ahead. Anyway, she didn't have any particular desire to befriend this stranger. He had information that was useful to her – that was all.

It was getting very late and Thandie wondered when they would rest. She wasn't going to mention that to Sander, though. He might think her weak. He had said that he wandered at night and slept in the day, so she would fit in with him.

She wasn't sure if she would be able to sleep now anyway, with the adrenaline rushing through her veins. She had never been on a journey like this, not knowing where she was going or how long she would be gone. Everything seemed new and fresh to her, as if there could be a hidden surprise around any corner. Thandie was beginning to wonder if she had been a little too impulsive in walking out into the night with this stranger, but then she had been the one to suggest it to him, not the other way around. He had looked ready to disappear into the night.

Perhaps it was an impossible undertaking. Perhaps they should be facing up to the unicorn with a whole army, or at least a sorcerer, rather than just the two of them. She had no idea where they were going or what they were going to do when they got there.

"So, where are we going to travel first?" She broke the silence.

"Why, to the castle in the clouds of course."

"I know *that* but how do we reach it?"

Sander scratched his head, under his hat. "There are various ways—"

"— And what do we do when we get there?" asked Thandie.

"*That* I do not know. I hoped you had a plan."

Thandie stopped walking. "Of course I have a plan. It just needs some refinement."

"May I ask what it is? I know I need to lead us to the castle, but how we will free the people when we get there?"

"The unicorn has taken away their memories, correct?"

Sander nodded. "Well, he took that first girl's memories so I can only assume he did the same to the others."

"Why does he want their memories?"

"How would I know? I barely spoke to the unicorn. He just threatened me – told me that he had spies and he would know if I told anyone."

"So the unicorn speaks?"

Sander sighed. "Why the interrogation? I have told you everything I know."

There was a pause and Thandie started walking again. Sander followed alongside her. Thandie wanted to know more but he seemed very defensive. He was probably frightened. She tried to imagine what it must have been like to stumble upon something like that. She wouldn't push him any further on the subject.

She glanced in his direction again. "Well, whatever he uses them for ... we need to give them back. Remind them of what they have lost: their families, their lives."

"How do we do that?"

Thandie pondered this. A real plan suddenly sprang to mind.

"That girl you saw: Linnell Redfern, wasn't it?"

"Yes." Sander didn't look at her and it was difficult to judge what he was thinking.

"She was from the village of Arvale, wasn't she?"

Sander sighed. "A small hamlet just outside."

"I think we should go there. Before we find the unicorn. Her family and friends may be able to tell us something about her. Something that will help bring her back."

"But what good will that do? She is just one girl out of many."

"Still, hers is the only name I know, apart from those who went missing from Essendor, and we can't go back there now."

Sander looked unconvinced, but Thandie continued.

"I really think it would help. If we find out everything we can, then that would be one person who we stand a chance of saving. And even if we just save Linnell – bring back one person – people would believe us. They would trust you and we could go back to the castle with more people, to fight the unicorn."

Sander seemed to be considering this. "Linnell lived with her father, I believe. It was just the two of them and he was an old man. He would be easy enough to track down."

"Then let's go there."

Sander looked resigned and turned in a different direction. "Very well. We will head in the direction of Arvale. But we will have to walk between the mountains. It won't be easy and it will make our journey much longer."

"It will be worth it," said Thandie.

THE NEXT STOP
Sander

Sander did not want to go to Linnell's home. He didn't want to meet her father or see her home. He wanted no reminder of the day he led her away or what she'd left behind. But any excuse he gave would only arouse Thandie's suspicion. Linnell's father was an old man, anyway. Perhaps he had died or moved away: it was possible that Sander would not have to see him. So he would go along with Thandie's idea and pretend that he had never set foot near Linnell's home.

"We will go via Arvale, but there will be no more walking tonight," he said. I haven't slept all night and as soon as we are far enough from the main road, I want to get my head down."

"Where will we camp?"

"Somewhere off the beaten track," said Sander, suddenly veering off the road into the fields. "We need to be hidden away in case someone comes looking for you."

CAMP
Thandie

"Looking for me? I don't think anyone is likely to do that."

"Why not?"

"Well, Madam Tilbury and Berwick both have their hands full with other things at the moment, and the guards are hardly likely to waste much time looking for a poor orphan. It's not as if I am a member of the royal court. They'll be happy to quickly forget about me."

As soon as Thandie had said this she regretted it. It probably wasn't a good idea for Sander to think no one would miss her, so she quickly added, "On the other hand, my foster brothers and sisters are very protective of me. I told them what I was doing. They can be trusted not to tell the authorities for a time but will no doubt change their minds if I don't return soon." She didn't usually refer to Hetty, Tib and Finch as her foster siblings, but it seemed more apt than, "the people I share a house with."

"Oh yes, of course. I see what you mean," said Sander, then he pointed into the distance. "I think if we head in this direction we should find the perfect place to camp."

They only had to walk for a few more minutes before finding a sheltered spot near running water. They stopped and threw down their bags. A suggestion of the sun appeared at the horizon.

"Are we going to build a fire?" asked Thandie.

"No," said Sander, rolling out his blanket on the ground right away. "The nights are so warm at the moment that we don't need one, and it would only draw attention to our whereabouts."

"We don't need one to scare off wild animals?"

"There's nothing very fearsome around these parts – just the odd choker snake."

"Choker snake?"

"It's just a name. They rarely choke anyone and anyway, I am always alert to any threat, even in my sleep. I have my pipe. I could charm any creature that ventured too close."

"Great," muttered Thandie sarcastically. "Our most fearsome weapon is a seven-inch fipple pipe."

Sander grinned. "It works, I promise. A shelter is unnecessary as well," he said, removing his worn leather boots and sitting on top of the blanket. "I do hope that you won't make a fuss about sleeping out in the open air."

Thandie unrolled her own blanket some distance away. She had camped like this down by the river with Hetty, Finch and Tib on a few occasions before the curfew had been imposed on them "Sleeping outside doesn't trouble me. I'm not afraid of much."

"Nor am I. Nothing, in fact."

"There must be *something*." She thought of the unicorn – Sander's defensiveness earlier and his tears back in Essendor. But it seemed a little unfair to bring that up now when he was chatting away with such breezy confidence.

"I have tamed wild bears and battled the elements," he said. "I have seen great sorcerers cast terrible spells. If I had been the fearful type then these things might have given me cause for alarm, yet they did not. I think I can safely say that I am scared of nothing."

He leaned back on his arms with exaggerated casualness and Thandie fought the urge to laugh. She thought of common fears. Her mother had disliked all rodents. "What about rats?"

"No. Fluffy little things. Mice and rats have run over me in droves during the night when I'm sleeping. They don't bother me. They are quite intelligent creatures and they have more to fear from humans than the other way around. I even worked as a rat-catcher for a while."

"Really?" Thandie couldn't imagine Sander holding down any job, especially such an unexciting one.

"Yes, I charmed them away with my music, led them to the river to drown. I was paid handsomely for that."

Thandie pulled a face. "Charming indeed. How about spiders?" Hetty feared spiders.

"No, also fluffy little things! Mind you, I've seen spiders as big as your head. As big as dinner plates. They are simply living things making their own way in the world."

It seemed highly unlikely to Thandie that he'd seen spiders that size, but she didn't challenge him as there was no way to prove or disprove it. She thought of Tib refusing to sit near the edge of the roof. "Heights?"

Sander shook his head. "I promise you, I fear nothing. Not heights, nor water, nor enclosed spaces. I have no internal voice telling me to be careful or to hold back. I have no family to worry about me: I can take risks knowing that there will be no one to mourn me when I'm gone. That is the secret to being brave: having nothing to lose."

Thandie thought for a moment. "I don't agree."

Sander grinned. "I suspect that you never do."

"Aren't you going to ask me why?"

Sander yawned. "Why?"

"I think real bravery is fighting *for* other people. To protect them or keep them from harm. That's why I can be brave. For other people. That's why I am on this quest. I want to make sure that Essendor is safe for others."

"Are you sure?"

"What?"

"Are you sure that's why you are on this quest?"

"What do you mean?"

"At least I am honest about my selfishness. Maybe you need to admit to yourself that you have your own reasons for wanting to go on this particular adventure—"

"—I do not have any hidden reasons!" objected Thandie.

Sander yawned. "Whatever you want to tell yourself. Anyway, I am far too tired to chat right now." He lay down on his blanket and put his hat over his face, ending the conversation.

Thandie gritted her teeth. She'd like to squash that stupid hat right into his face. Or strike him with one of those enormous spiders that he claimed to have seen. He was exasperating. What right had he got to question her reasons for being on this quest?

One way or another he still hadn't revealed what he was frightened of, and she knew there must be something, as well as the mighty unicorn in the clouds. They were going to be travelling together for days. Thandie suspected that by the end of the journey, she would know what that something was.

CHAPTER EIGHT

AWAKE

Thandie

Sander seemed to fall asleep within minutes. Thandie did not. She was so tired that she felt she had been awake forever and could no longer remember how to sleep. She lay on her back, then her side and then her stomach, but couldn't find a comfortable position. If she didn't get a couple of hours sleep, then the long walk the next day would be unbearable. But knowing that somehow made it worse.

When her mother had first gone missing, Thandie had found it hard to sleep. It had been night-time when she had disappeared, so seven-year-old Thandie imagined that she might also return at night. She had lain in bed, eyes wide open, trying desperately to stay awake, but sleep always crept up on her in the end. She would wake in the morning, cross with herself, and vowing to try harder the next night.

Now, lying out in the open air in the early hours of the morning, her weary eyes remained stubbornly wide and sleep did not come. Her mind drifted back to Essendor. In just a couple of hours, the Tilbury household would begin to awaken. Tib was always first, running down the stairs to use the outhouse, his feet banging on the wooden stairs acting as a morning wake-up call for everyone else. Would they keep their promise to wait until morning before saying anything, or would Hetty's naturally obedient instinct kick in before then? Perhaps she had alerted Madam Tilbury as soon as she left and they were already on their trail.

Thandie sighed. She didn't want to be thinking about any of this right now. She looked over at Sander, who remained flat on his back, hat over his face, snoring growing louder by the minute. So much for his claims that he would react if a choker snake came to investigate; he probably wouldn't notice until it was wrapped three times around his neck. It crossed her mind that she could get up now and tiptoe away. In about two hours, if she walked quickly, she would be back in Essendor in time to meet Tib running down the stairs. The thought was highly tempting. But she was here for a reason, and although she may have made her decision to leave on a whim, it was still an important reason: she would rescue the stolen ones. It would not be easy, but, like all challenges, it would be worth it.

Thandie just needed to sleep. She looked across at Sander once more. He was obviously used to sleeping outdoors. Maybe a hat over the face was the secret. Thandie didn't have a hat but she reached into her bag and pulled out a clean dress, which she draped across her face, over her lightly closed eyes. It was certainly darker, but she didn't like the feeling of her face being covered, and after a few minutes she removed it.

The sun was rising higher and it was unquestionably light now. Thandie decided to give up on the idea of sleep. She reached into the pocket of her dress for her little leather-bound diary and pencil stub. She sat up, still huddled in her blanket, turned to a fresh page and began to write. Words flowed easily. She had a lot to say: so much to record. Hetty's dare last night and her solitary walk through the forest, meeting Sander outside the castle walls, her decision to leave Essendor.

She looked up for a second, chewing the end of her pencil and trying to remember the exact journey they had taken to this point. It was important for her to get these details right.

Sander was awake, she realized suddenly. He had shifted his hat off his face while she had been writing and was now watching her.

She scribbled a couple more words to complete her sentence, then turned the page so that her writing was hidden away.

Sander continued to watch her. "Why do you write in that little book?"

"It's my diary."

"I guessed that, but why do you write in it?"

Thandie sighed. "A couple of reasons. One is that it clears my head. If I get my cluttered thoughts on to the page then they stop swirling around in my head and stopping me from sleeping. You should try it."

"I'm not much of a writer. Anyway, I don't have any problems sleeping."

"I'd noticed."

"What's the other reason?"

"I suppose … I like to have a record of what I've done each day."

"Why?"

"I don't always trust my memory. Memories fade, and people remember selective events. Sometimes it is hard to know if it is a real memory or just a family story that has been told so many times it feels real. I prefer facts. When it's written in this book, I know what's real and what is not."

"But don't facts sometimes depend on your point of view? My story of yesterday's events might be very different to yours."

Thandie considered this. "No! Our stories might be different but surely there are certain concrete facts that remain the same? You can't just argue them away. You really should try it, you know. You have plenty of stories to tell, do you not?"

"My stories are all stored away up here," said Sander, tapping the side of his head.

"But if I asked you what amazing sight you discovered last Wednesday, would you be able to tell me?

"Last Wednesday… Yes, it was a memorable day. I climbed the tallest tree in the kingdom. A splendid rare Bronzewood out by the coast, known by the locals as the Sun Giant. The first part of the climb – up the long trunk - was the most difficult. Once I was up in the leaves it was easy. I had such a view. I swear I could see the whole kingdom—"

"—Last Wednesday was just an example," interrupted Thandie. She didn't particularly want to hear another one of Sander's adventure stories when she was trying to make a point. "What about on just an ordinary day, when you're not climbing altitudinous trees?"

Sander gave a full body stretch, with his arms right out above his head, which made Thandie jealous of his good night's sleep all over again.

"I can tell you read a lot of books when you use words like *altitudinous*. But the problem is, ordinary folk like me don't know what you're talking about."

Thandie narrowed her eyes. She suspected that Sander knew exactly what she was talking about. "Tall, then. What about on just an ordinary day, when you're not climbing *very tall* trees?"

"The thing about the life I lead is that there is no ordinary day."

Thandie folded her arms. "But will you be able to remember all these exciting adventures ten years from now?"

Sander sat up. "The question is, will I want to? Some people want to record their life experiences so that they can look back in years to come and convince themselves that they had a life worth living. But I am not that type of person. I am much more interested in the here and now. I am interested in living life to its absolute fullest and I never plan to stop living it."

"You will do whatever you want?"

"Yes."

"Without a thought for anyone else?"

"That's right."

"So you are claiming to be an entirely selfish person?"

Sander laughed, stood up and replaced his hat back on his head. "I suppose I am. So what exactly are you writing about this morning?" He peered at her diary.

Thandie snapped the book shut and wound the leather thong around it. "At this very moment I am not writing a thing because my peace is being constantly interrupted by trivial questions."

Sander grinned. "Are you writing about me?"

Thandie shook her head. She was used to Hetty thinking that the whole diary was about her and now she had Sander thinking it was all about him. Really there were only so many pages in the book. She tucked it away in the pocket of her dress, under the blanket. "What I write about is my own business and need not concern you."

"You *are* writing about me." He grinned and crossed his arms.

Thandie clenched her fists, resisting the urge to scream at him.

"You really are self-absorbed, aren't you? Of course I

mention you in passing as you are my only companion on this journey. But I can assure you I don't dwell long on any people in my diary. I am more interested in events. I have finished writing for this morning, anyway."

Sander stretched one leg out in front of him, and then the other. "Well I'm glad, as we will be too busy walking for more writing."

"Good. I hope we will have limited time for talking as well, otherwise I may have a headache by this afternoon."

Sander laughed again. "It depends how fit you are feeling. If we keep up a steady pace, we should be in Arvale in three days' time.

THE DAWN CHORUS
Thandie

As it turned out, there wasn't much talking on their walk to Arvale. Sander kept up a swift pace, striding ahead, and Thandie concentrated on keeping up. He was presumably used to walking alone and didn't want to chat every step of the way. She still had questions she wanted to ask about the unicorn, like how he spoke and what exactly he had said to Sander that day he had discovered Linnell. But it could wait. For now.

Instead, Thandie focused on the changing scenery. It didn't take them long to reach the Grey Mountain. She had always gazed at the mountain from Essendor and wondered what it would be like to clamber on the rocks, and now she knew.

Although they weren't going up and over the mountain, but around, it was still exhausting. The path disappeared in places and they had to climb their way over the jagged rocks, stopping only briefly for lunch. As they progressed, the grey terrain became much greener, indicating that they had reached the other side. They were on one side of a circular mountain range, surrounding a lush green valley and a cluster of lakes.

They found a sheltered spot to camp on the green mountainside, by some low bushes. The sun had already disappeared behind the mountain peaks, and evening was upon them earlier than in Essendor. Thandie was ready to sleep almost as soon as she had eaten. That night she did not have any problems getting so sleep, and drifted off almost as soon as she lay her head down.

Despite her exhaustion, she woke early, practically as the sun rose, enjoyed the buzzing and chirping of the crickets, which grew gradually louder as she came to. She always woke early back at Madam Tilbury's but she was used to the sounds there – the crow of her neighbour's cockerel and the famers calling to one another as they left for the fields. But sleeping outside, the sounds of nature were ten times louder than inside Madam Tilbury's little cottage.

There was also the sound of Sander's pipe. He was playing so softly and strangely, that it blended in to the natural sounds, like a different bird. For a few moments, Thandie shut her eyes, just to enjoy the music. And then the real birds started singing.

After a while she opened her eyes and sat up, pulling her blankets around her. The view was the most beautiful she'd ever seen. The moon was still out, mysterious and white in the grey and cloudy morning sky. She could barely see the lake from where they were but the shape of the pine trees was clear, such a dark green that they were nearly black. Distant bird calls rang out in the mountain air. She tried to identify the chirrups and twitters and recognized the chiffchaff and the trill of a bluebird. Other than that, she couldn't untangle one sound from another. Finch would know. He even knew what the birdcall meant – whether they were singing a song to attract a mate, or as a warning. She wondered if Finch, Hetty and Tib were missing her as much as she missed them. She would like to tell them about this stunning morning.

It was a treat for her eyes as well as her ears. The sky was lightening, with yellow patches breaking the cloud cover, and a rose pink streak near the horizon.

Sander was silhouetted against the pink sky. He stopped playing and put his pipe down.

"Astounding," said Thandie. "The birds must sing because of the beauty of the sunrise."

Sander smiled. "No. You have it the wrong way around. It is the beauty of the birdsong that makes the sun rise."

Thandie took a moment to let this sink in. Sander really did love his music. "Where did you learn to play the pipe so well?"

"By listening to the trees, the birds and the babbling brook."

Thandie sighed, stood up and threw a pebble down the mountainside. "Can you please give me the real answer? Not your *I am an adventurer of the world* answer."

Sander raised both eyebrows. "That is the real answer. Well, sort of. Once I had learned the fundamentals – how to blow into the instrument and play the basic notes – I listened to the sounds of nature. To me, the rhythms of life provide the *real* music."

Thandie laughed. "What I meant was, who taught you to blow into the instrument and play the basic notes?"

Sander sighed. "One of my brothers."

"And do you have many brothers?"

"A handful."

"Do you get on?"

"We got on … like brothers, I suppose. Sometimes we got on very well but about half the time we wanted to throttle each other, you know?"

Thandie didn't know. She had no brothers or sisters. But strangely enough, Hetty jumped straight into her thoughts. She wanted to throttle Hetty more than half the time. Probably about eighty percent. But since she had been away, she missed Hetty more than she thought possible. Like a sister, perhaps.

"Are they older or younger than you?"

Sander sighed again. "That is not an easy question to answer."

"How can it be a difficult question?"

"I no longer see my family."

Sander picked up his pipe once again and began to play a complicated tune. Thandie guessed that was the end of this particular conversation. He was frustrating. But then she didn't say much about her family either. Maybe some of his memories, like hers, were too painful to discuss.

Moments later he lowered his pipe. "Do you play?"

Thandie laughed. "A little. My mother taught me. I can play some basic notes, as you would say, but that's about it."

Sander smiled and handed her the pipe. "In that case, I have an exercise for you. Can you play the notes B and A?"

Thandie nodded. They were the first notes she'd been taught. She played, just as her mother had taught her, pressing her fingers carefully over the holes so the notes didn't squeak. Her mother's voice played in her memory. *"Firm fingers, Thandie!"* She was quite pleased with the results, considering that she hadn't picked up a pipe in about three years.

But Sander didn't look unduly impressed. "Now, put that down and listen to the birds again."

Thandie put the pipe down. "They sound lovely – but I said that earlier."

"Shhh! Really pay attention. Find a single voice in the chorus."

Thandie listened. She heard one particular bird trilling in short bursts, sounding a little like a flute. "I can hear one. I think it's a blackbird."

Sander nodded. "He is in fine voice this morning. Now play those notes again. But this time don't think about how hard you are pressing your fingers into the holes or how hard you are blowing.

Just think about that blackbird up in the tree. Call to him."

Thandie laughed. Call to a bird? She felt a little foolish, but did as she was told and thought about the bird as she played. She played the notes more lightly, somehow. A new rhythm came to mind and she played it a few times and then stopped. The birdcall started up again, in the distance, as if in response. Thandie and Sander both laughed. Then the bird sang again.

"Play with him, this time," said Sander. "Don't try to copy his song. Play your own melody but don't get too absorbed in the mechanics of what you are doing. Listen to the bird."

Thandie could only remember one tune. The Essendor song. It had been popular before she was born, at the time of Queen Bia. A minstrel had written it especially for the young queen. Under the reign of Zelos the people had not been allowed to sing or play about the Midnight Unicorn, who had been a loyal protector of the queen and her people, but disappeared when Zelos came to the throne. Still, many sang in secret. Thandie's mother sang it to Thandie in her cradle and taught her to play it on the pipe when she was older. Later, after her mother had disappeared, Zelos had gone, and the unicorn had returned, people had started singing it in the open again. Everyone played it: in the schoolrooms and in the streets. Thandie had played it so often that her fingers remembered. The words looped in her mind as she played.

"In Essendor, at Wintertide,
Wrap up warm and come outside.
As the snow begins to fall,
The unicorn protects us all.
Midnight black against the white,
In the silence of the night,
Take my hand and dance with me,
In Essendor, we're all born free."

It was a strange song to play on an early morning in midsummer and she tried not to think about the memories it stirred. Her first winter at Madam Tilbury's, roasting chestnuts on the fire and eating them so hot that she and the others all got blisters on their fingertips. Learning to play the pipe with her mother by the hearth. Sitting on the roof with Finch and Hetty when Tib was too young to join them, staring into the woods and hoping to catch a glimpse of the Midnight Unicorn.

Thandie pushed the memories away, instead focusing on the tune and playing it for her new friend, the blackbird. This time she played it better than ever before.

When she had finished, Sander raised his eyebrows slightly and smiled. "See? Learning from the birds. Now give me back my pipe. I miss it."

Their music lesson became a regular occurrence, every time they stopped for a break, and at both sunrise and sunset. Thandie enjoyed it and knew she was improving fast, although she would never be as good as Sander. When Sander played, Thandie forgot she was even listening to music; the melodies shut out everything else. She did wonder if the pipe was enchanted, but her own squeaky notes when she blew too hard put paid to that idea. Perhaps it was Sander himself, with his strange ways, who was the enchanted one, not the wooden pipe.

HUNTING
Thandie

When they had finished the last of the food that Thandie had taken from Madam Tilbury's, they picked a few berries and mushrooms. Thandie trusted Sander to know which ones were safe to eat. He was the adventurer, after all.

But berries and mushrooms were not enough to sustain them and by the evening, Thandie's stomach was growling. "Where will we next be able to find proper food?"

Sander looked quite relaxed about it. "It's easy. How do you think I feed myself on most evenings? We will go hunting."

"With what?" asked Thandie. Sander was carrying a lot with him but she had yet to see a bow and arrow or other hunting weapon.

"I seem to remember that you are quite handy with a catapult," said Sander, reaching his hand to his bruised eye. The swelling had gone down but it was still a pale yellow and a little bloodshot.

This was the first time he had mentioned the catapult incident since it had happened. Thandie felt embarrassed, but she refused to admit it and held her chin high. She had been in the right. She took the catapult out of her pocket, immediately thinking of Tib. "I doubt I'd be able to hunt much with this. A sparrow perhaps, or a couple of caterpillars."

"Well then it's lucky I have my pipe. As I explained to you on our first night, I am able to charm most creatures, which will help in our quest for dinner. Come with me and you can watch me in action."

Sander left his bags where they were and pushed his way into some nearby bushes and closely-growing trees. Thandie followed him and they crouched down together, peering out through the branches.

"There is a lot of wildlife at this time of the evening if you know where to search," Sander whispered, pointing to the green slope, where a dozen brown furry creatures the size of beavers, but without the tail or the big teeth, were scurrying about.

They were not the most attractive animals, with large feet and stubby horns behind their rounded ears. Some of them scuttled about seemingly searching for food, while others rose up on their hind legs, alert to danger. "What are they?" asked Thandie.

"Grats. Short-horned grats, by the looks of things. "

"Grats?"

"Yes. They tend to come out at dawn and dusk to search for food. As you've noticed, not many travellers venture this way so they are not used to hunters. Also, they are not particularly bright."

Thandie peered at them. Poor things. "I see. And they're good to eat?"

"They're quite tough but surprisingly tasty."

The creatures on guard looked in the direction of their hiding place and gradually began to disappear behind rocks and into burrows. They were getting away! But Sander seemed unperturbed. He removed his pipe from the sheath on his belt and began to play. He left the cover of the bushes as he did so, ducking his head to avoid the branches, and sat in plain view.

One of the grats stopped suddenly in front of a rock and turned, ears pricked up at the sound of the music. Sander did not look up, did not pay it any attention. It was as if he had not even noticed; he just continued to play. The grat began hopping away from the rest of its pack, in a direct line to Sander. Sander still did not look up but he must have been aware that the grat was approaching, because his tune changed, mimicking the creature's ungainly hops.

It was only when the grat was just a few feet away that Sander made eye contact with the animal, which froze, nose twitching, as if bewitched. Sander continued to play with his right hand and rummaged in his pocket with the other one. He brought out something small and bright. Thandie couldn't see what, but it looked like a feather. He tucked it into the end of the pipe, stopped playing, covered the sound hole and blew hard.

The grat's nose stopped twitching and it fell to the floor, the feather sticking out of its neck.

Sander's tune stopped. The animal was dead.

"As easy as that." Sander turned and grinned proudly as he went to fetch their evening meal.

Thandie didn't grin back.

"I wouldn't concern yourself with it too greatly," said Sander. "The darts have a poisoned tip, so it would have been killed outright. Anyway, grats breed so quickly that their numbers are always increasing and the others probably won't even notice that this one's gone."

Sander had obviously interpreted her reaction as squeamishness, which wasn't strictly accurate.

Although Thandie had felt uneasy watching the encounter, it was not the creature's demise that bothered her. Rather it was the way that Sander had lured the grat to him. When she had watched him just now playing his pipe, sitting on the rock, and looking as if he had no idea there was an audience, she was reminded of the first time she had seen him, outside Essendor's city walls. She had thought that night in Essendor that *she* was the clever one, waiting in the shadows and biding her time to approach. But perhaps he had known all along that she was there and was just waiting for her to approach. Perhaps he had even chosen the most suitable tune.

Sander's music had a power that she was only just beginning

to understand. Perhaps he had lured her to him, just like a humble horned grat. The grat was destined for the pot, but what did Sander have in mind for her?

CHAPTER NINE

ARVALE

Thandie

They trudged around the mountain, following a similar pattern of pipe-playing, walking, resting, hunting and eating. With all the walking and only Sander to talk to, each day felt much longer than usual. They stayed off the road to avoid being seen and to keep shaded from the sun, and the routine seemed to work – they didn't meet a soul. The Grey Mountain gradually became greener as they moved around to the other side. On the third day, they walked all morning and for most of the afternoon. It was the perfect walking weather – dry but not too hot – and they made good progress. By late afternoon, Thandie could see the village of Arvale on the other side of the valley. Positioned by the edge of one of the larger lakes, it was a pretty little place with a church, a tavern, a village square and quaint wooden houses decked with flowers. Even from their position looking down on the village, Thandie could see that people were going about their daily lives, fishing in the lake, chatting in the streets, children playing. They wore colourful clothes and looked … normal.

"I expected Arvale to look sad," said Thandie.

"How could a village look sad?" It was the first thing that Sander had said in some time.

"I don't know. But Arvale has lost three young people to the unicorn – that must surely have an effect on a place of its size. I certainly didn't think it would have such pretty flowers everywhere."

Sander did not reply. He was definitely quieter than usual as he led Thandie along a smaller, higher winding path that bypassed the village and led up the mountain behind. He pointed to a cluster of dilapidated wooden houses nestled in the green slopes. "I believe that Linnell came from over there."

Thandie gazed at the houses. Even from this distance she could sense the melancholy atmosphere. Thandie tried to imagine what it would have been like for Linnell, living in such a place. The views were breathtaking, but there was absolutely nothing here: no tavern, no blacksmith, no shops. It was a lonely place, and looked to be over an hour's walk even from Arvale village. She could see why Linnell might have followed a stranger away, seeking a better life. Thandie herself had dreamed of adventure on numerous occasions but at least she'd had the whole city of Essendor to explore right on her doorstep.

The path grew steeper and they passed cattle grazing in the pastures, a cow barn, a well and an old iron cartwheel. But no people. Apart from the animals, which seemed well cared-for, this place felt abandoned. It was possible that Linnell's father had died – Sander had said he was old – or moved away, although this didn't seem to be the sort of place from which people would move. All the houses were in an unloved state, with broken shutters and peeling paint.

"Do you know which is … was … her house?" she asked Sander.

"No."

They continued along the path and Thandie was relieved when they reached the first house and saw an elderly woman sitting outside on the porch. The place was not abandoned after all. The woman had a woollen blanket over her knees despite the warmth of the day and looked up at them expectantly. Thandie looked at Sander but he did nothing, so she approached the porch herself. "Excuse me, Madam," she said, and the woman stood up with more energy and vitality than Thandie had expected, given her age.

She scrutinized Thandie, looking her up and down slowly. "Can I help you, my dear?"

"We, er..." Again she looked to Sander for support but he was a little way away, scuffing his foot in the dusty track. "We are looking for Linnell's father."

The woman hesitated. For a moment, Thandie thought she was going to give her bad news. Perhaps he *had* died.

"I see," said the old woman, slowly. "Yannick Redfern lives just opposite – right there."

"Many thanks."

"Have you come far?"

"From Essendor."

"I see," she said again. Maybe the woman thought that they brought news of Linnell. Thandie must be careful when speaking to Linnell's father that he didn't get the same impression.

Thandie followed the woman's directions to the house

opposite. Sander continued to hang back, which puzzled Thandie. Why come all this way and then show so little interest? He was probably feeling guilty about having seen Linnell and done nothing, but she wished he could put it aside and support her now.

"Knock loudly," called the woman. "Yannick is a little hard of hearing."

Thandie raised her hand to indicate that she'd heard. She walked up the wooden steps to the house, crossed the small veranda and knocked sharply on the door. She brushed herself down as she waited for someone to answer. She must look a state after travelling for so long. Nobody came. Thandie glanced back at the old woman, who was still watching them from the porch. Surely she would know if Linnell's father had gone out for the day. She looked like the sort of woman who knew everything.

Just as Thandie was about to knock again, the door opened slowly, revealing an old man with a grey beard and tired eyes. His expression was strangely blank and he barely seemed to register them.

"Farmer Redfern?"

The old man didn't respond; he just stood there, blinking. Thandie wondered if the effects of old age had set in. Would this poor man be of any help to them?

"It is nothing urgent," she stammered, not wanting to get his hopes up. "We were just hoping that we could ask you some questions about your daughter, Linnell?" Thandie turned to Sander for support, but although he was now standing behind her, he was looking off in the other direction. "Not that we know where she is," she added quickly.

At the mention of Linnell, something about the man's manner changed and his blue eyes filled with tears. He looked from Thandie to Sander as if seeing them for the first time and ushered them inside. "Come, come." It struck Thandie as a remarkably trusting act. He was still hospitable to strangers, despite everything that had happened.

The house was small, dark. It smelled of damp moss, polished wood, and lost hope.

He led them to the table, where there were only two chairs. "Please, sit."

Sander refused and stood near the door, resting against the wall. Thandie took the nearest seat while Farmer Redfern put a kettle on the stove. "Something to eat," he muttered, as if to himself.

"Please don't go to any trouble, Farmer Redfern," said Thandie.

"Yannick, please," he insisted. "I have some potted meat here. And some bread. Please eat. You have been travelling. You must be weary." He brought the items over with some tin plates and knives. Thandie thanked him and helped both herself and Sander to some food. Sander moved towards the table to eat his but continued to stand. Yannick took the other seat.

"So, you are trying to find my daughter and the others?" He looked interested but weary. "Do you know where she is – my girl?"

Thandie was surprised at how calmly he asked the question. Perhaps others had been to see him in this way before and his hopes had been dashed. She hesitated for a moment before replying. She wanted to tell him everything she knew. About the unicorn in the clouds and about the stolen memories. Thandie was sure she could trust him to keep it to himself; he would do anything to have his daughter back and he wouldn't compromise their quest by giving the information away.

She glanced at Sander, asking the question silently with a raise of her eyebrows, but he shook his head in response: a tiny but definite movement. Could he not speak for himself?

Thandie turned back to Yannick "I'm so sorry, I can't tell you anything about where we are going, but we heard of her whereabouts from a … trusted source. We think that she is still alive."

"I *know* that she is still alive," said the old man. "Many years ago, when my wife died, I knew she had gone. Something was taken from me along with her. But with Linnell…" Yannick trailed off, seemingly unable to put his thoughts into words.

Thandie wanted to say something to make him feel better. "We think – we hope – that we might know where to find them. Anything you can tell us will help."

"You want me to tell you about Linnell." The old man paused, clasping his hands together, eyes roaming around the room as if looking for answers. "Where shall I begin?" he asked.

"At the beginning, I suppose," said Thandie. She turned to Sander for confirmation or some kind of support but he said nothing. It was frustrating.

Yannick looked at his hands and coughed. "The beginning. We thought that we were not to be blessed with children, but then Linnell came along late in our lives. A little miracle. She was just tiny when her mother died. They told me I wouldn't be able to bring her up alone. That I was an old man and she needed a mother. My sister, who lives in the east of the kingdom, would have taken her. But I knew … or I felt … when I looked at her big blue eyes … that she needed me. Or maybe I needed her."

Thandie nodded, tears pricking at her eyes. She had never known her father and she knew what it was like to grow up without a mother. Yannick cleared his throat and continued. "As she grew, she became more like her mother to look at, with beautiful long fair hair, and the same singing voice. But there was always something about her that was her very own – a certain spirit that was pure Linnell. It was as if she were destined for something special—"

Sander's knife rattled on the plate as he placed it back on the table, interrupting Yannick. Thandie gave Sander a sharp look.

"Please, Farmer Redfern, talk us through the day she went missing," said Sander. His voice sounded strangely formal – not like Sander at all. Or at least not like the Sander that Thandie knew.

Yannick stared at him for a moment, as if he too were not taken in by Sander. But he obliged with the story of her disappearance, which he must have relayed countless times over the past two years.

"Linnell liked to take her schoolbooks to the woods, where it was quiet. I didn't mind – she needed her freedom and it had always been such a safe place here. I knew straight away when she didn't return for her noontime meal that something was wrong.

I waited a little and then sent Piet, our farmhand, to look for her. He searched in all the usual places: the barn, the woods, but she was nowhere. He went to Arvale to get more men. A big group came, looking everywhere and shouting her name. I wanted to go but they told me I must wait here in case she returned. They told me she would be back by nightfall.

"I hoped that they were searching properly for my little songbird – my pearl. Of course, I will never know now if I would have done a better job. Perhaps if I had been with them they might have found her."

"No – you did the right thing." Thandie knew those feelings of helplessness and guilt. This man had been too old to search for his daughter. She had been too young to search for her mother.

"When they came back from the search they brought these." Yannick shuffled over to a wooden trunk at the side of the room. He carefully lifted the lid, and with shaking hands brought out a few items. First, some schoolbooks. History. "These were found abandoned by the side of an old fallen tree." He placed them upon the table.

Thandie picked up one of the books with the reverence such an item deserved and leafed through the yellowing pages. The book was familiar to her. It was probably a set text for all the young people in the kingdom. An embroidered bookmark was tucked inside, presumably at the point Linnell had last been reading. Thandie looked at the bookmark first. Linnell's name, surrounded by birds and butterflies. The embroidery was untidy, the stitches large and coming undone. Linnell had presumably made it, and by the looks of things, she was not the sort of girl who enjoyed embroidery. Just like Thandie herself. Linnell had been fourteen when she disappeared – a year younger than Thandie was now. Would they have been friends? Linnell would be sixteen now, of course.

Next, Thandie turned to the page that Linnell had been reading just before she disappeared. A beautiful queen, resplendent in dark blue velvet robes. What had Linnell been thinking when she read this page? And why had she abandoned it?

"I let her go alone to the woods. I thought that she was safe." The old man hung his head, ashamed. Thandie patted his hand. "You weren't to know."

He nodded, as if he had heard these words before, and continued to remove items from the trunk. Another book. A pencil. And a circle of flowers. A flower crown. Brittle, dry and dusty now but five years ago it would have been bright and vibrant. Thandie held it briefly and resisted the urge to place it upon her head.

"They found no other trace of her. They swam up and down the river and all around the lake. They sent out the hounds to take up her trail. But there was nothing. They looked for days. Then they stopped looking. They told me that she had probably run away of her own accord, taken up with a sweetheart. But I knew that my Linnell wouldn't do that. She was ... is ... a good girl."

Sander remained silent, intent on the items on the table. He seemed so distracted and she guessed that his thoughts were at the castle in the clouds, the last time he had seen Linnell. He could not, of course, share this information with the old man.

Thandie nodded at Yannick, encouraging him to continue.

"She used to dream of better things, of course, but she would never have gone without telling me."

Thandie understood. She knew what it was like to have dreams of getting away.

"I thought something must have happened. I kept thinking this way. Then a few months later, Piet brought back the news from Arvale about *their* missing children. I knew straightaway when I heard. Three more children, all different ages, vanished. It wasn't just my Linnell any more. She was just the first."

THE LIST
Thandie

Thandie ran her fingers lightly over the flower crown and the books, objects which made Linnell seem real to her. She felt even surer now that Linnell was alive and that she would be the one to bring her back.

"Would it be acceptable to you if we took these with us? I promise that I will return them safely to you." Thandie did not say *with your daughter* but the unspoken words hung between them.

Yannick nodded and Thandie carefully placed the things in her bag.

"Is there anything more you can tell us about your daughter, Yannick? Any way that we would know her, or she would know us – so that we could show ourselves to be friends?"

The old man ran a hand over his face wearily.

"There was a song. A song she used to like. She would sing it all the time. I wrote it for her mother many years ago and then it became her own. Now that I have lost them both, it belongs only to me."

The man reached inside the trunk once again, and this time he pulled out a wooden fiddle. It looked basic, hand carved with four strings, but the moment he played a single note, Thandie could tell he was an expert. Even Sander came closer and looked as though he was finally listening. Yannick played a few experimental notes, tuning the instrument, then began a slow tune, to which he sang along.

"To me you are a diamond,
To me you are a pearl,
To me you are an emerald,
To me you are the world.

"I'd give you a diamond to shine the whole day long,
But I have no diamond, so I give to you this song."

Tears sprang up unexpectedly in Thandie's eyes. Yannick's voice was warm and rich with emotion, despite a few cracks due to his age. By the time he reached the second verse, the high-pitched, woody sound of Sander's pipe joined the deeper tones of the fiddle.

"To me you are the mountain,
To me you are the sea,

To me you are the forest,
You're everything to me."

Yannick looked sharply at Sander as they played. Then, when he had finished the tune, he lowered his fiddle and stared suspiciously at him. "You know this tune?"

Sander shrugged and smiled his most charming smile. "I always pick up a tune quickly."

Linnell's father kept staring as if he didn't quite believe Sander, but Thandie broke the tension by resting her hand gently on the old man's arm. "It's true," she said. The man's eyes softened once more and the suspicion fell from his face. He played a couple more sad, lilting songs, Sander playing along too.

When they had finished, there was silence. The absence of the music hung in the air.

"Do you know anything about any of the others who went missing? From Arvale, or elsewhere?" asked Thandie.

Yannick packed his fiddle away in its case. "You have all their names? Of the stolen ones?"

"No," said Thandie, surprised. "I don't even know the exact number of people missing. Do you?"

"Oh yes. I needed to know. Our farmhand, Piet, travels to all the nearby villages. He tells me what is going on and I take note. Would you like to hear their names?"

"Yes," said Thandie, excited at this new information. She expected Linnell's father to rummage in the trunk as he had done with the flower crown, but instead he closed his eyes and began to recite the list of names.

"Linnell Redfern, age fourteen, near Arvale.
Posy Tweed, age thirteen, Arvale.
John Fairton, age eleven, Arvale.
Ivy Medway, age eleven, Arvale.
Aldo Strood, age ten, from the Elithian circus camped near Essendor…"

"Stop a moment – let me get my pencil," said Thandie. She wrote down the names at the back of her book, scrawling them out as Linnell's father recited the rest, like a poem, or a prayer.

The old man, with his milky eyes and trembling hands, knew all forty-three names and ages by heart.

Just hearing their names made it all the more real for Thandie. Each one of these names was a real person, with a home and a family just like Linnell. Each one of these children deserved to be found. She glanced over at Sander to see what his reaction was to the list, but he was looking down at the tabletop and it was hard to tell.

When Thandie had finished writing, Yannick put his hand on her arm once again. "Just find her. If you can," he said.

Before meeting Yannick, Thandie had wanted desperately to find the stolen ones, but now she knew she had to. "If it's not too much trouble, do you think you could write down those words for me? The words from the song?"

Yannick obliged, using the pencil stub and a page torn from the old schoolbook. His writing was spidery and faint but legible, just. He folded the paper very small and tucked it into her palm. "Keep this safe, missy. Just for your eyes, you understand?"

LINNELL'S ROOM
Thandie

When they announced their intention to leave, Yannick shook his head. "You must shelter here tonight."

They didn't protest. They had already walked for a several days and it made sense to rest before continuing their journey.

Thandie was surprised that he should extend his hospitality so generously. She supposed that in a remote place like this there were no inns or boarding houses, so people just naturally offered up their homes.

Yannick directed Sander out to the barn, where he would have shelter and a warm hay bed. Thandie would have liked to have a private conversation with him, to ask him why he had been so withdrawn, but that would have to wait until they were on the road again.

Then Yannick showed Thandie to Linnell's old room and bid her goodnight. Her eyelids were heavy. The hour was still early and the sky not yet completely dark but, after her unsettled night under the stars, Thandie's missed sleep and early starts were catching up with her.

It was a tiny room, barely bigger than a cupboard, with the same wooden floors that ran throughout the cottage, a washstand and a single iron bedstead. There was a single shelf on the wall above the bed, which was empty, and a nightstand next to the bed which held a simple lamp. None of Linnell's personal things were here; Thandie supposed the Redferns didn't have many possessions in the first place and anything she did own was hidden away in the trunk that Yannick had shown them. Why had he locked them away like that? Maybe to preserve them, to keep them from dust, or maybe because he could not bear the constant reminders.

There was one item of interest: a small framed picture hung above the bed head. Thandie inspected it more closely. It was a watercolour, in rosy tones, which showed a young woman cradling a girl on her lap. The woman, who was leaning in towards the child as if to plant a kiss on her head, had fair hair, wound around her head in a thick plait. The girl was also blonde and reached a small hand up towards her mother's cheek. It was a pretty, touching painting , which Thandie assumed was of Linnell and her mother. Yannick had said that Linnell's mother had died when she was a young child. Perhaps this image was painted just before her death. Thandie wasn't sure if she would want such a reminder of her own mother hanging on the wall. She didn't have any images of her mother, anyway, apart from those in her mind, which she kept locked tightly away.

Thandie wanted to find out as much as she could about Linnell: to discover what had driven her away from her home on a whim. She felt that if she could understand that, then she would be a bit closer to being able to free her from the unicorn. She moved towards the washstand, in front of the oval wall-mirror.

She slowly unbraided her hair, running her fingers through the crimped locks as they loosened. It sounded from Yannick's description as though she and Linnell looked nothing alike. Linnell was fair and delicate; she was dark and strong. Yet there were similarities as well. They both braided their hair. They had both lost their mothers. Until Linnell's disappearance, they were also both stuck in places with no clear route out; they both wanted, one way or another, to find a better life.

Thandie took her brush and ran it through her hair repeatedly from root to tip, enjoying the tingling of her scalp. When her hair was brushed and shining, she stayed a little longer, looking at her own image in the mirror, and the framed picture on the wall behind.

Thandie was literally treading in Linnell's footsteps: looking in her mirror, sleeping in her bed. But how did their stories differ? And would the ending of Thandie's story be different to Linnell's?

Those were the question that whirled around Thandie's mind as she stepped across the creaking floorboards, between the cool sheets, and drifted into a deep sleep.

SUNBEAM
Thandie

It was just Thandie and Yannick at the breakfast table. They sat outside, on the wooden veranda. Thandie guessed that Sander would be awake and ready by this time, but he chose to stay away in the solitude of the barn, no doubt still avoiding any conversation. Thandie and Yannick each had a morning bowl of oats and creamy milk brought to them by the farmhand, Piet.

An old birdcage hung on a chain from the beam above. Thandie hadn't noticed it when they had approached the house the day before. It looked as though it had once been painted white, but the paint had chipped away in most places, and it was speckled with the beginnings of rust. The cage door was open; Thandie absent-mindedly gazed at it.

Yannick put down his spoon. "She had a pet canary she called Sunbeam. A sweet little thing he was – bright yellow with black beady eyes – and the singing! He used to chirp and whistle all day long. I used to say that they were a good pair and I didn't know who sang more – her or that bird."

"He sounds lovely."

"He was. She would let him fly around the place and he

162

would land back on her hand." Yannick smiled, remembering.

Thandie brought a spoonful of oats to her mouth and chewed. "It must have been sad for you when he died."

"Oh, but he didn't die, you see. The night that Linnell," he paused, "left, the bird stopped singing. All his trills and happy whistles just came to an end. He wouldn't come out of the cage, wouldn't do anything. I couldn't bear to see him sitting silently in his cage. It made everything worse, somehow."

Thandie continued chewing and nodded. She had been right that the reminders of Linnell were too painful for Yannick.

"I let the bird out and I shooed him away. He fluttered back a couple of times but I wouldn't let him back in the cage. I just kept on shooing. After a while, he took the hint and flew off. The last I saw of him, he was headed towards the mountains in that direction."

Thandie looked in the direction the old man was pointing as if she expected to see a pair of little yellow wings beating in the sky. "Maybe he went to find her," she said.

Yannick patted her hand. "Maybe."

They finished eating, then Thandie gathered her belongings and they waited for Sander on the porch. The days had been so hot but right now, the early morning air was fresh and the view was spectacular.

Yannick suddenly spoke, breaking the silence of the morning. "You are cleverer than my daughter, you know."

It was such a surprising thing for the old man to say, that Thandie didn't quite know how to respond. She waited quietly for him to explain.

"Linnell was … is … many things. Beautiful. Practical. Honest. Gifted: such a voice, you wouldn't believe. But … when she was here… I did sometimes worry that she didn't have the ability to think things through as she should. She accepted things at face value and was perhaps a little … gullible."

What exactly was he telling her?

Yannick looked at Thandie with his kind blue eyes. "I see that you are different. You have a spark about you. That is why I don't think that you will make the same mistakes."

He stopped and stared at the Grey Mountain.

"Go on," prompted Thandie, softly.

"Piet was working high up in the fields the day that Linnell went missing…"

"Yes?"

"…And he says he heard something strange coming from the woods."

"What was it?" asked Thandie, in a whisper, although she already knew.

"He heard someone playing a pipe. Beautiful music, he said, not like anything he'd ever heard before."

Thandie nodded. She understood.

She hoped that he was right and that she was cleverer than Linnell. She sensed that she might need to be, to stay ahead in this game. Just as when she played Merels with Tib, she should think about her own strategy, but she should never take her eyes off what the other person was doing, or there might be a nasty surprise ahead.

Sander appeared then, from around the corner, looking all ready for the journey in his patchwork jacket, bags slung over his shoulder. He waved from a distance, not looking as if he was going to come back and thank Farmer Redfern for the hospitability. Thandie raised her hand in response, although the sight of him made her skin tighten. She made her way to the porch steps, but Yannick caught her elbow.

"They're out there somewhere, you know. Linnell and all those others. There's something special about you, child. You'll find my little songbird, won't you?"

Thandie nodded. "I will do my very best."

Impulsively, she kissed Yannick lightly on his cold, wrinkled cheek and then followed Sander out into the sun.

CHAPTER TEN

CONFESSION

Thandie

As they left the Redfern's property, Thandie couldn't look at Sander. Yannick could have been wrong about the pipe playing – Piet might have heard something or someone else – but deep down she knew that he was guilty. There was no other explanation for the way he acted. He had left without saying a proper farewell to Farmer Redfern and had acted so strangely in the cottage last night.

She wanted his side of the story – she wanted him to tell the truth – but at the moment he was barely talking at all. She decided to start with a less challenging question.

"How was the barn?"

"Luxurious compared to what I'm used to. And your bed for the night?"

"Very comfortable. I feel ready for the next part of the journey."

They walked a few more paces, in the opposite direction from which they had approached the houses, towards the woods and the mountains.

"So, which way now? How does one reach a castle in the clouds?"

Her voice sounded strange, even to her. Sander kept walking. He seemed keen to leave Linnell's home behind him.

"There are different ways, all of them involve going up as high as we can. The castle in the clouds is above Mount Opacus over there, but the mountain itself is impossible to climb, with long stretches of vertical slopes and sections of rock that might collapse at any time."

Thandie stared hard in the direction that Sander was pointing, but she could see no castle or sign of a castle. Just a tall mountain and thick white cloud.

"So how *do* we reach it?"

"We have choices. We could climb the neighbouring mountain and pull ourselves across in a basket…"

"Sounds tiring."

"Yes, and it is hot weather for such an expedition… We could build a hot air balloon… Or we could climb the golden tree…"

"A golden tree! You're making this up now."

"I'm not, really."

The path forked ahead and they paused, putting their bags on the ground between them. Sander's brow furrowed and he clearly had something on his mind. He looked guilty. She couldn't put off her questions any more.

"Which way did you take Linnell?" Thandie's hands were shaking with anticipation but she asked the question gently. She wanted to give Sander a chance to tell her and she sensed that if she were too forthright, he would back away.

He looked down at his feet. Was he going to deny it? Or maybe he would be angry; she had already seen the way he reacted when he felt threatened. She reached in the pocket of her dress, feeling the reassuring Y-shape of Tib's catapult.

Sander took a deep, shuddering breath. The look on his face reminded her of how he had been the first night she met him, back in Essendor. He looked as if the truth was hurting him physically.

Then he spoke in a rush. "I didn't take her. She came willingly. But I led her to the unicorn. I had promised him that I would find someone…"

Thandie felt sick.

Sander carried on with his confession. He told her how he had met Linnell in the woods, about her wonderful singing voice and about the promises he'd made. He told her how they had walked up to the castle and how he had pulled her across in the basket and left her to continue alone while he waited on the other mountain peak.

"I felt so bad about what I was doing that I couldn't bring myself to go with her. I didn't want to see. But I waited there for hours. When she did not return, I knew that he had taken her. I went to the castle then. To see her. And the rest of it is just as I told you: he had taken her memories. She no longer recognized me or knew anything about her old life."

"Why?" Thandie whispered. "Why did you do it?"

Sander hunched over as if in pain. "The unicorn knows what people want. And I too wanted something very, very badly. A long time ago. Something that he gave to me."

"What? What did you want from him?"

Sander didn't answer and Thandie didn't press him further;

there were other things she needed to know first.

"So you weren't hiding from the unicorn that first night in Essendor. You were lurking – waiting in the dark for some likely prey?"

Sander nodded. "But as soon as we started talking, I knew that you were different. I wanted to tell you everything."

"But you did not. Why?"

"You would not have come with me," said Sander.

Thandie buried her face in her hands. It felt good. She breathed deeply. He was probably right. She wouldn't have done. And she wished he had not told her now.

Sander nodded. "It seemed too much. Too huge. Unforgivable. But I am sorry. So very sorry. I wish I had not done any of it. I wish I had never met the unicorn. And I do want to put everything right."

"And what about the others? Are you responsible for all those missing people – for taking them away from their families?"

Sander shook his head. "No – what happened afterwards is just as I told you. After I led Linnell away, I was so ashamed and filled with guilt. But the unicorn wanted more people. He was thirsty for more memories. I said I would. I promised him that I would lead more people to him, just to get away, but I wouldn't… I couldn't do that again. I escaped from him and I have been hiding ever since. But now, I am ready to face him again, whatever than means."

Sander couldn't meet her gaze. Was this because of his shame – or was he still lying to her now? It was impossible to tell. "Why didn't you tell someone before? You could have prevented all those other kidnaps. Forty-two people!"

"I know!" cried Sander, kicking out at a nearby tree. "I have been so weak and I hate myself. Seeing Linnell's father was the most difficult thing I have ever done. But don't you see, I couldn't tell anyone without confessing my part in the crime?"

"So who *did* steal the others away?"

"I don't know. He must have other people working for him now: people like me. Perhaps he did all along."

Thandie didn't know whether to believe this. Sander sounded as though he was telling the truth, but then he had sounded as though he was telling the truth back in Essendor. Could this young boy really be responsible for all those people going missing?

"Until I met you I didn't know what to do," Sander continued, "but you told me if I had done something wrong then I should try to put it right. If we free the people together then you can take the credit and I can fade away. I can go back to being a simple adventurer."

Thandie sighed. She was not sure she could forgive what he had done. People made mistakes, but leading someone away, into danger, was more than a mistake. It was an intentional act. Still, he did seem genuinely sorry. And the only way he could go even halfway towards putting things right would be to free the people.

Thandie's mind whirled with the impossibility of her situation. Yannick had said that she was clever. But to continue on her journey now, with a self-confessed kidnapper, was surely not the choice of a clever person.

On the other hand, she knew him now. Surely she was a good enough judge of character to know that the person she had spent all those hours playing the pipe with, had shared bread and conversation with, was not evil. He *had* confessed. And he did appear truly guilty. If she walked away now, Sander would disappear into the forest and the chance of finding the stolen ones would be gone forever. She thought of Yannick's weary face and the hope in his eyes as she left. She thought of Tib, and how proud he would be. She thought of her mother, who could be out there somewhere, just waiting to be found.

THE DECISION
Sander

Sander stared at her, awaiting her decision.

She raised her chin. "I will continue on this journey, but I have to know that any question I ask you, you will answer with complete honesty."

Sander nodded. "I promise you that." His insides leaped happily. This girl Thandie was either very brave or very stupid.

QUESTIONS
Thandie

"Where exactly did you meet Linnell?" asked Thandie.

Sander turned, frowning. "I just told you – here."

"But right here on the path? Or up by the house?"

"Why do you want to know?"

"I am trying to get the picture straight in my mind."

Sander sighed. "I met her in the woods."

"In the woods? So she was studying?"

Sander closed his eyes briefly and then opened them. He

looked pained again. "She was singing."

"Singing, of course," said Thandie. She knew enough about Linnell now to know that is exactly what she would have been doing when she should have been studying her schoolbooks. She would have been taken in by Sander's pipe-playing and his tales of adventure.

Thandie still had many more questions that she would like to ask: Did Sander spend long persuading Linnell to accompany him? Did he feel bad at the time about what he was doing? And what was the deal that he had made? But he stood hunched, hat pulled low, and she sensed that this was not the time to ask these questions. She would wait until a time when he was a little more relaxed.

"Which way from here, Sander? You were telling me the different ways – a golden tree, a flying balloon – remember?"

Sander seemed relieved by the change of subject and launched straight in to an explanation of the journey. "Climbing the neighbouring mountain is the most direct route from here – we could be there by the end of the day – but it is a hazardous climb."

"We're not in any particular hurry, are we? And we still have some planning to do."

"I suppose you are right. In that case, we could see if we

could find the flying wolves. We would have to go via Wending, which is a couple of days' walk around the lake, but it is more scenic and certainly an easier option. We would save our strength for when we meet with the unicorn."

Thandie laughed. "Did you say flying wolves? How could you forget to mention them before?"

"Well, it is the longer option, time-wise. But I take it from your expression that you like the idea?"

"Of course!" Thandie thought only how much she would like to see such an unusual animal. She would worry later about the practicalities of approaching them.

Sander smiled back, for the first time since they had been at Yannick's. "Well then, flying wolves it is. The most likely place to find them is in Wending, which is right here, down into the valley and around the lake to the other side."

They walked the rest of the way in near silence, commenting just occasionally on the view from the path or the sight of a rare butterfly.

OLD AGE

Thandie

And so the journey continued. Yannick had equipped them with the flower crown, the history books and the list of names but also generous supplies of food and water from the well. If all went to plan, then they would not need to hunt again before they reached the castle.

They walked.

Strangely, since his confession, Thandie felt more relaxed in Sander's company. The lie had always been there, like a wall between them, and now that it had lifted, Sander seemed less guarded. Thandie herself felt less suspicious and freer as a result.

They continued west on the lower mountain slopes, walking around Arvale to the north, and past smaller lakes. She spotted a waterfall in the distance. "Look over there, Sander – a waterfall."

Sander nodded. "Ah yes, I know that waterfall well. There is a magical helmet behind, guarded by a ghoulish skeleton army—"

Thandie was irritated with him all over again and interrupted his story. "—Of course you know the waterfall, how silly of me to point out a feature in the landscape to you. I shall remain quiet and let you be the tour guide."

Sander lowered his head, instantly quiet, and Thandie felt bad for her outburst. His superior way was not his fault and he *had* seen a lot of the kingdom. "I'm only joking," she said. "Do tell me about the waterfall."

He looked up again. "Really? Well I was just saying that there are giant sapphires there, guarded by a sorcerer's curse—"

Thandie stopped him again. "Which one is it: a sorcerer's curse? Or a skeleton army?"

Sander took off his hat and ran his hand through his hair. "I don't know – both! I haven't actually visited that very waterfall. There are so many…"

He trailed off and Thandie said nothing more. The waterfall had lost its appeal. They continued walking and she thought more about Sander and the inconsistencies in his stories. Yannick had said that Linnell had been gone for two whole years. Thandie had always guessed that Sander was about her age, but that couldn't be right; that would have made him only twelve years old when Linnell went missing and younger still when he met the unicorn for the first time. Possible, but unlikely. Sander must be older than he looked. Thandie supposed he could be sixteen or seventeen. Eighteen at a push. That would explain why he sometimes acted in such a superior way: a bit like Hetty with her extra six weeks.

"How old are you, Sander?"

He stopped in his tracks and turned around. "Why do you ask?"

"And why are you answering my question with one of your own? It is almost as if you are trying to avoid telling me."

He resumed walking. "No, I am happy for you to know my age – it's just you asked out of the blue and it seemed to me there must be a reason for your sudden interest."

"I was just thinking that you must be older than I'd first thought, unless you first met the unicorn when you were a small boy. I can't imagine Linnell being led away by someone much younger than her."

"I would rather not talk about Linnell. I have told you the part that I played – can't you be content to leave it at that?

There was a pause. Thandie could tell that Sander was uncomfortable but there was so much more she wanted to know. Since their visit to Farmer Redfern, Linnell seemed even more real to her and she wanted to understand how someone could abandon the one member of their close family who loved them dearly.

"What did you say to her, to persuade her to go with you?"

Sander did not look her in the eye. "I didn't have to persuade her. She wanted her wishes granted more than anything else."

"More than her love for her father?"

"I don't know what Linnell thought. I can only tell you what I thought."

Thandie sighed. "And what did you think, Sander? What did the unicorn give you to make it worth it?"

He looked at her with tears welling up in his eyes. "I don't feel I can tell you that right now. It won't help us find Linnell or the others."

"I just want to know as much as I can. It was so sad seeing such an old man on his own and missing his daughter."

"Old age is always sad."

"It doesn't have to be. Not if you have a healthy mind and body and you're surrounded by love. I just hope that when I am that age I have people around to take care of me."

"I will never grow old."

"We all have to grow old, Sander. Animals, plants, trees, even. We have a finite time on this earth."

"Not me. If I find myself in danger of growing old then I shall throw myself off a high mountaintop."

"Don't say things like that. What about the people who care about you?"

"There is no one I care about. And no one left who cares about me. And that is the way I like it."

Sander strode off ahead, putting some distance between him and Thandie. Which was fine. The conversation was a little too intense and if this journey was going to continue, she needed to find a way to walk with him in relative peace.

It was only after they had travelled another mile in silence that Thandie realized Sander had never answered her questions; she still didn't know how old he was, or the deal that he had made with the unicorn.

CHAPTER ELEVEN

THE LAUGHING LAKE

Thandie

The sun shone high and white in the sky and Thandie's bag weighed twice as much as usual. Her feet were hot, her legs were dusty, her face glowed with sweat and her head itched.

It was the hottest it had been since they left Essendor. They walked a few miles without talking, looking down through the trees on to a still blue lake. She was grateful when Sander finally suggested they rest for a while. They found a perfect spot, a clearing sheltered from the trees, and Thandie lay flat on her back enjoying the shade.

"I am so roasting, I could jump in that lake," she said.

"Why don't you? We have time for an hour's break. A swim will revive you and then we can still manage a few more miles before we set up camp. We are making good time and should be at Wending by tomorrow night. I will stay here and plan the route. There is no one around."

Sander didn't look half as hot as she did. He still had his coat on.

A swim was highly tempting. Thandie took a blanket from her bag, then moved the diary and reading book from her pocket to just inside the flap to keep them dry. She threw her travelling cape over the top. She kept her catapult with her just in case.

She walked down the hill, through the trees and towards the lake.

A bird flew past and she caught a bright flash of yellow before it disappeared into the trees. She thought of Sunbeam, Linnell's canary, and wondered if he was out there somewhere, singing away with his new bird friends.

Down by the lake, she found a cluster of bushes that would provide good cover. She stripped down to her underclothes, confident that nobody could see, and unplaited her hair. An outcrop of flat grey rocks would provide the perfect platform to launch herself into the water. She made her way there and sat with her knees drawn up, watching the water gently lapping against the rocks. She dipped her toe in tentatively. It was warm, heated by the summer sun. Even when she lowered her leg in up to her knee it was cooler but not cold, so she screwed her eyes tightly shut and jumped in. Her heels slid against the slimy surface of the submerged rocks and she kicked away from them out into the open water. *Now* it was cold. She kept moving, swimming with her head out of the water as she had learned to do in the river at Essendor. Soon, her body had adjusted to the temperature and she swam more freely, wetting her face and her hair and trying not to let the water boatmen and other insects bother her. She swam more freely now, enjoying the cleansing feeling of the water. Pockets of the lake were warm from the sun and she swam to those, avoiding the cooler, shadowy areas. She felt her worries and anxieties wash away along with the grime she had accumulated on the journey.

After a while, she turned on to her back and floated, squinting up into the sun. This was her very favourite way to be in the water, lying on the surface of the lake as if it were a flat meadow, or a mattress. She hadn't been able to swim until very recently. Her mother could not swim herself and had a fear of being close to open water. But Madam Tilbury insisted that all four children should learn. "There's enough for me to worry about with you noisy rabble without thinking you might fall into the river and drown. The Midnight Unicorn cannot always be there to fish people out."

She had set up a stool in the kitchen and they had taken turns to lie on top of it, belly down, moving their arms and legs like young frogs. This had been the cause of much merriment, but Finch, who could already swim, had insisted that the only proper way to learn was in the water.

In the woods just outside Essendor, the river ran into a still pool, deep enough to swim in but shallow enough for Tib's feet to reach the bottom should they need to. Finch had taught them all to float first, lying on their backs with their arms stretched out like stars. Hetty had struggled, floundering and complaining about the water going up her nose, but Thandie found it easy. She could even lie with her arms folded behind her head, or with her knees tucked up to her chest.

"Once you can float on the water, then all you have to do is move your arms and legs a little and you're swimming," said Finch. He was right, and Thandie had become a good swimmer, although floating like a star was still her favourite thing. She didn't get much of a chance to do it back in Essendor, though. If she relaxed for too long, then one of the others – usually Tib – would stage an underwater attack.

But here, in the shadow of the mountains, there was no Tib to prevent her floating for as long as she liked. She may have been on a life-risking mission to save dozens of missing people, but she had never felt more relaxed. She laughed aloud at the thought.

And then the strangest thing happened.

The lake laughed back. She heard giggles and felt the water rise and fall beneath her, like a soft belly jiggling with laughter. It was a fun sound but, still, it shook her from her relaxed state. She splashed into an upright position, treading water and looking all around. She didn't know what she was looking for as it hadn't sounded like a person laughing; it had sounded like the lake itself. Perhaps the sound came from fairies or water sprites. Now, a low hum emanated from under the water.

"He-llo?" she questioned tentatively, continuing to look around her.

"Hello!" called a voice, or what must have been a dozen voices. High, pretty voices. Maybe it was fairies. The noise was friendly but still, Thandie didn't trust anything that kept itself hidden when it spoke to her. She turned on to her front and began swimming back to the water's edge, pulling back hard with her arms.

The water shook with laughter again, this time rippling so forcefully that Thandie was sent riding backwards on a wave. Before she had time to recover, a group of colourful creatures burst out from the water and into the air, zipping past her ears and over her head. She ducked and then turned around to watch them swoop and dive into the water. Fish! There were maybe fifty colourful, giggling fish and the humming sound was coming from their tiny, reverberating wings. Thandie treaded water, admiring the rainbow sheen of their scales and their speed and agility in both the air and the water. They seemed to want to be near her. A group of them encircled her at waist level, arching out of the water and splashing back in. She reached out a hand to stroke one as it flew by and it screeched delightedly and squirmed like Tib did when she tickled him. Then the others wanted to be tickled and swarmed around her crying "Me! Me! Me!" and all Thandie could hear was humming and giggling and high fishy voices and all she could feel was delicate wings fluttering on her arms and it seemed as though she had been transported to their magical watery world. Every time they laughed, she laughed, which made them laugh harder.

After just a few minutes, another shout went out among the fish "Rain! Rain! Rain!" and Thandie realized they were right; the sky had darkened and it was raining. Sudden, heavy raindrops that plopped from the sky into the lake, causing beautiful spotted patterns on the water's surface. The fish swooped down under the water and disappeared from view, without saying goodbye. She wondered why they minded a drop of rain: weren't they used to water? Thandie found it refreshing. She turned her face towards the sky and enjoyed the gentle massage of the raindrops on her skin. But then the rain grew heavier and almost painful and Thandie understood why the little fish, with their delicate wings, would prefer to hide underwater. She stayed in the lake until the rain had stopped but the fish did not return and she felt strangely lonely.

She swam to the edge and heaved herself out on to the flat rocks. Almost immediately she began shaking violently. It was strange to feel so cold on such a hot summer's day. She wrapped herself in a blanket and huddled under a tree. She was glad she'd been for the swim. It was just what she'd needed and would rejuvenate her for the journey ahead. She dressed, her numb fingers fumbling with the fastenings, and walked back to the camp. By the time she got there, the rain had cleared.

Sander had packed everything neatly away and kept it all dry under some bushes. Now he was cleaning his pipe.

He looked up at her. Her hands were still shaking violently and she squeezed them into her armpits.

"Your lips are blue — are you cold?"

Thandie nodded, teeth chattering.

"Lets get moving straight away," he said, handing her bag to her. "It is possible to get ill from a drop in temperature, even on a summer's day.

Thandie laughed. "I am just a little cold."

"Still, it is best not to sit still for too long."

HUMMINGFISH
Sander

On the way, Thandie told him what she had seen. "Those will be the hummingfish," he said. He had seen them plenty of times. "They are attracted to human laughter. Were you laughing?"

"I'm not sure," said Thandie, looking embarrassed at the idea she would be laughing on her own.

"Did they swim around you in a circle?"

Thandie looked disappointed that he had guessed this detail, and stopped her excited chatter. That was a shame. Sander felt he had seen everything there was to see and heard everything there was to hear. Hearing Thandie talk about it made him feel as if he were experiencing it for the first time all over again. He wanted her to continue.

"I've never seen them myself," he lied. "What were they like?"

Thandie told him about the laughter that made her laugh, the echoing that sounded like it was coming from the trees and he nodded, interested, as if he had not seen this himself countless times before. He liked to see her in animated storytelling mode. Her enthusiasm reminded her of his own, when he had started on his journey. When everything was new and everything was an adventure. Now he felt he had seen it all. Maybe he would never have that feeling of newness ever again.

DIARY
Thandie

After the sudden downpour, the sun soon returned and she was warm again. They walked for a couple of miles, Thandie plaiting her hair as they went. They were both hungry and so they stopped in a grassy clearing for another short break. While they ate, Thandie reached into the pocket of her dress for her diary. She had been planning to write an account that evening, but decided to do it now instead, as she could hardly wait to describe her lake swim. She knew that Tib would ask her to name all the colours of hummingfish and she wanted to record them while they were still fresh in her memory.

As she felt in her empty dress pocket, she remembered her diary wasn't there: she had put it in the top of her bag when she went for her lake swim. She opened the top flap and her reading book fell out, but not the diary. She ran her hand underneath, feeling for the soft leather cover in vain.

She felt a creeping sense of dread. She knew she couldn't have lost her diary: the flap of the bag had been tightly buckled. She ran her hand around the insides of the bag and then tipped the contents out on to the floor.

Sander looked up. "What are you looking for?"

"My diary." Thandie scrutinized his face. Sander was always very interested in what she was writing and he had been left alone with it for a good hour.

"Ah, the precious diary. Perhaps it has been taken by elves who will fastidiously copy out your wise words and distribute them to all four corners of the kingdom. *Thandie's Thoughts*, it could be called. You will be rich."

Thandie was not in the frame of mind for teasing of this nature. The diary was precious to her and couldn't be replaced. She continued to search through the pile from her bag, shaking out her clothes one by one. "It's not here. I know I left it here when I went for a swim."

"Perhaps it fell out along the way, or when I moved our things into the bushes," said Sander, more concerned now.

Thandie shook her head. "The bag was tightly fastened and the reading book is still here. It could not have done. Did anyone else come to the camp while you were there?" She knew they had not, as he would have mentioned it.

He shook his head and she felt herself beginning to shake again, as she had done when she had emerged from the cold water, but this time it was anger. There was only one explanation for what had happened to the diary: Sander had stolen it. The idea of him reading her private thoughts incensed her. "Did you take it?"

Sander laughed. "No, I did not."

"This is not a laughing matter!"

"And I am not amused."

Thandie put her hands on her hips. "Then prove it. Turn out your own bag."

Sander raised an eyebrow. "Really?"

Thandie nodded. "You've always been interested in what I'm writing." Sander upended his bag so that the contents spilled on to the ground. He did not have many possessions. A money pouch, a comb. No book of any kind.

"It's not here – see?"

Thandie crumpled and sat on the grass. She felt suddenly broken. She didn't know what to believe. "It's not just my diary. The people's names were in there and the song from Linnell's father was tucked inside. How are we going to free them without all that information?"

Sander shrugged. "I'm not sure that all of that would have helped, anyway."

Thandie ran through some of the names. " There was Linnell

of course, and Posy Tweed from Arvale. Then there was a John or a Jack. And an Ivy. The boy from the circus – Aldo, or was it an Eldo? And then the Essendor ones: Clover Malling, Lilith Grain and Tonno Green. But that's about all I can remember. Only about six or seven names out of forty-three! Why didn't I memorize the list?" Thandie put her head in her hands and mumbled. "What are we going to do?"

"Why don't we retrace our steps – see if it's fallen out along the way?" Sander suggested.

Thandie shook her head. "I won't find it that way. We have been walking cross country – we'd never find the same path again."

She was still struggling to believe that this was as simple as a lost diary. She studied her feet, trying not to look at Sander's innocent expression. If he had taken it – what then? Would she stay on the journey with him? Or make her way back to Essendor alone? Her mind raced like the hummingfish speeding around her in the lake. Why had she even gone with him in the first place? Hetty never would have. Nobody she knew would disappear into the night with a strange man.

Even before she found out about Linnell, she had never been really sure that she trusted Sander. Even now, as he protested his innocence, there seemed to be something a little strange about him. She opened her mouth to tell him all of this. To pour out everything that she felt. After all, she had nothing to lose now. But just as she was about to speak, he put his hand on her shoulder.

"Thandie, I've got something to confess."

Her heart raced. She had been right all along!

He shook his head. "No – I didn't take your diary. But there's something I should tell you – the reason that I didn't take your book. There would have been no point."

"Why?

"I can't read."

READING
Thandie

"You can't read?" Thandie tried to imagine a world without books.

"No. I was never interested in schoolwork and books. I wanted to see the real world. When I was a youngster my mother and brothers tried to make me go but I wouldn't stay in the schoolroom. I found all sorts of ways to escape. Once I climbed up inside the chimney while the schoolmaster was writing on the board. I know my letters – that's about it."

"But you seem so knowledgeable."

"Perhaps so, but nothing I have learned has been from books. My classroom is the world around me."

Thandie sighed and sat down heavily. Sander might have done one bad thing but that didn't mean he was guilty of everything. And she had accused him with no proof whatsoever. "I am sorry. But I don't know where it can be. I am so sure that I didn't take it into the water with me. And I really can't lose that book."

Sander sat down next to her. "That book is probably bobbing about somewhere in the middle of that lake, the pages washed clean. Anyway, what can possibly be inside that's so precious to you? As I said, I'm not sure those names would have helped us."

Thandie sighed again. "My memories." The memories of her mother that threatened to evaporate. The memories that she couldn't seem to share with anyone else.

Sander looked at her for a long time. "Your memories aren't kept in a book, Thandie. They are in here." He tapped his temple. "And in here." He put a hand to his chest. "I can't write my memories down but they are still always with me. Even when I wish that they weren't."

Thandie nodded. She knew this was true. She knew that the memory of her mother wouldn't leave her just because her book was missing but still, she really wanted it back. Perhaps it wasn't really lost. Perhaps it was caught in the lining of her bag or hidden inside a garment. She would have another look in a moment.

She felt bad that she had accused Sander, and wanted to offer an olive branch.

"I could teach you to read, just as you've been improving my pipe playing."

Sander shook his head. "I am too old to learn a new skill like reading. Besides, it is not the sort of skill one can master in a day or two, and our journey is nearly at an end."

"I know lots of people who learned to read at our sort of age," said Thandie, thinking of Finch, poring over his schoolbooks with Madam Tilbury. But Sander didn't reply, so she said no more about it.

CHAPTER TWELVE

WENDING

Thandie

They approached the village of Wending in the middle of the night, after the ordinary folk had gone to bed but before the shepherds and bakers had risen for the day. This suited them, because they could take the quick route through the village to the mountains without the risk of being seen.

The heat had quickly dissipated when the sun went down and it was cold and dark. The village was smaller than Arvale and there was enough moonlight for Thandie to tell it was just as pretty, set on a steep slope with all the houses clustered around the main road. At this hour, all the people were safely tucked up behind shutters and closed doors, and there were few sounds in the cobbled streets. Perhaps there was a curfew in Wending, just like in Essendor.

A dark shadow scuttled past their feet. Thandie started.

Sander didn't flinch. "Just a rat," he said, and she was reminded of what he'd said about being scared of nothing.

Thandie wasn't scared of rats but the unexpected movement put her on edge and she half-expected one of the doors to swing open, or for someone or something to jump out of the shadows. She quickened her pace, wanting to get through this sleeping village and into the mountains beyond.

A low, distant howl sounded. Thandie couldn't tell if it was the wind in the mountains, or an animal. "Was that the wolves?" she whispered.

"Perhaps," said Sander, "although I would expect them to be asleep at this hour. They normally howl just before hunting."

Thandie had heard wolves howling in the forest at Madam Tilbury's although they were just the ordinary type, without wings. "Do the people of Wending know about the flying wolves?"

"Of course. The flying wolf is their sacred animal. But the

villagers do not talk about them widely. If they were to boast about their wolves then no doubt everyone would be here wanting to see them. Some things are best left unspoiled."

They were through the main part of the village now, by an old inn at the edge of the woods, called *The Full Moon*. Its name and a wolf howling at the moon were painted on a sign, which swung from an iron bracket on the side of the building. The place looked deserted, although it was possible the innkeeper and his family were all upstairs in bed.

"I can't quite remember the route from here," said Sander. "It's one of these two paths ahead. Let me have a quick look."

He disappeared into the darkness and Thandie sat on a low bench outside the inn. They had been walking all day and night and she was grateful of the chance to put her feet up. She gazed into the darkness of the trees, where Sander had vanished, and concentrated on listening out for the wolves, but all she heard was the creaking of the sign above her head.

After a time, she stretched her arms and turned her head to relieve some of the tension in her neck. A printed notice nailed to the inn door caught her attention.

WARNING

She got up and moved closer to the door so that she could read the words below.

Sketched roughly under the warning heading was a man or boy in a patchwork coat and pointed hat. The face could have belonged to anyone.

Thandie read the print.

A traveller in brightly coloured garments, playing a pipe, has been reported in these parts. He speaks of unicorns.

There may be a connection to the stolen ones.

If seen, report immediately to the village council and DO NOT APPROACH.

Thandie ripped the notice down and read it twice more. The sounds of a twig breaking behind her made her turn sharply. She folded the notice and stuffed in her pocket, her heart beating quickly.

"What are you looking at?" Sander stood a few yards behind her. She was not sure how long he'd been there.

Thandie's mind raced for a plausible explanation. "I was

wondering if … the tavern was uninhabited or just shut for the night."

"And?"

"I think there are people there." Thandie spoke in a low voice and walked away from the building.

ACTING STRANGELY
Sander

Thandie was acting strangely and he could have sworn that she had something in her hand. She was keeping something from him, but he wasn't going to press her on the matter. No doubt, in time, he would discover what it was.

ONE STEP AHEAD
Thandie

The obvious assumption was that Sander was not just responsible for Linnell's disappearance; he was responsible for the disappearance of all the stolen ones. But Thandie didn't want to jump to conclusions as she had with the diary. She could ask him about it but then he could just deny it, whereas if she kept this to herself then maybe she would be one step ahead. She needed to live with the information, understand it a little better.

Not for the first time, Thandie asked herself the question: if he turned out to be guilty, would she go home, having been so close to the castle in the clouds?

She made the only decision she could. She would follow Sander on the last part of the journey, knowing that if she got this wrong, she might never return. But she wouldn't trust him. She would stay on her guard and be aware of every little thing he said and did. She may be with him, but she was on her own.

FLYING WOLVES
Thandie

The next step was to find the flying wolves.

Sander had explained that the wolves were more likely to be active at dawn or dusk, so they decided to approach them that very morning. There were just one or two more hours of darkness left, and they would catch as much sleep as they could in that time. They climbed further up and looked for somewhere sheltered on the mountainside, near where Sander expected to find the wolves at sunrise.

They rested behind some rocks, wrapped in two blankets each. Thandie was so tired that she managed to sleep in fits and starts but woke as soon as the sun came up.

By the time she got to her feet, Sander was already walking around. He dangled a furry creature by its leg. Another grat victim by the looks of things. Thandie hoped it wasn't for breakfast. The last grat she had tasted was just about edible but she would be happy never to taste one again. She was content to stick to the dry bread they'd brought from Yannick's.

"What's that for?"

"A peace offering. We can offer it to the wolves to show that we don't mean them harm."

"Don't they know you?"

"They do, but food gifts are always gratefully received by wolves."

Sander tied the grat carcass to his bag so that it dangled behind him. "We don't have far to climb. And we are early enough so we don't have to rush. See the plateau just up there? The wolves are bound to appear if we are patient."

The mountains were inky against the salmon-coloured sky and the air was crisp. Thandie tried to ignore her tiredness and the aches in her legs as they trudged up the mountainside. As they got higher, her boots crunched on little patches of ice, which was strange in midsummer.

Thandie had loved the idea of flying wolves. They sounded mysterious, magical. But now that the thought was about to become reality, she was less sure.

"Do the wolves have sharp teeth?" she asked, a little nervously. Sander looked amused. "Yes, they have extremely sharp teeth, designed for ripping through flesh. And strong back teeth for grinding bone. How are you with animals in general?"

Thandie thought for a moment. Back home, there were farmyard animals all around, but they were just part of the scenery. There was the usual livestock at the market. Madam Tilbury had a bad tempered nanny goat out the back. And then there were the animals that Tib brought home. Usually small, bedraggled things that didn't last long: a mouse, a shrew, a hedgehog. But a wolf? That was a different beast all together.

"I don't know. I am from the city, remember. I haven't had too much to do with animals."

"You've ridden a horse though?"

"Yes…" Thandie had ridden a horse, maybe three times in her life and not in the past five years. Hetty was a much more proficient horse rider.

Sander continued to smile. "How funny. You were so keen on the idea of meeting the wolves that I had you down as an animal lover. Not to worry, they will warm to you."

"I hope so," muttered Thandie, pulling a face.

"Just remember that they are wild animals and if they want to kill us then they will." Sander seemed quite cheerful about the idea.

"Thank you for your words of reassurance. I feel so much better now."

"I am merely trying to prepare you as best I can. I've ridden one of the wolves many times before and he knows me, but I've never taken anyone else with me. If you remember just a few simple rules, then no harm will come to you."

"Simple rules. Very well. Tell me once we're settled."

They reached the plateau, which was covered by moss, patches of snow and low green shrubs. They crouched down behind some boulders so that they would not be seen. Sander pointed to a dark archway at ground level in the rocky mountainside a few yards away. "That's their den," he said. "Don't take your eyes off it.

They should venture out soon."

Thandie removed the bags from her back and tried to move in to a position that was comfortable while remaining shielded from view. Sander seemed quite happy to crouch there indefinitely.

"So tell me, what are these rules?" asked Thandie.

"However friendly they appear, these wolves are wild animals. Humans may have mistreated them in the past so they may not trust you. Remember never to turn your back to the wolves so that they don't attack you from behind and keep your eye on them at all times."

Thandie grimaced.

"And don't show fear. They will sense it if you are afraid."

"I'm not afraid, I am not afraid," repeated Thandie in an attempt to convince herself. She breathed on her hands to warm them. "I can't see anything yet."

"They'll be here. You just have to be patient."

Then, just as Thandie's fingers were freezing solid and she was ready to give up and opt instead for the basket pulley system, a little beige-faced, black-nosed animal poked its face out into the world. Thandie nearly squealed with delight at the sight but instead, turned and grinned at Sander. "A cub!"

He nodded, as two more faces joined the first. They sniffed

the morning air for a little while and then ventured out into the clearing. Three playful wolf cubs, with stocky legs and rounded paws. They rolled and tumbled over one another, remaining close and moving as a pack.

"Just the cubs. The adults must have left early to go hunting. We won't need this after all," said Sander, gesturing to the dead grat hanging off his bag.

Another five cubs followed, popping out of the den one by one. They had light beige bodies – darker on the back – and all looked the same, although they clearly had different personalities. One lay on the ground, happy to have the others clambering over it. Another was more dominant, biting its siblings and standing over them. Thandie noticed that they didn't stray too far from the den.

She had never been this close to wolves before. If wolves got too close to the livestock on the farms, they were taught to raise the alarm and chase them away, not to watch from a hiding spot. But now she saw how appealing they were. How like the stray pups that Tib fed in the evening, thinking of them as pets.

"This is the first time I've seen these cubs," said Sander. "The last time I was here they weren't even born; they must only be a few weeks old."

Thandie watched them playfully snapping at each other, and it was a while before she noticed: these little cubs were just normal wolves. There were no wings or even signs of wings on their backs. She turned to Sander, eyebrows raised. "You promised *flying* wolves."

Sander smiled back at her. "And *flying* wolves are what you are looking at. They just don't develop wings until they are mature. Wait until you see the adults."

Thandie narrowed her eyes. Another lie from Sander? She didn't know what to believe.

They continued watching the cubs play for a few minutes until they stopped, ears pricked up, and ventured further away from the den. They seemed alert to some movement and looked towards the hillside where two older wolves, with long, lean limbs, emerged from over the horizon. These creatures were different from the tumbling cubs. Whiter, sharper, narrower eyes. And it was hard to tell from this distance, but they seemed bigger than normal wolves. One held a dead animal – a hare by the looks of things – in its jaws, and blood was smeared around its muzzle and down its front.

"The alpha – the older one with more fur around is face – is named Conan and his partner – the female – Kemi," Sander whispered excitedly to Thandie. "At least, that is what I call them – I have no idea what they call each other."

"Do the cubs belong to them?"

Sander shook his head. "They belong to different mothers but they are all brought up together by the alpha pair."

"Like Madam Tilbury!" blurted Thandie, thinking of her own pack back home. She instantly felt foolish for mentioning it, but Sander ignored the comment anyway: he was too busy watching the wolves.

The cubs were very interested at the sight of their breakfast, and ran yapping towards the older wolves, tripping over one another. The adults came nearer and circled their offspring. Thandie was excited to notice the large, bulky wings folded up on their backs. She couldn't see them very well from her hiding place but they looked white, feathery, like swans' wings. Her heart skipped a beat. Could these creatures really fly? And would it really be possible to ride such wild animals?

The wolves dropped the animal carcasses on the ground and nudged the cubs into position so that each received a share. Bones cracked as the little ones tore at the meat. Thandie shuddered. Different teeth for ripping flesh and grinding bone, Sander had said. If the cubs' jaws were that strong, then what could the adults crunch through?

"We're safe. The adults will have already eaten on the hunt," explained Sander, as if reading her mind.

Immediately after eating, the cubs lay down on the ground between the paws of the older wolves. They groomed one another, licking, nuzzling and nibbling. The female seemed to pay more attention to the cubs and the male groomed the female's folded wings. When they bit each other's faces and tails, it looked almost aggressive, but Sander assured Thandie that this behaviour was essential for bonding.

Now that the atmosphere had calmed, Sander prepared himself to approach them. He took out his pipe. "I will approach Conan and you go to Kemi. I will play to them first – it calms them down and lets them know it's me. They like things to be familiar."

"But I am *not* familiar. What will they think of meeting a strange new person?"

"They should be content enough with me here. Be confident and don't make any unexpected movements. Watch me."

Sander grinned. He stood and emerged from their hiding place before Thandie had a chance to ask him any more questions. Like, what would happen if Kemi attacked?

Sander shuffled slowly in the wolves' direction. The whole group stood almost instantly, ears pricked up. Then he dropped down on to one knee, in an unthreatening pose. He slowly brought out his pipe and began to play. His music was slow and haunting, the notes deep and long.

Thandie knew by now the effect that the music would have, and was not surprised when the wolves began walking towards them. She kept her distance a little, walking behind Sander. The music calmed her as it did the wolves, and she was just about relaxed enough to enjoy the sight of the cubs following along bravely behind their parents. But the adult wolves turned around and nudged the cubs in the opposite direction, obviously unsure of the situation and wanting to keep them safe. The cubs got the message and tumbled back to the den.

Sander stopped playing and lowered his pipe. The male, Conan, bounded towards him like a dog, mouth open and tongue lolling. Kemi, the female, followed behind, and both wolves circled Sander, licking him and nosing at his feet. He greeted each of them in turn, stroking them and letting them lick his hands.

Then they noticed Thandie. Kemi stared directly at her, her eyes yellow and bright.

"Try not to stare back at her," whispered Sander. "She might think that you are challenging her position."

Thandie was sure that Sander had advised her to keep her eyes on them at all times, but now was not the time to argue about it: she most definitely didn't want to challenge any wolves. She quickly averted her eyes, trying to look friendly but not confrontational. It was not an easy balance to strike but she must have done something right because Kemi sauntered over towards her, with small light footsteps, stopping about a yard away.

Thandie saw that she was definitely bigger than a normal wolf. Kemi's head was at the height of her shoulders. Thandie's heart beat rapidly. Was she showing fear? She hoped not, although her body was telling her to run in the opposite direction. She looked up and Kemi flinched, ducking down slightly as if she were about to bound away. Despite her size and sharp teeth, she was nervous. More nervous than Thandie, even.

Thandie tentatively held out a hand, inviting the wolf to approach, and Kemi did so, sniffing at her for a long time, using her strong sense of smell to assess Thandie. She seemed to approve, and stood by her side, looking relaxed.

Sander was making a real fuss of Conan – stroking him around the ears and head as if he were a domestic pup. They clearly had a deep connection. That went some way towards easing Thandie's concerns about Sander. Animals were supposed to be good judges of character, weren't they? At least, that's what Tib always said.

Kemi glanced back at Conan and then ducked her head towards Thandie as if asking to be petted in a similar way. Thandie ran her hand along Kemi's back. Her fur was far thicker and coarser that it appeared. Thandie was careful to stroke only in the direction it grew. Then Thandie stroked around Kemi's head, which was softer. Kemi didn't respond to Thandie's touch in quite the same way as Conan did to Sander, but she enjoyed the stroking for a few moments before stepping away.

Thandie was particularly interested in Kemi's wings, which were folded up close to her body like a bat's, but she didn't dare to touch those. After a few moments, Kemi trotted back to Conan's side. But Thandie was left feeling proud of the moment that they had shared. Kemi liked her, she was sure.

"Well done," said Sander. "You're nearly ready for the next step."

"Flying?" The muscles in Thandie's arms and legs twitched with nerves and excitement. She could still barely believe that these wolves could fly by themselves, let alone with human riders.

"Watch me first," said Sander. He held the fur by Conan's

neck and swung his right leg over Conan's back as if he were a horse. Once he was sitting astride Conan, he bent his legs at the knees and leaned forward.

Kemi trotted back a few paces, towards Thandie, as if to give them some space. Conan threw back his head, opened his mouth and barked: a long series of yaps that sounded like some sort of code. Kemi joined in and Thandie laughed. "They looked as though they were going to howl."

Sander shook his head. "Wolves howl before they are about to hunt, but they bark before they are about to fly."

Conan continued yapping, then he bent his legs and unfolded his wings, which were over double his size. The pure white feathers were things of beauty. With his wings outstretched, Conan's proportions changed and he looked like a completely different animal. His sinewy legs, which had seemed so strong and capable, now looked like useless little sticks compared to the giant and powerful wings. There was a moment where he stayed crouching, as if gathering his strength. Then, like a spring releasing, he pounced into the air and beat his wings steadily. He was flying.

Thandie shielded her eyes from the sun and watched them go, Sander sitting happily on Conan's back. Conan reminded her of an owl: one of the silent white creatures that Finch would sometimes spot from the back of Madam Tilbury's roof. They flew like that for a minute or two, once around the nearest mountain peak, flapping and swooping, showing off for Thandie.

Sander shouted something to Conan – she couldn't hear what – and they flew down to land on a rocky ledge a few feet away. Sander dismounted and stood next to Conan, one hand on his back.

"Now it's your turn," shouted Sander from above.

Thandie looked again at Kemi's narrow body and slender legs. She reached out and put a hand on her back as she had done before and the wolf leaned in towards her. There was not much bulk under all that fur.

"I can't," called Thandie. "She will never be able to carry me."

"You'll be surprised: these creatures are stronger than you think. They are bigger than normal wolves, remember. You cannot ride them, running on the ground – their backs arch too much – but it is different in the air. They adopt a completely different position. Besides, it's why we are here, is it not?"

Thandie swallowed and Kemi looked warily at her, perhaps sensing her unease.

"I don't know where to begin."

"Just show her what you want to do. She will respond."

Thandie walked towards Kemi and stroked her, just as she had done before, more firmly this time. Kemi seemed happy enough, so Thandie reached her right arm across Kemi's shoulders as though embracing her. Kemi felt surprisingly warm in the chilly morning air.

Kemi lay down, on her right side with head up, her forepaws on the ground and her hind legs stretched out in front of her. Thandie kneeled on the ground next to her so that she didn't break contact. It felt quite an awkward position but at least they seemed to be bonding. Kemi smelled of the forest and of something strong and wolf-like that Thandie would have found hard to describe. She wondered what she smelled like to Kemi. At least she had been for that swim in the lake; she must be reasonably clean.

"Well done," called Sander. "By lying down, she's telling you she's happy to carry you. You can sit on her back now."

Thandie still felt a little uneasy. Minutes before she hadn't been sure whether the wolf wanted her for their next meal and now she was contemplating climbing on to her. But she had to do it. After all, as Sander said, that was why they were there. So from her bent over, kneeling position, Thandie threw a leg over

Kemi's right flank. Now she was nearly lying on Kemi, but it felt wrong – as though she might squash the poor she-wolf.

"Shift your weight back and put your legs behind her wings," said Sander.

Somehow, Thandie managed to do as he had instructed and her position instantly felt more comfortable as her weight shifted into the correct place.

Kemi stood up, front legs first, followed by back legs, and unfolded her beautiful wings. Thandie was close enough to see the pattern of feathers, smooth and even, without a mark or a gap. Then Kemi lowered her rear end and Thandie slid back, lying flat and clutching Kemi's shoulders.

Then Kemi jumped.

At least that was what it felt like: a jump. Not even a high jump, but a travelling jump, like a frog's, that would take them maybe another wolf's length across the ground. At first Thandie was disappointed and wondered what she had done wrong, but then she realized that Kemi had not landed. The jump continued. It turned into a glide, which swept them off the mountainside into nothingness.

Thandie clung on as Kemi soared faster. The cold wind whipped her plaits around her face. Thandie gasped. She couldn't see, or hear. The scenery around her blurred into a swirl of greys, whites and dull greens. Sounds stopped making sense. She squeezed her eyes firmly shut and gripped as tightly as she could with her arms and legs. Kemi tilted to the left and she slid suddenly and shrieked. She wished she'd watched Sander more carefully when he was riding Conan because she felt as if she was doing something wrong; she might fall off or hurt the wolf by gripping too forcefully.

Then Kemi slowed. The wind stopped roaring in Thandie's ears and she dared to open her eyes. They were in the air above the mountains, gliding in and out of the clouds.

They were flying.

Kemi threw back her head and made a high barking sound as she had done on the ground. Thandie did the same, yapping and barking along with her. It felt like the right sound to make: somewhere between laughter and excitement

Thandie breathed in deeply, relishing the exhilarating cold air. She no longer felt too heavy for Kemi. Thandie loosened her grip very slightly, confident that Kemi wouldn't let her fall. She felt as if she herself were flying. Wouldn't that be something – to be able to sprout wings and fly whenever the mood took her?

She heard the beating of another pair of large wings behind

her and then Conan and Sander swept into view. Conan came as close to Kemi as their great wings allowed, and she could hear the male wolf panting loudly.

"You're a natural!" called Sander.

"Thanks to Kemi," answered Thandie, patting the she-wolf on her side.

The two wolves flew companionably alongside each other at a relaxed pace. The wolves seemed to know where to go – possibly Sander was steering Conan – and Thandie was able to admire the view below. There was the circle of mountains, standing like a group of friends sharing secrets in the schoolyard. Between them were the lakes, and the little villages. Thandie looked for places she knew, tried to plot out the route they'd taken, but it was all so small, she wasn't sure she could identify anything.

"You and Conan look good together," she told Sander.

"I've known him since he was just a cub," said Sander. Sander said it as though that had been years ago.

"Has anyone ever flown on Kemi before?"

"I don't know," said Sander. "Many years ago, the villagers from Wending tried to tame them – to keep them in stables like horses – but that didn't turn out well. They are wild creatures, meant to be free."

"They don't seem so wild now," said Thandie, stroking the short fur at Kemi's shoulder.

"True, but this flight is on their terms only. If Kemi wanted to throw you off into the valley then she could without too much trouble."

Thandie held on a little tighter and Sander laughed. "You know what I mean: they are not tame. The people of Wending know that and keep a respectful distance. But I wouldn't be surprised if some of the more adventurous children trek up here and fly. I know I would have done at their age."

Thandie nodded. She could well imagine children daring one another to approach a wolf, just as, back in Essendor, they had dared one another to break the curfew. But that wasn't quite what she meant when she had asked if anyone had flown on Kemi. "I meant the stolen ones. I wonder if any of them reached the castle this way."

"I wouldn't know," said Sander, looking at her sharply.

Thandie hoped that she was the only one to have ridden Kemi, although she wasn't quite sure why. Perhaps she wanted to feel that Kemi was her wolf, just as Conan was Sander's.

They flew higher into the clouds, the features below shrinking, until Thandie could make out nothing at all. It was colder too, with flakes of snow blowing in the air. Thandie's cheeks felt raw and she had to narrow her eyes to stop them watering. "How far is it to the castle?"

"Not far now," said Sander, reassuringly. "That's Opacus, just up ahead."

But Thandie hadn't asked because she was impatient to get there. She had asked because she wanted to stay up here, flying on Kemi's back, forever. The closer they got, the more this difficult mission became a reality. There was so much that Thandie still didn't know. Somehow Sander seemed to have avoided talking very much about the unicorn or the castle. But now she needed to find out.

"Sander, does the unicorn speak?"

"No, he uses an interpreter. Another powerful sorcerer – a woman. It might seem strange at first but you will quickly grow used to it."

That did seem strange. But at least Sander had answered her directly this time. And there was so much more she wanted to know. "*Why* is the unicorn taking these people? I know you said he takes their memories, but what does he use them for?"

Sander glanced at her. She felt like he was assessing how much he should tell her.

"The unicorn knows a great deal about magic but he does not have the energy that it requires. Spells and sorcery sap his natural energy and he needs positive emotions, like love and nostalgia, to direct into his magic."

"But if he is collecting memories, then why has he been taking children? Surely older people would have years more memories to steal?"

Sander shook his head. "Young memories are the best. They are crisper – clearer – and the emotion is stronger. Particularly those people on the cusp of adulthood. As people grow older, the memories fade, details get jumbled and they are not as powerful. They become like well-told stories: memories of memories rather than fresh experiences full of emotion. It is the emotion that the unicorn needs."

Thandie knew only too well how powerful emotions could be in a not-quite-adult brain. Particularly when they were kept suppressed. Just thinking of her mother brought all sorts of raw emotions bubbling up inside her: mainly pain and heartache at her loss.

They were flying through thick white cloud now, and could only see their wolves and each other. They didn't speak for a time and the only sound was the wolves' giant wings beating.

Up here, Sander had told her more about the unicorn than he had on the rest of the journey put together. She felt he would answer anything now.

"I have one more question for you," said Thandie. "What was the deal that you made with the unicorn?"

She held her breath, waiting for the response.

And after a few seconds, Sander's voice broke the silence.

"It's over there."

"What?" The cloud cleared and Thandie looked to where Sander was pointing. The castle. The sight made her temporarily lose her grip on Kemi. She gasped and grabbed back on to her fur, heart beating fast. Any more questions would have to wait.

Right at the very peak of the tallest mountain were some steps, leading into the clouds up to a castle, which was built in the very clouds themselves, like an impossible drawing that Thandie had seen in the schoolroom when she was small.

Thandie had only seen one castle before: Essendor. She couldn't imagine Essendor without its pointed stone turrets. The stone steps at Essendor had been worn down by countless important people through the ages and the very walls were steeped in story and legend. But this place, this castle that Thandie was looking at now, was different indeed.

Perhaps it was because they had come upon it so suddenly, but it looked as if it had only just come into being, as if it had sprung up from the clouds themselves. It was white and gleaming, with coloured glass windows and spindly towers. Who would build such a castle? And how? Thandie suspected that magic had been involved. But the big question was why? Why put a castle up here, where virtually no one could reach it? There was nothing to defend and no people to protect. Just one unicorn, living with just an old interpreter, according to Sander.

What sort of creature would want to live out here in this strange grandeur? Someone who saw himself as literally above the rest of the world. Someone who wanted to look down on people, like a god. Of course, the castle's main purpose now was as a prison, so this isolated location was perfect. Somewhere in those ice-white towers, or down in the dungeons, dozens of children remained locked away, without even their memories for comfort.

Sander stared at her, smiling. "Impressive, isn't it?"

That was not what Thandie was thinking. The sight of the castle made her feel a little sick. "I suppose it was as I expected," she said. "It is as you described."

Then it crossed Thandie's mind:

225

Most of what Sander said was true. She had been sceptical about flying wolves and a castle in the clouds, yet here she was, flying on Kemi's back towards the great fortress, just as he had said they would. But he had lied about other things. To Yannick, in his cottage. And to her, when she first met him in Essendor. Thandie could not shake the feeling that something about Sander was not quite right. She felt in her pocket for the notice from the inn door. *DO NOT APPROACH* it had said about a person who looked a lot like Sander.

Most of what he said was true. But not all.

And how did she tell which parts?

CHAPTER THIRTEEN

THE WHITE CASTLE

Thandie

Thandie didn't know where Kemi would land, because the ground itself looked like fluffy cloud. The wolves knew better, though, and Conan landed a few hundred yards away from the white castle, with Kemi just behind. There was something solid underneath the swirling whiteness.

Thandie climbed down from Kemi's back tentatively. Her legs felt weak and shaky, even though the whole flight must have lasted only a few minutes. Really, all they had done was to head directly up and a little to the east. Kemi lay down and folded up her wings, looking tired and spent. Thandie stroked her down the length of her back. "Thank you, Kemi," she said.

The place was eerily quiet. Thandie stared at the castle, and the steps leading up to the front door. It looked strangely unreal, like a model or a toy. They were close to some other steps, one or two just visible above the next layer of cloud. Thandie went over to investigate, walking tentatively. She half-expected her feet to fall straight through the cloud-covered ground at any moment.

She stepped down on to the first stair and noticed that they carried on, curving around like a spiral staircase. "Where do these go?" she called out.

"Down," said Sander, simply. "Back home."

That was a strangely comforting thought. Thandie now knew where the escape route was, should she need it.

She walked back to Sander and the wolves.

Sander untied the dead grat from his bag and threw it down for the wolves, who were instantly upon it. They obviously needed to replenish the energy they'd used on the journey. Thandie watched Kemi attack the meal, tearing at the flesh. How different she looked to when she was flying: more like a dog now than a bird.

Thandie stretched out each of her legs, rotating her foot at the ankle. Then she untied and re-braided each of her plants, which were coming loose after being whipped about so viciously in the wind.

"How do you feel?" Sander seemed amused. He had of course travelled on the back of a flying wolf many times. But it was new to Thandie and she may never have another experience like that for as long as she lived. She wanted him to understand that.

"I feel that ... if I never return from the castle in the clouds, then at least I have done this. I have flown on the back of a flying wolf and seen the most spectacular view I will ever see."

His smile fell from his face. "Don't say that. You will return, I know it. And you will see many more spectacular sights than this in your life. You are still so young."

"Sometimes you sound like an old man. You are young yourself, don't forget!" Thandie realized that he never had answered her question about his exact age.

Sander had that distant, inscrutable look about him once again. "Sometimes I feel like an old man. I have seen so much."

Thandie wondered what he had seen. She thought that maybe it wasn't all good.

The wolves finished their meal in seconds. They stood side-by side, looking re-energized.

"They are ready to go home now," said Sander, reaching out

to rub the fur around Conan's sharp face.

"To go home? Won't they wait for us?"

"No. They need to get back to the cubs."

Of course they did. Thandie wouldn't want to keep them away. But still, it would be hard to say goodbye. And how would they get back again afterwards? She wouldn't think about that now. One step at a time.

Kemi gazed at her intently with those amazing saffron eyes. Then both wolves turned their backs to Thandie and Sander, and trotted towards the mountain's edge without a backward glance. Then they spread out their great white wings and soared into the whiteness of the clouds.

Thandie's heart soared with them. Maybe she would never see Kemi again. Maybe she would never see a flying wolf again. But, whatever happened, she had this afternoon to remember.

Thandie wanted to write about it, so that she didn't forget the feeling. Her fingers twitched instinctively for her diary in the pocket of her dress. There was no diary of course, just the warning notice that she had taken from outside the tavern. She removed it from her pocket, suspicion rising up in her as it had before.

"What is that?" asked Sander.

Thandie silently handed him the notice and watched him smooth it out.

"It looks nothing like me – apart from the coat," he said.

"And is it you?" said Thandie.

"What do you mean?"

"What I *mean* is that if the only person you stole away was Linnell from near Arvale, then why do they have your picture up near Wending?"

Sander scratched the back of his neck. "Ahhh, like I said, the unicorn must have other people working for him now."

"All wearing patchwork coats?"

He held out his arm, pointing at the coat sleeve, which was faded and frayed at the edges.

"They're not actually brightly coloured garments, so they have that wrong," he said, passing the notice back to Thandie.

They both stared at it in Thandie's hands for a little while longer. Blood rushed in her ears. She couldn't think straight.

"I thought you couldn't read," she said quietly.

TELL HER EVERYTHING
Sander

Thandie knew. He was sure of it. He thought quickly. "I can't read – not really – I get stuck with longer words."

"You said you knew your letters and that was about it."

He hesitated.

Sander could make an excuse, try to smooth things over, but Thandie was not stupid. He felt the sudden urge to tell her everything.

She stared at the notice for a second or two, then she scrunched it into a ball and handed it to him. She turned to the castle. "There is no time to lose."

Sander put out an arm to stop her. "Wait! There is something more I must tell you!"

A SECOND CONFESSION
Thandie

Thandie sighed. A second confession. He could only be about to tell her about her missing diary, or the other people. Either way, she didn't want to hear it. She thought of the way he was with the wolves, the way that Conan trusted him. Animals had an instinct for these things, didn't they? She would rather cling to the shreds of hope that Sander was a decent person.

Thandie raised her hand in front of her. "No. Don't tell me any more."

She didn't want to have this conversation. She wanted to get on and do what they had come here to do. She turned away from Sander and continued walking in the direction of the castle.

She was about to enter a forbidding castle with a self-confessed kidnapper who had brought at least one girl and possibly forty-two other young people to this very spot. Not one of those people had ever been seen again. It was already highly questionable whether she should go any further on this journey, and if there was anything else that Sander had done, any other crimes he needed to confess, then Thandie would rather not know. This was the only way she could think of to protect herself.

For now, there was no turning back, whatever Sander had done.

ADVICE
Sander

This was usually the point at which Sander would abandon Thandie and leave her to face the unicorn alone. But not this time. Thandie was different and he had to be there with her.

He wanted to tell her everything, to explain how it had all happened. She didn't realize the magnitude of what they were about to do. He needed to somehow make her understand – prepare her.

"Thandie, will you please listen to me for a moment?"

Thandie sighed. "No more confessions, please. I need to think about the future, not what has gone before."

"No more confessions," agreed Sander. "But still, I want to give you an idea of what to expect."

Thandie nodded and he continued.

"The unicorn is very powerful. He understands the way that human minds work and he will try to trick you."

Determination was written on Thandie's face. "I am not so easy to trick, Sander. I am not going to be deceived by a unicorn's clever words. I am focused. I am here to free the missing ones and to go home."

Sander sighed. Underestimating the unicorn's power was the worst thing that she could do. "Do not give him anything. He cannot take anything from you without your permission." Sander had offered that piece of advice forty-three times but nobody had ever heeded it. The unicorn had a way of preying on people's weaknesses and using their hopes and fears to control them. He hoped Thandie was different.

She was looking around her now and seemed keen to carry on with their quest. "I'm here to take back, not to give. I won't give the unicorn a thing."

"Please remember that," said Sander. If she took his advice then perhaps there was a way for them both to succeed. Thandie could free the people and he could still keep his part of the bargain.

Thandie scrutinized the castle. "I've been thinking – is there no back way into this place? Can't we bypass the unicorn all together and go straight to where the stolen ones are held?"

"No. You are underestimating his power. We cannot hide from him. He undoubtedly knows that we are here – he probably knew about our journey to him. We have to face him. I have to face him," said Sander.

And who knows what will happen? he thought.

"What the unicorn doesn't know, is that this time, I am on

your side. He will expect me to act in a certain way, say certain things. From the moment we cross the threshold of the castle, I will be acting as though I am loyal to the unicorn. You must remember that it is an act."

Thandie nodded. He hoped she trusted him.

"You must prepare a story to tell the unicorn- something that you want – something that would be worth travelling this distance for and taking this risk. Do you understand?"

Thandie nodded again.

They walked up the frosty steps together.

$\mathcal{C}$HAPTER FOURTEEN

WAITING

Thandie

Sander pulled on the bell pull and the doors swung open. They walked through the great doorway, the vast shining hallway, and up the stairs to a set of black quartz doors. True to his word, Sander's demeanour changed as they got closer to the throne room. He stopped looking guilty – stopped looking at her at all.

"The unicorn will want to see me on my own first. You wait here and follow when you are called." He pushed open the door and went in without glancing back. She tried to peek in as he went but the doors began to swing shut straight away and all she could see was ice-white walls and high windows. From deep within the room she heard a woman's voice.

"Welcome, Sander. I have not seen you for some time."

This must be the interpreter.

She heard Sander's familiar voice next. "No. I have been busy. It is getting harder to find what you want."

And then she couldn't hear any more – they must have moved further away from the doors. Thandie supposed they would be reasonably quick and that she should wait where she was. She didn't like waiting, especially when she didn't know how long for. She sat down in a cross-legged position directly in front of the double doors, wondering if she would be able to hear any more through the gap, but she could not.

Prepare a story, Sander had said. A plausible reason that was important enough for a girl her age to risk everything. Her mother flashed into her mind. Her mother – her reason for everything. Maybe even her reason for being here now. But she certainly wasn't going to tell the unicorn about her mother. No, it had to be something else. She tried to imagine what someone else her age might wish for. What had the stolen ones wished for? Love? Friendship? Riches? She knew what Linnell wanted. She had seen the pages marked in the book. Beautiful dresses, jewels. When … if … the unicorn asked her, that is what she would tell him.

Thandie soon tired of waiting where she was, alone in the silent castle. She stood and looked over the balcony to the doors through which they'd entered. She had never been anywhere so quiet. Or so big. Did anyone really need this amount of space? No wonder he felt the need to steal others away from their own lives and families. Perhaps he just wanted the company. He wanted their memories because he had none of his own. But if they- the stolen ones – were here, somewhere, why couldn't she hear them? She knew how noisy the four of them could be at Madam Tilbury's. There were ten times that number here; there should have been ten times the noise.

Perhaps the people were locked away in a dungeon somewhere. Or perhaps worse – perhaps they had not survived the experience.

She had waited long enough now and was growing desperate to find out. If only the doors would open. She studied them. Black quartz when everything else was white and heavily engraved. She ran her fingers across the patterns and then pushed gently. They didn't move. What kind of place had doors without handles?

Thandie disliked how her heart beat and how her hands sweated, despite the stark coldness of the place. Her head told her that there was no reason to be nervous. This unicorn might have convinced others that he was something special – Linnell, the other stolen ones, Sander even – but he would not convince her. She knew what he really was: a thief, a cheat, a kidnapper, maybe worse.

When it came down to it he was a creature, an animal. She thought of the horses that she saw in Essendor pulling carts and carriages. Dull, plodding animals, not like the wolves she'd just met. She would not be nervous about meeting an Essendor horse, so why should she be nervous about meeting this one, who was just the same but with a few magic powers. Worse than a simple creature, he was a beast, without a heart or soul. Her enemy – whom she was here to defeat.

She was suddenly filled with resentment at the whole idea of waiting here, outside these doors, as if she were some messenger girl seeking the great one's favour. If they were going to ignore her for so long, then she would go exploring. Perhaps she would find the stolen ones by herself. She turned away from the doors, but just as she was deciding whether to slide down the left-hand or the right-hand banister, the quartz-studded doors swung open behind her. It was time.

THE THRONE ROOM
Thandie

Sander met her in the doorway, avoiding her gaze and shifting from foot to foot. Thandie recognized this now as his guilty expression.

"Is there anything more I need to know?" whispered Thandie, but Sander did not reply and simply led her into the throne room. Sander could be acting this way for the benefit of the unicorn, but if it was an act, it was a good one.

An eerie, icy room lay before her, lit by candlelight. It was ostentatious, with ornate ice sculptures and glittering pools. Thandie tried not to look at any of it; she didn't want to appear impressed.

And the unicorn walked towards them.

Thandie had to steel herself not to gasp. This was a creature very different to those carthorses of Essendor. He may have been a beast, but he was a beast of great beauty, and, despite herself, her skin tingled with excitement at the sight of him. He was like an ice sculpture that had been magicked into life but so very alive, his muscles rippling and tail swaying. He stood proudly, head held high, sharp golden horn pointing towards the ceiling, breathing steadily through his nostrils. She wanted to hate him, but his breathtaking beauty made it difficult.

When she had looked at the wolves earlier, her first instinct had been to run, knowing that the animals could overpower her if they chose. Yet, looking at this majestic creature, she had the opposite reaction. She was drawn to him and could not run away if she'd wanted to.

"Welcome," said a voice. Thandie turned to look and saw an elderly woman, dressed in white, standing towards the back of the room. The interpreter. What was she doing in this castle? Did she work for the beast? Or was she a prisoner here like the stolen ones? How did she interpret the unicorn's words? The interpreter must have powers of sorcery of her own.

"You look cold."

Thandie knew that the interpreter was the one speaking but still, the voice seemed to come from the beast himself. He was somehow eloquent, even though he couldn't speak. This female voice, alongside his magnificent appearance, gave the impression of softness, goodness. He didn't look or seem like a monster. She had to keep reminding herself what he was – the enemy – and looked away, in an attempt to break the spell.

"I am the perfect temperature," said Thandie, gritting her

teeth to stop them chattering. She would show no weakness. She would keep control. She would tell him nothing, show him nothing. He could not take anything from her that she did not freely give – Sander had told her that – so she would tell him as little as possible. She was here to rescue the missing people and she would keep reminding them all of that fact.

"Where are all the others?" Thandie directed her question to Sander, but he stood back, away from her, and would not meet her gaze. Not for the first time, she thought what a good actor he was, pretending to be on the unicorn's side. If, indeed, that was what he was doing.

"The others are quite safe," said the interpreter, eyeing Sander suspiciously. "They don't normally require bringing all the way here, do they?"

Sander smiled mischievously like he had done when they had met outside Essendor castle. "Some are trickier than others, but I like the challenge."

Some were trickier than others. So that was confirmation. There was nobody else working for the unicorn: it was Sander who had led all the young people away and she had walked right into his trap like a clueless grat. Perhaps Linnell, with her dreams of material things and wishes for a better life, was easy to trick, but she, Thandie, required a more complex web of lies. He had tried to gain her trust by confessing to some of his crimes, and appealed to her sense of heroism. But all of it was to get her to the place in which she was currently standing.

Sander had taken her here to betray her.

THE REAL REASON
Thandie

Thandie's swallowed hard. There was a possibility that Sander was *pretending* to the unicorn that he had lured her here with cunning lies. It was confusing, but either way she couldn't rely on him. She would have to just do what she had come here to do.

The unicorn walked slowly up to Thandie. He was standing on what appeared to be a circular pool of frozen ice, the blue sky visible below its surface. He looked her up and down and snorted, clouds of steam billowing into the icy air. The interpreter spoke.

"His Majesty would like to know the reason for your visit."

Thandie scrunched her hands into tight fists. What was she supposed to say? Sander had told her to lie but now she wasn't sure if she should trust his advice. Her thoughts were racing and she wasn't even sure that she could remember the lie she had prepared. Her mouth was dry. But she was here, in front of the unicorn – this was her chance.

"I have a question for him – a request. I am told that he grants wishes."

The unicorn stopped and stared at her, hooves scratching the icy surface of the pool.

"This is true. What is it that you truly desire?"

What did she truly desire? An image of her mother flew unbidden into her mind. Thandie was resting her cheek on her mother's shoulder while she read to her at bedtime. Thandie could almost feel the warmth and familiar smell of her, her long hair gently tickling her arm. But why was this coming into her mind now? She would not share this with the unicorn.

Thandie tried to bring to mind her cover story of wanting riches – beautiful things – but she couldn't seem to find the words. She would have to think quickly. She gazed all around at the fine room. She thought of Linnell's book, marked at the page of kings and queens, and found her voice.

"In my city, Essendor, the rich people live protected behind the city walls, whereas the ordinary folk live in humble cottages outside. Sometimes they sleep four or five to a room. This is not right. I desire to live like a queen. I want to dress in fancy clothes and to sleep in a soft feather bed. To live in a fine palace. Just as you do."

Thandie spoke passionately, her voice rising. She felt sure that these were the things that others would have asked for.

The unicorn paused for a moment, studying her, and then shook his head slowly, his mane ruffling. He lifted his chin and made a neighing sound. To Thandie, it sounded like a laugh. The interpreter spoke the unicorn's words again.

"An ardent speech, Thandie. Quite believable. Yet I do not believe you."

She had thought she had been so convincing. What now? Thandie's hands began to tremble and she shoved them into her pockets. She tried to sneak another quick look at Sander but he had backed away again and was loitering behind the interpreter. Thandie was on her own.

"His Majesty suspects you are trying to trick him. You are really here because of the other children, aren't you, Thandie?"

She had to speak and she had to show that she was not afraid. She stared into the interpreter's eyes, ignoring the unicorn all together. The woman's eyes were creased at the edges, like a kindly grandmother's, yet Thandie could detect no warmth.

"Why do you call him 'His Majesty'? The creature is no king."

The woman laughed. "He is king of this world in the clouds."

"But he has no subjects. What use is a king in an empty castle?"

"He has over forty subjects and is gaining power all the time. Before long he will no doubt be king in your world, too, and you will be calling him by his true title."

"Subjects! They are not his subjects. He kidnapped them!"

The unicorn made a sound, like a deep neigh, in his throat. The interpreter translated.

"No one is a prisoner here. Every single one of these people came willingly, just as you have done today. The doors are unlocked and everyone stays here through choice. You shouldn't believe everything you hear."

Thandie stopped pretending. It was obvious that the unicorn wasn't going to believe a word and she was no good at acting anyway. She looked around the room, noting the door at the back. "Where are they?"

"They are just over there through that door. They are well looked after. I am no monster." Here, the interpreter pointed behind them. "You will get to meet them and see for yourself. First, why not talk a while? Why not explain what you really want – why are you *really* here? Everyone has something that they really desire. In the end, that always matters more than anything."

Thandie put her hands to her head. She was so tired. Her thoughts felt muddled and she wished she could think straight. Who had told her that the unicorn was evil? It had been other people who had told her a monster was kidnapping children; Thandie had suspected all along that they might be leaving of their own accord.

Why was she really here? It was to free the people, wasn't it? But more thoughts of her mother leaped into her mind, uninvited. She closed her eyes lightly and breathed in deeply through her nose. The air was cold and crisp. "The lives of these children and their families matters more than just me. I am just an individual. They are many."

It was true. Thandie tried to remember Linnell's father – the trust in his kind blue eyes. He was putting all his faith in her. He wanted his daughter back. He was why she was really here. He and countless others like him.

"I know why you are really here," the unicorn continued. She no longer noticed that the interpreter was speaking for him; it was as if he spoke directly to Thandie. "You may be telling yourself that you are here to free all the missing children, but you are really trying to find a missing person of your own, aren't you?

Thandie's heart thumped in her chest. "How do you know about my mother?"

The unicorn laughed and continued. "Do not concern yourself with how I know. I know a lot of things. All this energy from these young minds! You were young when she went away, weren't you?"

Then Thandie's attention was drawn to something in the interpreter's hand. A book. A familiar-looking book, dog-eared and bound in leather. Her heart hammered in her chest.

It was her diary.

THE DIARY
Thandie

Of course Sander had stolen her diary. Why had she ever trusted him? Thandie wanted to reach out and grab it but she refused to show how much it meant to her.

For some reason, this betrayal felt worse to her than his lies about the number of people he'd led away. Her diary was her everything. The only link now to her mother. The record of what had happened and all her memories.

This was how the unicorn knew her desires. He had read her secret thoughts scrawled in black ink.

Seven. She had been seven years old when her mother left. It was during the reign of the evil King Zelos. People were hungry and there was no food. Crime rates were high. People were desperate. And people were going missing. It was a bit different to this time around: most of the missing were adults, and they all seemed to be people who had upset Zelos in some way. Zelos was arresting people for small misdemeanours but instead of putting them into prison he was recruiting them as his spies. Or so the rumours ran.

Thandie hadn't considered that her mother might disappear. Her mother was brave and creative and it was just the two of them; she wouldn't let herself get arrested in the middle of the night. But that, of course, was exactly what did happen. Thandie went from being half of a close mother and daughter pair to being on her own. For a few years she was passed around from house to house: some better than others but never finding a home of her own. At least she was not left to fend for herself as some other children were. Then Madam Tilbury took her in.

Thandie was not going to tell the unicorn any of that. She was not going to tell the unicorn anything. She never spoke to anyone about her mother. But fragments of memory flooded into her mind, as much as she tried to push them away.

Her mother's hair tickling her as she leaned over to kiss her goodnight. The smell of rosewater. The pain of a grazed knee vanishing when her mother kissed it better.

The unicorn was so close now that she could feel his warm breath on her icy arm. "I know where your mother is. She is alive. I can bring her here."

Thandie did not react. He was lying to her – trying to draw her in. But still the memories kept on coming.

A green skirt at just the right height for Thandie to hide behind. The emptiness she left in Thandie's life when she went away. Thandie aged ten when Queen Audrey defeated King Zelos and took the throne. The rumours that spread slowly around the market square and beyond. All the missing people who came suddenly back. Berwick Tilbury, the Harding brothers, all no doubt with stories to tell but all keeping quiet. But not her mother. Never her mother. The endless not-knowing that continued to this day.

"I can take those painful memories away," said the unicorn.

"Just nod your head and I will take them so they don't hurt you any more. You can have your mother – be with her once again."

Thandie screwed up her eyes, trying to block the voice out. She knew she must resist his words, but could no longer remember why. What could possibly be bad about a deal that brought her mother back to her? She felt herself softening, preparing to let the bad memories float away. It would be better for her – better for everyone. And she could be with her mother again. They could make new memories.

Thandie opened her eyes and stared at the unicorn. "Where is she?"

There was no answer, but the unicorn walked back a few paces and lowered his head to the frozen pool. The ice didn't crack, as Thandie expected, but seemed to melt, golden warmth radiating from the unicorn's horn. The water itself appeared golden, and it waved and rippled then stilled. Deep in the pool, but quite clear, was the image of a woman in a long green dress swimming underwater. The person was not here, in this pool, but somewhere out in the world. It was as if Thandie were looking through a spyglass to a faraway place.

Thandie held her breath in anticipation. She thought she recognized the long red hair, the dress, but she needed to see her face. The woman swam away, her feet splaying out like a frog's, and Thandie worried that she wouldn't turn around. Thandie kneeled down by the pool. The woman continued to swim in a large circle and then round to face Thandie, as if she were swimming directly towards her. It was her mother. She was sure of it. Even underwater and seven years older, she knew it.

"Ma," called Thandie, although she knew her mother couldn't hear. She reached her hand into the water. It was so icy cold that it bit her fingertips and she withdrew immediately. As she did so, the pool iced over once again, creaking and cracking into a frosted layer. The image of her mother had gone.

Thandie felt warm tears on her cheeks and wiped them away. Her mother was alive. Somewhere in the kingdom. She had no idea where, or why she was swimming, but the unicorn knew. He could bring her to Thandie. They could live here together, in this castle in the clouds. Could it really be true? Would she really feel the warmth of her mother's embrace?

She walked on to the circle, which was solid again, and looked down as if she might see her mother beneath her feet, but all she saw was the sky and clouds moving silently past.

The unicorn began to walk around the edge of the icy circle.

Thandie remembered her last words to Tib: *I will come back*

– I promise. They were the same words that her mother had said to her, seven years ago. Her mother hadn't kept her promise. Did it really matter if she kept hers? Tib would survive. He would find someone else to rely on. Losing parents at such a young age just made you hardier.

The unicorn cantered faster and faster around her, but strangely, she could hear no noise. Perhaps his feet were not even touching the floor. Perhaps he was flying, like the wolves had done. Everything was a white blur. The smell of perfumed smoke filled her nostrils, warming and comforting.

"Think only of your mother, Thandie." She was thinking of her mother, with a desperate need. She was ready to leave this unpredictable, frustrating, difficult life behind her and step into a new, simpler world, where she would have the comfort of her mother's embrace once again. If the unicorn wanted her painful memories, then he was welcome to them. She would be free.

But every time the unicorn galloped past, she saw another face. Sander's face. Without his usual smile. He was serious. Shaking his head.

"Don't do it, Thandie," he said. His voice was distant. "Don't give your memories away."

She tried to block out the words. She wanted her mother now

so badly. She would listen to the unicorn, not Sander. Sander was not a true friend; he was full of secrets. He had taken her precious diary away. But she didn't need it any more – not if she had her mother.

A scuffle broke her concentration. The interpreter cried out. Sander was wrangling with the old woman: taking something from her. Thandie tried to focus on the unicorn and her memories once again but Sander leaped in front of the unicorn's path. He joined her on the frozen pool, put a hand on her shoulder, shook her gently, rousing her from her dream-like state.

"Thandie," he cried. "Listen to me." Sander held something up in front of him. Something oblong shaped and bound in leather. Her diary.

HAPPY MEMORIES
Sander

Sander opened the diary and began to read. Loudly. He wanted Thandie to hear him above the unicorn's words. Above any thoughts running through her brain. These words were important.

He read the first entry in the book. Thandie's writing was

large, childlike and untidy. She must have been just seven or eight when she wrote the words, possibly writing by candlelight in a temporary home.

My Mother

Her hair was long and red. She wore it swept up in the day but down at night. Her nightgown was old and worn but very, very soft.

She said she would be twenty minutes but she never came back.

I keep part of her always in my middle name – Maybeth – her first name made up of the month of her birth and her own mother's given name.

She had a scar on her knee from toppling off a stool when she was a little girl. Still, she didn't mind me climbing on stools. We have to make our own mistakes, she said.

She loved to make music, to read, to grow things. She loved me.

I will write down all my memories. I must write in this book every day.

<u>*I must always remember.*</u>

The book was full of entries like these: memories of her

mother. Even her daily record of events – everything – was connected back to her mother. Sander didn't need to go on. The words were reaching Thandie, he could tell. She looked at him, tears welling up in her eyes and lower lip trembling. She was not lost to the unicorn yet.

"Don't give your memories away, Thandie. They are too precious."

Thandie opened her mouth slightly as if to speak, but no words came. She looked bewildered, as if she had no idea where she was.

The unicorn slowed to a walk and finally a standstill. He stood close to Sander, breathing hard.

"This is unwise, Sander," said the interpreter, although it was unclear if these were her own words or the unicorn's.

Sander ignored her and flicked through the diary to a page towards the back. The writing was much neater and tiny, as if Thandie realized she was reaching the end of the book and wanted to fit in as much information as she possibly could. He read aloud again.

My journey to free the stolen ones is underway. Sander is

still strange and I doubt I will ever trust him entirely, but I am finding that I am enjoying my journey – my adventure.

Today, I set about rediscovering how to play the pipe, during the most beautiful sunrise I have ever seen. Today, not everything is perfect but, for the first time, I feel I can go on, even if I never discover what happened to my mother. Today, I feel glad to be alive.

Sander closed the diary carefully and handed it back to Thandie. She held it in her hands as if it were delicate and breakable, like a baby bird. "You can live without her, Thandie. You are strong enough and young enough. You have your whole life ahead of you."

Tears streamed down Thandie's cheeks. She put both her hands to her face but the tears kept coming. "But I need her."

"If she is out there, then you may find her … *will* find her. But trusting in the unicorn is not the way. Even if the unicorn finds her, even if he brings her to you, without your memories, how will you recognize her? She will be nothing to you."

Thandie was sobbing now.

She was back. Sander was certain that she would not give her memories away.

The unicorn knew it too. The offer came one more time. "This is your last chance, Thandie. Give up your memories now or regret your decision forever."

But Thandie looked up, just shook her head and said, her voice wobbling but loud, "No. My memories belong to me alone. They are the most precious treasures I have."

ALONE NOW
Thandie

When Thandie's mother first disappeared, Thandie repeatedly dreamed that she had returned. The dreams always varied slightly but she would be in an ordinary location: in the woods, at the vegetable market, or even in the schoolroom. Her mother would turn and smile, pleased to see Thandie. She might stretch out an arm. But just as Thandie ran to her, went to grasp her hand, she would wake up.

She felt now as if she were wakening from such a dream: confused, disorientated and as if she had lost her mother all over again. She shivered, noticing her surroundings. This room was so cold. The unicorn, interpreter and Sander stood around her, glaring at one another. She put the diary back in her apron pocket, feeling reassured by the familiar weight.

The unicorn stood tense, head lowered and ears pinned back. He was angry, but not with Thandie. His sharp horn was pointed directly at Sander. For a moment, Thandie thought he might attack, but he did not. He just stared at him, perfect blue eyes glinting with intent. The interpreter spoke for him. "So, Sander, you have made a choice. An unwise choice. It seems that an agreement has been broken."

Sander barely acknowledged the words. Instead, he turned to Thandie.

"Listen to me, Thandie." There was urgency in his voice but she wasn't sure that she could comprehend it. There was so much that she didn't understand. Had Sander taken her diary to save her from the unicorn, or had he planned to betray her and then changed his mind? She had so much she wanted to ask him, but there was no time.

For now, he had asked her to listen. She nodded her head.

"You will find them through there," he said, pointing to the double doors at the back of the room. It took Thandie a few seconds to realize he meant the stolen ones.

"I can't come with you. You have to do this by yourself." He unbuckled the pipe in its holder from his waist and handed it to her. She took it, her stomach tightening. She had never see him parted from his pipe and she wasn't quite sure what it meant. It was as if he was giving up.

"Are you sure?"

Sander nodded. "You will need it."

Thandie was confused. Wouldn't he need it himself? She felt the tension in the air; angry looks were exchanged, a fight was brewing. Couldn't he use some of his own musical magic against the unicorn? But as he turned away from her to face the unicorn, he didn't look scared; he was smiling in true Sander-like fashion. He must have a plan.

Thandie looked between them all, and she realized that this was not her fight.

She threw Sander's pipe in its holder over her shoulder like a sash, and darted off towards the doors.

She felt a cool, claw-like hand on her upper arm.

"You, girl, stay. You may not wander where you please," said the interpreter. But the unicorn snorted. The interpreter turned to him and nodded briefly, then back to Thandie. "My master says you can go where you please. He has no interest in you."

Thandie didn't wait for them to change their mind. She

darted off, feet sliding on the strange frozen floor, towards the double doors.

She left Sander to face the unicorn alone. She couldn't think about Sander now. She had come here to free the stolen people and that was what she would do.

CHAPTER FIFTEEN

A BROKEN DEAL

Sander

Sander watched Thandie run through the double doors. There was nothing he could do to help her now. He hadn't planned it this way but he was sure that, finally, he had done the right thing. If anyone could free these people, it was Thandie. At least, he thought she could and he desperately hoped that he was right.

MANY YEARS AGO

Sander was the son of a cobbler. The youngest of seven brothers. A tumbling wolf pack of which he was the favourite pet. He soon discovered that the world was his for the taking. He was not the tallest brother, or the strongest, but he was fast, agile and brave. He had a handsome face and a quick smile. From an early age, he fully expected everyone he met to warm to him and for people to do things his way. His older brothers, his teachers, his friends.

"That one could charm the birds down from the trees and the fish from the seas," said his mother's friends.

"That's what I worry about," said his mother. Somehow, he always seemed to have the biggest piece of cake at the table. The biggest slice of luck, you might say.

Sander watched as his brothers settled one-by-one. His eldest two brothers trained with his father, as shoemakers, the middle two stayed in their small town and worked in the fields. The younger two went to seek their fortune in Essendor. He saw them all grow tired, their faces lined with worry and lack of sleep. When Sander reached adolescence, some of the prettiest girls in the village showed a romantic interest, but he would not marry. Not now, not ever.

On his sixteenth birthday the family came together and sat around the kitchen table to celebrate his coming of age. Each brother had suggestions for the life he might lead: a suitable occupation, a suitable match. But Sander dismissed them all.

"That life is not for me," said Sander.

"But what other life is there?" asked his mother.

"I'm going to see the world. I am going to travel to the farthest reaches of the kingdom and discover new sights. People will remember my name for years to come. They will write about me in their books."

"You remind me of myself when I was younger. I shared your thirst for adventure," said his oldest brother, "but as I grew older, I realized that a man cannot live that way forever. He needs people around him, a family, a community."

This particular brother had transformed over the past few years from a slim young man to a middle-aged one, with a growing paunch and an arthritic limp. The thought that Sander might grow up to be anything like him filled him with horror.

His brother laughed, hands on his wide belly. "I give you just a couple of years of this lifestyle before you are back in the village, with a family of your own, content to live an ordinary life."

That was when he knew. Sander was not scared of scaling

mountains or leaping across ravines but he had one real, deep fear. Sander did not want to grow old. He left the very next day and did not return home for several years.

He discovered many new sights, just as he had promised, and had adventures in all four corners of the kingdom. One of the happiest was when he met the flying wolves of Wending. It took time to gain their trust, but soon a bond was established and, for the first time, he was able to have adventures up in the sky as well as down on the earth. When he discovered the world above, where the castle now stood, it seemed like a dream – a creation of his imagination – but when Conan had lain down and rested on the very clouds themselves, he had known it was real. He felt sure that this was the big discovery – the one that for which he would be remembered.

It was in this uninhabited, cloud-filled world that Sander first encountered the unicorn.

In those days, he had not yet begun to adopt the form of a unicorn – he was still a sorcerer. They were as surprised as each other to meet another person in this hidden land. The sorcerer recognized Sander was special. Sander had a drive and a charm about him that he did not possess himself. The sorcerer would have been a fool to let someone with such qualities walk away, for he knew that in time, they would be useful to him.

So he made Sander an offer: he would use his magic to give him anything in the world he wanted. In return he wanted only two things. Firstly, Sander should not tell a soul about this hidden world in the clouds. There was no castle back then, but he had big plans for this world. Secondly, Sander must agree to work for him. Not now, not the following year or the year after that. But he should come when he was called and be prepared to do whatever it was that was asked of him.

"What is it exactly you want me to do?" asked Sander.

"I don't know. Yet," was the sorcerer's reply.

"I wouldn't need to ... hurt anyone, or ... kill anyone, would I?"

"No, I promise that nothing I ask of you will ever involve physical harm to yourself or another."

So Sander agreed. After all, if it didn't involve hurting another, then it couldn't be so terrible, could it?

He whispered his wish, his heart's desire, and the sorcerer made it real for him. The deal was done.

Working for the sorcerer was easy. He never seemed to need Sander, although Sander continued to enjoy the benefits of his wish. Whenever he asked if there was anything he could do, the reply was, "Not yet. I shall tell you when the time is right."

The world in the clouds grew. Sander never saw how it was built but every time he visited, it was bigger and better. Humble buildings to begin with and then the castle, rising up as if from the clouds themselves. The sorcerer's magic was great indeed. When Sander was tired of camping out under the stars, he could stay there in luxury for a time.

Then, three years ago, everything changed. The sorcerer was angry. Everything he had so carefully planned was under threat. It was then that Sander saw him as a unicorn for the first time. The Greatest Unicorn. As a unicorn, his powers were ten times that of a common sorcerer. That was how he had managed to build the castle. But at the moment, he could only transform for short periods of time.

He could achieve great things and lead whole cities, but he needed to harness that power. He needed more emotion: Sadness, compassion, anger, love. He had limited access to these feelings himself but he had begun to wonder if there was a way he might be able to use the emotions of others, for his own purposes. And that was where Sander could help him. Finally, it was time. Sander had work to do.

Sander had protested, of course. He did not want to lead people away, knew that it was cruel to tempt them with the promise of wishes granted, but by then of course, it was too late.

It was only now, after spending time with Thandie, that he realized he had a choice. He didn't have to live this way any more.

So now he turned to face the unicorn, fully aware of what he was doing.

"I have worked for you for years. My debt is paid. Undo the sorcery. I take back my wish. I wish now only to be free from you – whatever that means."

The interpreter spoke for the unicorn once again. "So, you think that the girl is special? You think that she can free all these people by herself?"

Sander said nothing.

"She may be brave and self-assured but she is not special. Before you intervened, she was about to give me all her memories. She was no stronger than any of the others. Weaker than them, even, because of all that emotion she keeps stored up inside."

"Thandie is not weak," said Sander. He had never met a braver person. He wished that he could say the same about himself.

"Sometimes we are drawn to those who have the strengths we desire for ourselves. I once thought you were special. You have charm, a way with people and a gift for music that I do not possess. I thought that you would support me in my goals: that you would be a loyal servant. But I was blind to your weaknesses. You are, it seems, too easily swayed by others. I cannot trust you. And an untrustworthy subordinate is of no use to me. You have betrayed me and now I will take back what is mine."

$\mathscr{C}$HAPTER SIXTEEN

THE STOLEN ONES
Thandie

Thandie flung open the double doors. She didn't know what she had been expecting – a dark prison, a fight with some guards – but it certainly hadn't been this.

As she stepped into the room and closed the doors behind her, the warmth struck Thandie. The throne room had been icy and dark but this room was golden and cosy. And it was full of people. Happy-looking people, dressed in fine clothes. They didn't look like prisoners. It was the most beautiful room that Thandie had ever seen. Light streamed in from high windows and lower windows were free of bars. There were paintings and tapestries of beautiful beasts: a dragon, a phoenix and some snowy white flying wolves. There was even a set of glass doors, leading out into the mist.

Long, rectangular pools like the ones in the throne room ran along both sides of this room. There were toys, puzzles and other playthings. For a moment, Thandie wondered if she had come to the right place. These people could not be the stolen ones. But then she looked more closely. They were smiling and seemed content, but their eyes were not engaging with the world around them or with each other. No one turned to look at her: a stranger entering the room.

Maybe all was not as it first appeared.

Thandie looked at each face in turn, hoping to see someone she recognized. As she did so, she realized she had been doing this for years: every time she entered a room full of people. She was looking for her mother's face. But she had to stop looking. She would not find her mother here. Instead, she must free these people and take them home. For Linnell's father. For Linnell. For Sander. For Tib. And, most importantly, for herself.

Besides, her mother could not be here. There was nobody here over about the age of eighteen – they were all on the cusp of adulthood. The stolen ones. They didn't know it, but they were about to be free.

Thandie breathed deeply, trying to calm her panic. She reached into her pocket and felt the worn cover of her diary. This would help her, just as it helped Sander to save her from the unicorn. She needed to find Linnell. All she had to go on was Sander's description and her father's. So she knew she was looking for someone beautiful (although that may have been a loving father's biased opinion) with blonde hair, who must be one of the oldest here. It was so hard to tell. Countless girls had fair hair and it was so difficult to tell their ages. She would just have to approach people one by one.

She began walking through the room, looking at each individual face. One boy with freckles – a bit younger that her – pushed a little model sailboat along the sparkling water. Two smiling boys in close-fitting blue outfits were juggling, throwing wooden batons to each other and expertly catching every one. Another girl absent-mindedly unwrapped candies from coloured papers in a glass dish. Another looked so like Hetty from the back that she had to walk around and stare at her, just to check. She ran up to the first girl. The one with the toffees. She dispensed with any formal greetings and launched straight into an explanation of why she was there.

"I am Thandie and I am here to rescue you. I am looking for Linnell Redfern. What is your name?"

The girl did not reply at first. She popped one of the sweet treats into her mouth and chewed slowly, looking almost at Thandie but not quite. "I'm not sure," she said, through the chewing.

Thandie took out the little leather book and read a few of the female names aloud.

"Marietta? Posy? Flora? Fay?"

There seemed to be a glimmer of recognition and the girl sat up straighter and smoothed down her skirts. But then the blank look came over her once again. "Would you like one?" she offered, pushing the dish towards Thandie.

Thandie shook her head. This was a waste of time. She stood up and called into the room, "I am here to free you all." Her voice wasn't particularly loud but nobody else was making any noise and the sound echoed alarmingly around the room.

A couple of people glanced at her, smiling softly, but not one replied. They were all caught up in their own mundane activities. Thandie shuddered. It could have so easily been her, if Sander hadn't pulled her back. She would have been like these people:

mute and blankly smiling.

She walked slowly around the room, hands clasped to her mouth. What was she going to do now, if nobody even remembered their own names? This wasn't going to work. And if it didn't work, what would she do? Run away on her own? She took another deep breath to compose herself. If she couldn't find Linnell, she would search for the Essendor people. Although Essendor was a big city, it was still small enough that one started to see familiar faces, especially those of a similar age. She knew little Clover Malling – the youngest to go missing – had red curly hair. Perhaps Thandie would recognize her.

She continued scanning the crowded room, and then she saw a face that she was sure could only be Linnell. The girl was really quite beautiful, with straw-coloured hair braided tightly around her head, a deep blue dress and pearls in her hair. She sat in a high-backed gilt chair, hands clasped in her lap, gazing up at one of the high windows. Most people in the room were silent, or talking to themselves, but this girl was singing. Or rather humming a pretty but meandering tune, as if she couldn't remember the words. She had a sweet singing voice.

"Linnell!" called Thandie, rushing to her, but the girl did not turn around. Still, there was a definite resemblance to the portrait that she'd seen in Linnell's bedroom, which must have been her mother. And the singing, of course. Thandie stood right by her and said her name again: "Linnell?" The girl smiled politely and looked faintly puzzled, gazing around as if there was a Linnell in the room but she just couldn't identify her.

She seemed to want to help. "I think I knew a Linnell once," she said, her brows knitting together. Her voice was clear and high.

"Yes," said Thandie, rummaging in her bag and bringing out the flower crown and the books. "These belonged to her."

Linnell held the dried flower crown flat in her hands like a dinner plate. Then she reached for a brown stalk that had come loose and tucked it tidily back in place. She hummed again as she did so, and then stopped, gazing up at Thandie with wide blue eyes. "Did I make this? A long time ago?"

Thandie nodded. As much as she wanted to shout at Linnell, shake at her, get her away from this place, she sensed she shouldn't rush her.

Linnell frowned. "There were some woods. Some flowers…" she began. She stared towards Thandie, but not directly at her, as though she were trying to recollect a dream.

"That's right," said Thandie gently. "Some woods, and a

farm. Your cottage with just you and your father. A little yellow bird called Sunbeam. Do you remember?"

Linnell reached her hand forward and looked up, as if expecting a little yellow canary to fly over and perch there. But then she stopped and lowered her hand. The memory had fluttered away. But Thandie could help retrieve it, she knew it. "You went to the woods with your schoolbooks, and you met a boy. He brought you here, do you remember?"

Linnell shook her head but Thandie continued. "The boy played a pipe. You liked the music. He played along to your song."

The pipe. It was still slung in its holder across her shoulder. She brought it out, put it to her lips and began to play, steadily and carefully. She played the same notes that Sander had played at Linnell's father's house. It was a simple tune and she could do it if she concentrated.

The girl knew the tune. Her eyes looked into Thandie's, properly this time. She looked sharper, and her blank smile dropped away. She began to hum along, but this time there was a shape to the tune. She followed the notes perfectly.

"Words. We need the words," said Thandie. She put the pipe away and opened her diary. The loose paper covered in Yannick's handwritten lyrics was still tucked inside. Thandie unfolded it.

She was not a great singer but she had to do this: it was a way to break through to Linnell. She took a deep breath and sang, as loudly and in tune as she could manage.

"To me you are a diamond,
To me you are a pearl,
To me you are an emerald,
To me you are the world.

"I'd give you a diamond to shine the whole day long,
But I have no diamond, so I give to you this song."

Some of the other children in the room stopped and stared at her but the thought of an audience listening to her questionable singing voice didn't concern Thandie as it might usually. Because the song was working its magic.

Recognition shone in Linnell's expression like a lit lamp. She was coming back. As if to prove Thandie right, she joined in with the next verse.

"To me you are the mountain,
To me you are the sea,

To me you are the forest,
You're everything to me."

Thandie picked up the pipe again and played the melody, her fingers finding the notes easily. And Linnell sang the next words without prompting.

"I'd give you a diamond to shine the whole day long,
But I have no diamond, so I give to you this song."

At the end of the song, Linnell stood quite still, her mouth slightly open. "My song," she whispered. "My mother's song. My father's song. My father…"

She turned slowly and gazed around, as if expecting to find him, but instead, seeing this room and all these people for the first time.

"Why am I here?" she asked softly, tears filling in her eyes.

Thandie found it difficult to watch her struggling. "There was a unicorn, do you remember?"

Linnell nodded slowly and looked down at her clothes. She smoothed out the skirt with her hand. "Yes, I remember the unicorn. He granted my wish. But then—" She trailed off and closed her eyes.

"The unicorn is evil," explained Thandie. "He takes people's memories from them to stay powerful and strong. Every person in this room has had their memories – their life – stolen from them. But I am here to help. My name is Thandie and I am a friend. Do you want your memories back?"

Linnell nodded again. "My father—"

"He's waiting for you back home," said Thandie. "Your old life awaits as it always has. But you can't have both. It is your memories or your wish, do you understand?"

Linnell began to cry. "My wish was foolish. I don't really care about fine clothes. Not if my sacrifice must be so great. I choose my memories. I want them all back."

Thandie stared open-mouthed at Linnell's hair and clothes. They were changing. "I think it is working. All you had to do was to take back the wish."

Linnell looked down at her skirt and stroked the embroidered fabric. The detailed gold embroidery unravelled and shrank back into the material of the skirt, as if someone were unpicking it from the wrong side. At the same time, the vivid colour of the dress faded before their eyes, turning from a deep blue to nondescript beige. Her bodice loosened and the pearls fell from her hair, bouncing on the marble floor and disappearing like raindrops.

At the same time, some colour returned to Linnell's face, and some lucidity to her expression. Linnell was back. She was still as beautiful as ever, but now she looked like an ordinary peasant girl rather than a member of the royal court. Thandie thought she might prefer her this way. She looked like someone who might become a friend.

Then Thandie's heart leaped as she realized exactly what this transformation meant. The spell was undone. It had worked. As long as no one followed her in and stopped her, she could save everyone in this room. The thought made her heart beat faster in panic. She couldn't let that happen. She ran to the double doors. If she wedged something between the two handles, then it would prevent them from opening and give her time to free as many people as possible.

She looked around for something to lodge there but could see nothing suitable. Then she remembered the Y-shaped stick that was Tib's catapult. It was the perfect size and shape. She slid it between the handles so that the upper part was caught between them and they couldn't open.

Thandie turned and Linnell was behind her, following her like a stray pup.

"How long have I been here?" whispered Linnell softly.

Thandie put a hand on the other girl's arm. "Later. I will tell you everything later. But for now, I need your help. We need to free all these other people."

BACK IN THE THRONE ROOM
Sander

The unicorn suddenly flinched, as if under attack from an invisible source. Sander smiled. Was this a sign that he was losing power? Perhaps Thandie was having some success in the other room "Some of the memories have been returned to their rightful owner, haven't they?"

The interpreter spoke for the unicorn again.

"Of course the girl will be able to communicate with Linnell. She knows about her, from you and Linnell's father. But there is no way she will do the same with the other young people in that room. All she has is their names, which they will not even recognize."

Sander's smile faltered. He feared this might be true.

The interpreter continued.

"She will fail, then she will come back and see you for who you really are. She won't be interested in your explanations. She will be defeated, vulnerable and still searching for her mother. Then, one way or another, she will give up her precious memories to my master. There will be forty-four people in that room and the Greatest Unicorn will be greater still."

"But what then? If you don't have me, how will you find any more young people?"

"My master does not plan to stay up in this castle forever. With just one more young person's memories, he will be strong enough to execute the second part of his plan to take over the kingdom. And Thandie's memories are so powerful, so emotional, so perfect! You picked a good candidate, Sander."

Sander was filled with hate.

"We will start with the city of Essendor. They are weak without their precious queen and her sister. There is no Midnight Unicorn to protect them.

"The Greatest Unicorn will appear in a golden haze – delivering their precious children to their homes. The people will hear how the evil Midnight Unicorn kept the stolen ones captive and will be eternally grateful for their return. They will look for a new saviour. The poor Queen Audrey will die of her mysterious sleeping sickness, her sister will be banished, and the throne will be free for the taking."

Sander's heart beat faster. Could a fourteen-year-old girl really undo all these years of planning? He hoped so.

"Had you waited, had you continued in your work, then you would have been able to share in that power. Now, you will be nothing."

Sander would be nothing. Yet the thought that he was finally doing the right thing made him feel stronger and braver than ever before.

He turned to face the unicorn, ready to accept his fate.

THE OTHERS
Thandie

Thandie made a sweeping gesture to the other people in the room. "We need to help these people. They have all had their memories taken, just like you. Can you tell me any of their names?" asked Thandie.

"No." Linnell hung her head. "I have been here for a long time but I don't think I have ever spoken to any of the others…"

"Don't be ashamed. None of this is your fault," said Thandie, putting her hands on Linnell's shoulders. Linnell's eyes darted to the doorway, which was now temporarily locked by Tib's catapult.

"Where is he?" she whispered. "Does he know you're here?"

She was talking about the unicorn, of course. Thandie could tell how scared the poor girl was. "Yes, but don't worry, my friend is keeping him occupied." She tried not to think about Sander, about how he was getting on. Or about what would happen if Sander's plan failed. "Try not to think about the unicorn. We need to concentrate on taking back the stolen memories."

Linnell looked around at the door again and clasped Thandie's hands "Let's not. Let's just lead the people out of the castle to safety. They will come with us, I'm sure. They will do anything they are told."

Thandie looked at the boy with the boat and the girl with the toffees. She was sure that Linnell was right, and that the stolen ones would follow, but Linnell didn't have the full picture. "You don't understand. The unicorn is using the memories to gain power. With every memory we take back, he weakens."

"It doesn't matter how powerful he is if we escape! We will tell those in power and they will send some soldiers to fight him."

Thandie shook her head. "We need to free them properly – restore their memories. Are you sure there isn't anything you can tell me about any of the others here?"

Linnell shook her head, her eyes welling with tears. She still looked so confused. "I just want to go home."

"It doesn't matter," said Thandie. "We'll get you home." She knew it was not Linnell's fault. Her memory had been stolen; it must have been traumatic. But still Thandie wished there was something – anything – Linnell could tell her about these people. She opened her book and read out some of the names at the back.

"Posy Tweed, John Fairton, and Ivy Medway, all from Arvale. That is your closest village. Do you recognize any names or faces?"

"Ar-vale, Ar-vale," repeated Linnell dreamily, staring into space. Thandie looked around hopelessly. Any one of these people could be a Posy, Ivy or a John. She couldn't tell from the way they looked. She shouted out a couple of names from the list but nobody paid any attention. She had literally nothing to go on.

Then she noticed that Linnell was humming again. A new tune this time.

"What is that? What it the tune you are humming?"

"'Ar-vale, Our vale.' It is a song from Arvale, I think. The

Arvale harvest song…"

"Sing it! Sing the words!" shouted Thandie excitedly.

Linnell looked surprised but began to sing.

"Arvale – our vale,
Harvest time again.
Arvale – our vale,
Celebrate the rain…."

It was a simple tune with just four notes. Thandie could follow along on the pipe, even if it sounded a little clumsy. She wished Sander were here. He would have picked it up instantly. But still, she was pleased with the job she was doing. She heard his voice in her head as she played. *"Don't think about how hard you are pressing your fingers into the holes or how hard you are blowing. Just think about that bird in the tree… Listen to the bird."*

Right now, Linnell was the songbird, singing sweetly and Thandie was accompanying her morning song.

The two girls walked around the room, until four pairs of eyes gradually turned towards them. Thandie noticed that same spark in their eyes that she had seen with Linnell. These were surely the four missing people from Arvale. Linnell confirmed it. "I think I recognize them. Yes. But they are so much taller now. Thandie, how long have I been here?"

Thandie couldn't bring herself to answer this question. "I will tell you everything I know, but now is not the time. We need to give these people their memories back and escape from this place. You understand that, don't you?"

Linnell nodded and continued to sing as Thandie read their names aloud from the page. Gradually, the mist began to clear for them and the four Arvale youths sang along to their song, tentatively at first and then with passion.

That was when it hit Thandie: if the Arvale harvest song worked for the Arvale people, then why not the Essendor wintertide song? She left Linnell to talk to the Arvale group, picked up the pipe and went to find Clover Malling and the other Essendor children. It didn't take her long to identify them, and she piped the Essendor song, the same tune that she had played that beautiful breaking dawn when Sander had given her first real pipe-playing lesson.

Back then, she'd fought against the memories the song stirred, of eating chestnuts at Madam Tilbury's, and learning to play the pipe with her mother. This time, she let the memories flood back to her. Snow falling in Essendor square as Queen Audrey was crowned, the reds and greens of winter foliage hung in boughs on people's doors and the honeyed smells of festive baked buns. This song brought back so many memories of her birth city. Surely it must be the same for anyone who had grown up in Essendor? Thandie saw the lights flicker behind their eyes as the music stirred something deep within them.

Linnell was by her side again, cheeks flushed. "It's working! The Arvale group have remembered who they are."

"Well done, Linnell. It is working here, too, but I think we need the words as well as the music. Will you sing along?" She scribbled down the words and passed them to Linnell. This time, as Thandie played, Linnell sang along in her sweet way.

"In Essendor, at Wintertide,
Wrap up warm and come outside,
As the snow begins to fall,
The unicorn protects us all,
Midnight black against the white,
In the silence of the night,
Take my hand and dance with me,
In Essendor, we're all born free."

The Essendor children began to come back, little Clover Malling the first to start singing along. That was when Thandie realized: her plan was actually going to work.

CHAPTER SEVENTEEN

THE TRANSFORMATION

Sander

Sander faced the unicorn, no longer afraid.

"I don't care about the deal any more. I don't care about promises I made or promises you made. I refuse to work for you any more." Sander felt lighter, freer, just saying the words.

The unicorn turned back his ears, showed his teeth and swished his tail violently. He was angry, Sander could tell. But Sander didn't care.

The interpreter was angry, too. She raised her staff.

"My master has made life extremely easy for you. For the past eighteen years you have been free to roam, to adventure, to do as you please. All he expected in return was your loyalty: a small price to pay. But you have let him down."

Sander held his hands to his head. "No. It was not a small price to pay; it was the greatest price of all. I have put aside all my morals, all my beliefs, to work for you. What you have both done to those young people is pure evil. You have used part of their very souls for your own gain, without caring who you hurt."

The interpreter laughed loudly, the sound echoing around the room. "You talk as though you were not part of this. As though it were not the three of us, working together."

Sander shook his head. "None of this was my idea. I would never have agreed to the deal if I had known what it meant."

"If you really believed that, Sander, you would have never brought Linnell to my master two years ago. Yet you did. And you brought forty-two other people after her. Quite a long time to change your mind, wasn't it?"

"I thought it was too late for me. But I realize now that it is not."

"Why? Because of that girl, Thandie? She might talk about selflessness but she has her own wants. She is not really here for the others. She wanted to find her mother. We all just want to help ourselves."

"Maybe to begin with but then most of us come to realize that we cannot live in isolation. My time of selfishness has come to an end. I have grown up. So undo the wish that you granted and let me be free."

MANY YEARS AGO
Sander

The one thing that Sander couldn't find at the top of a mountain or on a deserted island was youth. He couldn't bear the thought of losing his youthful looks, his charm or his fit and healthy body. And that was the great prize that had been offered to him twenty years ago. As long as he worked for the unicorn, Sander's skin would remain smooth and unlined, his eyes bright, his hair lustrous and the skip in his step would be as energetic as ever. He would not age.

While the sorcerer perfected his skills of transformation and the castle grew in size and splendour, Sander's quests and adventures continued. He realized that, with youth on his side, he really could be the best adventurer; there was nothing to hold him back. At first he returned home every six months or so, but then the time between his visits lengthened until he stopped visiting at all.

He thought little of his family and the life he had left behind, until one day just three years back.

Sander was in a marketplace near where he had grown up when he heard two old women gossiping: his mother was ill.

He hadn't seen her for over five years. He had to see her now.

He came to the village at night-time and sat by her bedside in the cottage where he had lived as a boy. she was unwell, struggling with her breathing, her speech laboured.

She reached to him with her frail hand, and he stroked its papery skin. The illness had aged her, which was a pity: she used to be so beautiful. He held her hand between his own.

"Sander? Time has not changed you at all. How can it be? You are nearing thirty and yet you do not look a day over sixteen."

"It is just the fresh air and exercise, mother. They are good for the mind and body."

But she knew. Even in this weak light and battling ill health, she knew. She didn't know how he had done it but she knew that some kind of spell or enchantment must be responsible. Sander realized that he could not keep returning here, to this village where people knew him. They would grow and change but he would stay the same. If he chose to keep his youth, then he would have to give up all emotional ties and lead a lonely and selfish life. Or he could return to the unicorn and ask for his old life back. He could come back to the village and lead a normal, happy life.

He made his decision: he said a tearful farewell to his mother and left the village without contacting the rest of his family. Shortly afterwards, he heard that his mother had died. He didn't return.

After his mother's death, the unicorn came to him. By this time he had almost forgotten about his part of the deal. No, not forgotten, pushed it to the back of his mind.

But now the unicorn told Sander exactly what was required of him.

He needed people. Young people, with fresh memories.

"No," said Sander. He was no kidnapper.

But the unicorn was adamant. "You promised to do anything as long as it didn't involve hurting anyone," he said.

"But taking people from their families... It would be hurting them. Not physically but... It would be wrong," said Sander. "It is something I cannot do."

"Then our agreement has come to an end," said the unicorn.

"I will give you back all the years that I have saved you."

And Sander realized what that meant. He stretched his arm out in front of him and looked at his hand, trying to imagine it as his mother's had looked. He would age overnight. He would be a different person. An older person. Uglier, weaker. This was something he wasn't prepared to do. He had achieved what he had always wanted: eternal youth. And if all he had to do was to lead some people here, to this grand castle, then it was a small price to pay.

"I will do it," he said.

He had cut all ties with his family; he had no distant relations and no friends. And if there was no one to answer to, then what did it matter if you did wrong?

Except now, since meeting Thandie, there *was* someone to answer to.

IN THE THRONE ROOM

TRANSFORMATIONS
Sander

The interpreter laughed a loud cackling laugh, and the unicorn lowered his head, pointing the sharp tip of his horn towards Sander.

Back when he had made his wish, he was so sure of his chosen path, so sure that youth was the most important thing in the world. Back then, the sorcerer had cast the spell from a wand. The spell had felt good, like golden sunlight flooding his body.

This time, the magic came from the unicorn's horn. It shot out towards him and pierced his chest. Twenty years of aging hit him at once, the pain spreading through his body. He felt it in his hands first. They stiffened, like claws. He couldn't bend them. His knees, his elbows, all his joints, felt as though they could do with a good oiling. His head hurt, his eyes were dry. Even his hearing was deadened. He ran his tongue along his teeth. They were more crowded, crooked. All those niggling ailments he had avoided for years came at once. His head ached. He ran his hand through his hair and found it sparse.

Sander inspected his hands, which until a moment ago had been smooth and unlined with even, pink nails. Now they were wrinkled around the knuckles, with thick, ridged nails. He turned them over and felt the calluses on his palms.

"That is just your hands, Sander. Would you like to see your face?" the interpreter sneered, and the unicorn stepped towards the central frozen pool, dipping his horn towards the ice.

Sander knew he should look away, put off this moment until he was alone, but curiosity got the better of him. He gazed into the pool at his face, which was no longer the young, tanned, sixteen-year-old face that had been such a pleasure to inhabit for the past twenty years. The face that gazed back at him from the pool was unfamiliar, lined, puffy. His eyebrows were bushier and lower, and his eyelids sagged above bruise-coloured smudges. His hairline grew further back. Even his nose seemed larger. His face but not his face. The face of an aging man.

The unicorn stepped back and met his gaze. "Your handsome looks opened doors for you, did they not? Meals and journeys given for free, beds for the night. Many were taken in by your attractive appearance and charming mannerisms but we will see if this continues. Now you are a man with average looks at the onset of middle age. Perhaps you will understand the limitations that we have faced, as aging sorcerers in an unforgiving world."

Sander forced a smile. "I am perhaps not as shallow as you imagine. Life will be different, but it will go on."

"Think of the future, Sander. What do you have to look forward to? You abandoned your family long ago, Thandie will be disgusted by you and you will be known throughout the kingdom as the man who stole children away from their families."

The interpreter laughed again but stopped suddenly when the unicorn flinched, side-stepping as he had before. She looked at her master with concern and then continued speaking for him.

"Perhaps you will continue on your adventures, staying fit and fighting as hard as you can against the inevitable aging process, but there will come a time when you are too weak to haul yourself up a rope, too frail to walk long distances. What will be waiting for you then, Sander, apart from creeping old age and death? Perhaps then, you will regret your betrayal and the choice you have made."

Sander looked away from the pool and met the unicorn's gaze. He refused to give in to these defeatist thoughts. "I will never regret doing the right thing. And I may be weakened with age, but I notice that you are also weakening. You are losing your power."

It was true. The unicorn stood still, no longer stamping or running but breathing hard, breath rattling. His power was dwindling.

Despite the transformation and his newfound vulnerability, Sander laughed. "It's working!" he cried. "Whatever Thandie is doing in there is sapping your strength. People are regaining their memories. You are no longer the Greatest Unicorn."

The unicorn's eyes flashed with anger and a dark green mist crept up around him, starting from his hooves and travelling higher.

Sander blinked and stepped back, fearful that it was a toxic spell.

The unicorn reared up, slowly. There was so much mist now that Sander could barely see, but he concentrated hard on the unicorn, who was shaking his head vigorously and moving his limbs as if running on the spot. The figure began to look less equine and more human. The mist slowly cleared, dissolving into the air, and the Greatest Unicorn was gone. In his place, stood a man. A man that Sander recognized, older and more tired than the last time they'd met, but still tall and slim with dark clothes and a deep yellow hat. The sorcerer.

"So I am not the only one who has aged," said Sander.

As well as looking old and tired, the man also looked angry. Like a man whose dreams had been thwarted and who would not give in easily. He narrowed his eyes at Sander.

"You think you can beat me but you are very much mistaken. Remember that without my unicorn powers I am still a sorcerer – the greatest sorcerer in the kingdom! You and that girl are no match for me."

The interpreter stepped towards the sorcerer, with concern in her eyes, but he turned on her, raising his voice. "Why are you still standing there? I no longer need you – I can speak for myself! Find that girl and stop her!"

RATTLING DOORS
Thandie

It was working. With music, familiar local songs and the few facts she knew, Thandie and Linnell managed to bring the young people out of their living slumber. And the more who regained their memory, the easier and faster it became. Everyone knew somebody or someone. People sung snippets of local songs that their cousin had shared with them, or described the hair colour of someone who had disappeared from the next village.

Thandie ticked them off one by one.

She didn't have time to speak to them, to discover their stories, but it was fascinating to see them return to the real word.

One girl had striking black ringlets but as she regained her memories, the perfect curls unfurled until they were poker-straight. Still glossy and healthy-looking, just straight. Had she really given up everything just for curly hair?

Another girl gave up an adorable mahogany coloured puppy with big black eyes to have her memories back again.

But the ones that really stuck in Thandie's mind were the juggling boys. She guessed that one of them must be Aldo, the missing circus performer, so she played the famous Elithian circus march. The younger boy immediately stopped juggling and listened to its fast tempo. But as recognition lit up in his eyes, the older boy faded, ghost-like, and then vanished. The pain in the younger boy's expression was so acute that Thandie had to look away. She knew what it was like to get so close to finding someone you loved, only to lose them again.

As people returned, Thandie's excitement grew, but with it, the jangling of her nerves increased. She wondered what was happening on the other side of the doors. As the stolen ones recovered their memories, did the unicorn grow weaker? Or was he just biding his time, waiting to attack? Her gaze darted towards the double doors, expecting them to burst open at any time and for an angry unicorn to rush in. She had no idea what she would do if he did.

The atmosphere in the room changed. When she had walked in, it had been quiet and tranquil, like a room full of ghosts. But now, people were talking to one another, helping one another, explaining what was happening.

She had now met every person in that room. Everyone from the list was there. Everyone was recovering their memories, although some were slower than others.

Thandie began to realize the scale of the problem. There were dozens of people here. And they were all beginning to look to her – the leader – with a single question: "Can we go home now?"

She just needed a moment to think. She would get the people out of this castle and as far away from here as possible, then she would stop, breathe, and formulate a plan. But there was no time. A rattling sound drew her attention to the double doors.

The handles were rattling as they twisted and turned.

Someone was trying the doors from the other side.

Tib's flimsy catapult jiggled between the door handles, which would not hold for more than a few minutes. If it was the unicorn, then he would undo all the good that she had done here. Unless it was Sander. Thandie ran to the doors and pressed herself against the left-hand one with all the strength in her body.

"Sander?" she called, just in case, but there was no answer. There was a possibility he couldn't hear her, but she couldn't risk it.

"Linnell!" she shouted, "we need to get these people far away from the castle. Open the back doors. Get everyone out."

Linnell hesitated, looked around at the sea of confused people. Her eyes were welling with tears again.

Thandie wanted to scream. She knew how confused Linnell must feel, but if the unicorn managed to get in, then they could all be recaptured. Or worse. The quest would fail and they would never be found. "Open the back doors," she shouted to Linnell. "Now!"

Linnell ran to the glass doors and opened them easily. The unicorn had spoken the truth: they were unlocked. An icy blast of air swept into the room. "This way," she said to the Arvale group, who wandered outside. Thandie was relieved that some people were escaping, but they were going so slowly, as if they were browsing for fruit at the market, not running for their lives.

"Hurry up, please!" she called. "I think the unicorn is coming."

Linnell wrung her hands in front of her. "I can't do this by myself. Help me, Thandie!"

But Thandie didn't want to abandon her place by the door and, anyway, she couldn't leave without Sander – not after he had saved her. She thought desperately what instructions she could give Linnell. She didn't have a rulebook; she was making this up as she went along. And then she remembered: the steps that they'd seen outside the castle, leading back home, Sander had said. "The steps! she cried, "Go around the castle, find the steps and I will meet you there."

At this clear instruction, Linnell seemed to find renewed purpose, and sprang into action. Thandie was too far away to hear what she was saying, but Linnell sped up, moving urgently from group to group, ushering the people through the doorway, pointing them in the right direction.

But the doors kept rattling. Thandie could feel the jolts as whoever was on the other side pushed heavily. They were going to break through – Thandie knew it – but she would be ready for them. Just as Linnell ushered the last of the stolen ones out into the swirling clouds, Thandie reached for the catapult. She freed the door handles but armed herself. The double doors burst open and Thandie was sent staggering sideways. She took a couple of steps to right herself and aimed her recovered weapon at whoever was coming through the door.

As she had suspected, it was not Sander.

But it was not the unicorn, either.

It was the interpreter.

THE INTERPRETER
Thandie

The interpreter strode through the doorway and stood, looking around at the empty room. She was taller than Thandie and her head reached nearly to the top of the doorframe. With her near-white hair, stern eyes and gauzy white dress billowing in the cold air, she made a formidable figure.

"Where have they gone?" she asked, her voice icy. Her question was aimed at Linnell, who was standing petrified by the door. The stolen ones had made it outside and Linnell could be out of the door and with them in moments. She would be free.

But Linnell just stood there.

"Just go, Linnell!" screamed Thandie. "Follow them!" but Linnell continued to stand as still as one of the ice sculptures in the throne room, staring at the interpreter.

The interpreter took a few paces towards Linnell, her long dress giving the impression that she was gliding across the floor. "You didn't think you could get away with this, did you? My master will not be beaten by a couple of young girls. Not this time."

The interpreter banged her staff on the floor, muttered some incomprehensible words, and pointed her staff towards the open door. This seemed to bring Linnell out of her trance, but too late. Thorns sprouted from the floor and began to grow over the doorway – thick, wiry black thorns. Linnell rushed to the door and tried to push past them but they were immovable and growing thicker by the second.

Thandie held Tib's catapult tightly, like a charm, thinking of how effective it had been against Sander that night in Essendor. She raised it, pulled back the string and aimed it directly at the interpreter. She spoke in as loud and threatening a voice as she could muster. "Let us go now, or I will use this."

The old woman stared at Thandie and the corner of her mouth

twitched. At first, Thandie thought it was in anger, but then the interpreter threw back her head and laughed.

"Do you really mean to fight me with a child's toy? It is clear that you do not understand my power."

Thandie didn't delay any further: she let the missile fly towards the old woman. It was a powerful shot that flew straight and true but the interpreter was too quick for Thandie. She raised her staff to meet it, deflecting the shot and sending it flying straight back at Thandie. No ordinary staff could do that: it was her magic at work. The shot hit Thandie on the head, just above her right ear, and she staggered backwards, falling to the floor and clutching both hands to her head in pain.

The interpreter laughed again and pointed her staff at the catapult, breaking the string.

Then the old woman focused her attention entirely on Linnell. "You have been quite ungrateful and abused my master's hospitality. He is busy now, dealing with another betrayal, but you will come with me and answer some questions."

She grabbed Linnell by the arm and began to pull her towards the door.

Thandie lay sprawled on the floor, helpless, her bag and all her belongings scattered all around. Instinctively, she reached for her most treasured possession, her diary, and Tib's catapult which she tucked into the pocket of her dress. Then Sander's pipe, which she slid back into its holder.

She was only dimly aware of what was happening around her. Linnell was shouting, crying out as the interpreter dragged her towards the doors.

Sander's hunting darts were also scattered on the floor and Thandie reached out to gather them up. There were two within her reach and she picked them up with her fingertips, slowly, softly, not wanting to attract the interpreter's attention.

She picked up the pipe and, with a shaking hand, positioned the red-tailed dart into the end. Taking careful aim, to avoid causing any harm to Linnell, Thandie covered the sound hole and blew into the pipe, just as she had seen Sander do.

The dart flew swiftly, hitting the interpreter in the side of the neck. She turned, mouth falling open, and raised her right hand to her neck.

Then she crumpled to the floor.

BODY
Thandie

Linnell stood open-mouthed, eyes fixed on the prone body of the interpreter. "What happened?" she asked in a whisper. "Is she – dead?"

Thandie ran towards the old woman. The dart stood out of the side of her white neck like the last feather from a plucked chicken. Thandie twisted and pulled hard on the dart to remove it, and held it up for Linnell to see. The interpreter's arm hid her face but her back seemed to be moving up and down, so she was still breathing. Thandie had no idea if she would survive. Sander had said there was enough poison in a single dart to kill a grat outright, but Thandie wasn't sure what that meant for a fully-grown woman.

"She's alive," said Thandie. "We have to get out of here – away from the castle – before she awakes." Linnell didn't protest. Thandie held her by the hand as the interpreter had done, and they ran through the double doors.

CHAPTER EIGHTEEN

THE BATTLE
Sander

Sander had thought that he was safe. Had the sorcerer meant to kill him, then he would not have bothered to reverse the spell: he would have killed him on the spot.

But now that the stolen ones had their memories returned and he was weakened, Sander knew that the sorcerer could change his mind. He wouldn't want to risk Sander getting away now. Although the sorcerer was losing strength, he was still a great mind that had managed to create an entire world up in the clouds. And Sander faced him without a weapon, or even his treasured pipe.

Sander's body may have just aged twenty years but he was as alert and quick-witted as ever. He could wait for the sorcerer to attack, or he could take the initiative. He turned away from the sorcerer and raced up the steps to the throne. Either side of the throne was a flaming torch, set in a sconce. He took first one, and then the other, not because he needed two, but because he didn't want to leave the second one unattended.

As he took the torches, the light in the room changed and long shadows swung eerily up the pale ice blue walls. He strode back towards the sorcerer with a torch raised up in each hand, the sulphurous smell catching in his throat.

The sorcerer raised an eyebrow. "What do you think you are going to do – fight me with those? I can extinguish them both in a heartbeat." But the sorcerer did not extinguish them and Sander suspected that in his weakened state he could not. He looked pale, with dark shadows under his eyes, and was trembling. He didn't look like a powerful adversary.

Sander was just trying to decide what to do next, when the double doors burst open and Thandie and Linnell burst into the throne room. Relief washed over him. He was right: Thandie had somehow succeeded in her quest. Even the interpreter had not stopped her.

"Thandie! Linnell!" he called happily. He would have waved or run to them but was somewhat restricted by the torches.

But neither girl responded.

They both stared at him with confusion in their eyes.

TWO UNFAMILIAR MEN
Thandie

As they ran into the throne room, Thandie held the pipe near to her mouth, a dart in position. She expected to see Sander and the unicorn battling each other, or worse, the unicorn standing triumphant over the body of Sander. Instead, she saw two unfamiliar men staring at each other, one by the throne, half hidden behind two blazing torches, the other at the end of the walkway, in front of the circular pool.

One of them shouted but she wasn't sure which, or why.

She had no idea what was going on.

At least the unicorn had gone and she could get Linnell to safety before he returned. Then, she would find Sander and follow.

"Go, Linnell. Find the others and lead them down the steps

to a safe place – I will join you as soon as I can."

To Thandie's surprise, Linnell kissed her on the cheek. "Stay safe, Thandie." Then she ran down the stairs and towards the front door.

Thandie turned back to decide what to do next.

She took a proper look at the two men, who seemed on the verge of a fight.

One was tall and thin with a floppy yellow hat. He looked tired and stern. She felt that she seen him in the streets of Essendor, but not for some time. Then she realized something that she had been too slow to grasp as she raced into the throne room.

She knew the other man.

He was old – maybe in his mid thirties. He had fawn skin and sharp features, marked around the eyes with crow's feet. He was looking at her as if he knew her. At first, she couldn't place him. Perhaps he was a market stallholder from Essendor or someone she had encountered on Linnell's farm. But then she took in the stranger's unusual clothes – the colourful patchwork jacket and the red hat – and recognition quickly dawned on her. Her first instinct was to laugh – a quick barking laugh – although she didn't find it funny.

It was Sander. Not his father, brother or uncle, but Sander

himself. An older Sander.

If he was Sander, then the other man must be the unicorn. The unicorn, but also a man of magic and sorcery.

And Thandie finally understood the deal that Sander had made.

A BLAZE OF ICE
Sander

Thandie stared at him for a long time. He saw the realization dawn and her lip curl as she figured out who he was. Maybe she didn't mean to look at him with disgust but that is how it appeared.

"Thandie, I can explain!" he shouted. "There is so much I have been unable to tell you."

The iron torches were heavy in his hands; he could not hold them both for long. Spurred on by Thandie's appearance, he lifted the torch in his right hand and threw it, hard, in the sorcerer's direction.

The sorcerer remained completely calm, merely moving his head a few inches to the left to dodge the torch. It flew, a blazing streak, over the sorcerer's shoulder, past his ear and behind him, into the frozen pool.

Sander expected the torch to fizzle out, possibly the ice to melt, but instead, the icy circle caught alight instantly and flames shot out of the pool to head height. An intense heat took the chill off the air in the room and green smoke, like the smoke which had surrounded the sorcerer during his transformation, began to fill the room.

OLD
Thandie

Thandie stared at the flames, the green mist, the sorcerer and Sander.

She finally understood so much: the peculiar feeling that she had sometimes felt around Sander that he was an old soul in a young body.

"You are … old," she called out, above the roar and crackle of the flames

"I am," he replied. "I have been young for a long time – for twenty years – but I am old now. This man takes the shape of a unicorn. I only worked for him in return for the spell he cast."

So Sander had made a great personal sacrifice in the end: he had given up eternal youth to save her and the others.

"Go! Keep yourself safe!" he called, the way Thandie herself had called out to Linnell, earlier.

He seemed to be in control. She would leave and he would follow later. Thandie turned and raced towards the door.

THE REMAINING TORCH
Sander

The flames in the pool burned right through the thick layer of ice, if that was what it was, leaving a gaping hole in the centre of the room.

Sander held the remaining torch in both hands. He walked down the steps swinging it wildly to one side and then the other, as though keeping a wild animal at bay. If he could force the sorcerer back, then he would fall right into the open circle.

The sorcerer remained calm, barely registering Sander's efforts with the torch. He muttered something under his breath that could have been a spell and whenever Sander managed to get close to him, he held up an arm, blocking the fire, deflecting the flames.

The sorcerer was stronger than Sander had realized. Sander

wasn't sure that he could win this fight after all. But he had to. If Sander died, and the sorcerer survived, the sorcerer would take Thandie. He would take back Linnell and the others. The sorcerer would win and begin his attempt to take over the kingdom. The chances were that nobody would ever find this hidden world.

AT THE DOORS TO THE THRONE ROOM
Thandie

Thandie reached the doors to the throne room. She could leave now but it felt wrong to abandon Sander to his fight. She turned, just to check that he still had the upper hand. The green smoke partly obscured her view but it seemed that Sander was retreating: the sorcerer had moved away from the pool, and was nudging Sander closer and closer to the pillared wall.

Fight back, she willed him.

But he continued edging backwards until the sorcerer had Sander pinned against a pillar, holding him there with his left upper arm. Then the sorcerer began to wrestle the flaming torch away.

Thandie couldn't leave now; she had to do something.

BURNING HAIR
Sander

The sorcerer was so close that Sander could see the pores in his nose and the faintly bloodshot whites of his eyes. He had one arm pressed up against Sander's throat and the other on the flaming torch, trying to prise it from Sander's right hand.

They both had a grip on the torch and each did their best to gain control.

The sorcerer pushed the flame close to Sander's face. He could feel its heat on his cheek and smell hair burning. A steady drip of water fell on his shoulder; the heat from the torch must be melting one of the ice sculptures above.

The sorcerer narrowed his eyes. "You are a mere piper, no match for me. But if you admit defeat and turn the girl over to me, I will let you escape with your life."

"Never," said Sander. He found strength from somewhere and pushed the torch towards the sorcerer. He refused to concede this battle; there was too much to lose.

THE LAST DART
Thandie

There was one dart left. With trembling hands, Thandie placed it in the end of the pipe and took aim. She visualized the path that the dart would take, imagined it shooting straight to the sorcerer. If she had managed to hit the interpreter then surely she could do the same again. It would hit the sorcerer in the side of the neck and he would collapse, giving them both a chance to get out of this castle and away to safety.

Thandie blew.

The dart flew.

It missed.

LOST FEATHER
Sander

A dart whistled past Sander's right ear, hit the hard wall behind him and clattered to the floor. It was enough to momentarily distract the sorcerer from their fight and he looked away.

Sander saw the dart lying on the smooth floor, like a bird's lost feather. If he could just reach down and grab it, he could jab its sharp end into the sorcerer. The poison would immediately take effect and he would be free to get away.

He leaned down, his fingers almost within touching distance of the dart.

But, just as he got closer, the dart slid just a few hand's lengths away from him across the floor. He looked up sharply to see why.

The ice in the room was beginning to crack and the whole floor was shifting.

THE FLOOR
Thandie

She had not expected the dart to miss. She looked around desperately for another way to save Sander. She considered running back to the room where the interpreter lay, and gathering the remaining darts.

But then she noticed the floor in the throne room.

The flames in the central pool had burned out, and all the ice had melted. There was no longer anything there, just a gaping hole to the outside world. Even from where she stood, she could clearly see the blue sky.

Radiating from that circular hole were jagged cracks, which were growing longer and wider by the second.

"You have to get out of there!" yelled Thandie. "The floor is breaking!"

FISSURE
Sander

Sander heard Thandie call out. Two of the fissures in the floor widened and a giant slab of floor cracked away, sloping in to the middle of the room. He grabbed the pillar to stop himself from falling and managed to secure himself, but the sorcerer slid away, dropping the flaming torch and holding on to Sander's legs, just above his knees.

"Help me, Sander," called the sorcerer, looking up at him with pleading eyes. Sander could reach out and save them both or he could kick the sorcerer away, and watch him slide down into the swirling clouds.

UPPER HAND
Thandie

Sander had the upper hand in this fight once more. He had a firm grasp on the pillar and the sorcerer was losing his grip on Sander's legs. He fell a few inches and clasped Sander's calves.

"He's slipping! Let him go, Sander, save yourself!" she shouted. "Use the pillar to climb out!"

PUTTING IT RIGHT
Sander

Maybe Thandie was right. If Sander kicked out, he would be able to send the sorcerer sliding towards the centre. But maybe the sorcerer was still capable of using magic, and Sander could not take the risk of the sorcerer surviving.

However, there was one thing that the sorcerer would not be expecting: something that would definitely work.

Sander had done some dreadful things. Some would say that he had led a bad life. He had helped to take so much from so many. Now was his chance to do something honourable – he could rid the world of the Greatest Unicorn.

Sander looked at Thandie and smiled.

"You've done it," he shouted. "You don't need me any more. Keep playing the pipe!"

And he let go of the pillar.

LETTING GO
Thandie

Sander let go. It was a deliberate act, Thandie was sure. She gasped and ran a few metres back into the throne room, despite the instability of the floor. Both men slid rapidly towards the centre of the room, towards the gaping hole leading to nothing. The sorcerer's mouth widened in shock and he tried to turn on to his front, hands and feet scrabbling on the slippery slope, searching for a handhold but finding nothing.

Right behind him, Sander closed his eyes and stretched his arms out. He was so controlled and graceful that Thandie half-expected him to turn into a bird, but he did not. Both men slid down the slope, fell through the hole in the floor, into the clouds, and were gone.

TIME TO GET OUT
Thandie

Thandie ran to what had been the pool, and looked over the edge. All she could see were clouds and nothing beneath that, except, presumably, the mountains that they had climbed to get here. She half-expected Sander to peek back out from underneath, with his mischievous grin, to tell her that he was joking. But he did not.

They had gone. They had both gone.

Thandie shivered. The flames had gone and cold air blasted out of the hole in the floor.

She took a few steps away from the edge. The floor she was standing on began to creak. She had seen how rapidly part of the room broke away. She wasn't safe here.

She had to get out.

Somehow she managed to move her feet and stumble away from the gaping hole. She pushed her way out of the throne room doors, ran down the wide staircase, out of the front door with its beautiful coloured glass and out into the deserted cloudy landscape.

She ran as if she were being chased, although she wasn't sure who would be chasing her any more. The interpreter might awaken and come after her. She still felt that the unicorn might come after her, even though she had just seen the sorcerer disappear; she didn't know what to believe. All she knew was that she had to put as much distance between herself and the castle as possible.

She had told Linnell to head to the steps and that's where she must go, but for a moment, Thandie didn't know where the steps were. It seemed like a long time since the flying wolves had brought her to this land and she couldn't think which way to turn.

But then she saw a grat skull and shards of bone on the ground: the remnants of Conan and Kemi's meal. That gave her a sense of positioning and she remembered that the steps were close by. She ran, half blind in the thick cloud, in their direction. She ran, and she didn't look back.

CHAPTER NINETEEN

RUNNING

Thandie

Thandie found the steps easily, as if it was meant to be. She hurried down them, her feet going so quickly that she struggled to keep up. Finch always said that he preferred walking uphill to down, that going downhill hurt his knees, but after climbing up mountains, Thandie was relieved to be travelling downhill at last.

As she ran down, thoughts whirled around her mind.

Sander was gone. She had never been quite sure whether she could trust him but in the end, he had shown his loyalty. He had saved her and given up his own life. Was he really gone? Perhaps he had known something that she hadn't. Perhaps Conan had flown out and caught him in mid air.

She was sure that he had meant to fall but she was unsure why. Couldn't he have kicked the sorcerer away and saved himself? Perhaps it was Sander's way of giving up – giving in. He could have done so much more with his life. He could have had a family of his own, or taught children to play music, or continued on his adventures or … anything.

His voice came back to her: *"If I find myself in danger of growing old then I shall throw myself off a high mountaintop."*

Did he really mean that? Did he choose to die rather than face the aging process? It was such a sad fear. He did not allow himself the wisdom that came with age, the prospect of children or grandchildren: all the wonderful things about growing older.

She began to cry, all the pent up emotion of her experience rolling down her cheeks as fat tears. She cried for Sander, and for her mother and even for the sorcerer who was no longer part of this world.

But when her vision became too blurry, Thandie had to stop and wipe her eyes. She must concentrate on the steps. She didn't want to lose her footing. Wouldn't that be a shame – to travel all these miles and have all these adventures, only to trip and fall down some stone steps at the end. What would have been the point of it all?

She tried to think of other things, like what would be at the bottom of these steps. She remembered the options that Sander had given her. In reverse order, it had been flying wolves, a golden tree and some sort of basket across from the mountain.

But she didn't know, and what was the point of trying to guess what lay ahead? She just had to keep going.

BALANCE
Thandie

Just as it felt the steps would go on forever, Thandie heard the murmur of voices and knew she must have finally caught up with the stolen ones. Her feet emerged from the white mist before she did and she thought she heard Linnell's voice shout, "Thandie!"

It *was* Linnell, looked visibly relieved. She greeted Thandie with a warm hug.

"You came," she said. She looked over Thandie's shoulder, as if expecting to see somebody else emerge from the mist. "Did you find your friend?"

Thandie shook her head briefly, breathing hard from her long climb down. She needed to catch her breath and didn't want to talk about Sander to anyone yet. Linnell seemed to understand, and rested her hand briefly on Thandie's arm.

Thandie took in her surroundings. They were all there, the stolen ones, gathered together on a large, flat rocky ledge, only just big enough to hold them all. They sat huddled in subdued groups, their faces pale and drawn. Their eyes all swivelled hopefully towards Thandie, unsure of exactly who she was but certain she could lead them to safety.

"I'm glad you came – I didn't think I could get them home without you," said Linnell

Thandie shook her head. "You could have done it. You are stronger than you think."

Linnell didn't look convinced. It was strange; Linnell must be seventeen now – three years older than Thandie, but she seemed so much younger.

"It's not that easy," said Linnell. She showed Thandie the rudimentary pulley system, which was fixed to a wooden post. A rope stretched away from it out into the mist. Linnell pulled at it but it was stuck fast.

"There is a basket to ride in, but Sander, the boy who led me here, brought it back to the other side. He must have secured it in some way and now I don't know how to get us back across."

Thandie flinched at the sound of Sander's name. She examined and pulled on the rope as Linnell had done. It did seem to be fixed in place and she didn't want to yank it too hard for fear of breaking the rope. She sighed. She felt as though all these people had faith in her and she should somehow be the one to come up with an idea.

A high, accented voice rang out from the group. "There is a way across."

Thandie turned to see who had spoken. It was a boy, one of the youngest of the group, only ten or eleven. He was small and wiry and wore unusual clothes: blue stretchy tights, a matching top and flexible slippers. Thandie ran through the names in her mind. She remembered this boy. It was Aldo Strood, the Elithian circus performer. He had been juggling with the other, older boy, who had disappeared.

"What do you suggest we do?" asked Thandie.

"Walk across," he said simply.

Thandie looked at him. "Is this something you … do?"

"It is. I am a tightrope walker."

"And are you good at it?"

"Of course. I told her," he said, indicating Linnell, "but she didn't think it was a good idea."

Linnell bit her lower lip uncertainly. "I don't want to be responsible for any accidents... The boy's family ... all our families ... they've lost so much already."

Thandie gazed out into the clouds. It was impossible to tell how far the rope stretched. "Linnell, do you remember how far it was – how long the crossing took in the basket?"

"I don't know. It felt like forever but maybe a minute?"

Thandie looked back at Aldo.

He smiled. "I am sure I can do it. I have been up on the high wire since I could walk."

The resolve on his face was encouraging. Thandie had faith that he could do this. People didn't normally volunteer for anything that was beyond them. Also, she could think of no other plan. "Can we attach you to any sort of harness or rope, to keep you safe?" she asked.

Aldo shrugged. "I see nothing we could use. Besides, I need no harness. It is a short walk, no?"

He took off his slippers and stockings. "I go barefoot. This gives me more grip, see?" He wiggled his toes.

Linnell chewed on her lip a little more, shaking her head. They couldn't do this if they weren't all in agreement.

"Linnell, do you think we should do this?"

"It is the only way." She looked pale and tired.

Aldo nodded and stood up very straight, in performance mode, perhaps. "I go now. I ask you all to please be very quiet."

He hardly needed to make that request. The children were a subdued group in the first place, but now they held their collective breath as Aldo climbed on to the wooden post and sat on top of it, preparing to walk across. Still sitting, he put one foot on the rope in front of him, then the other ahead of the first. He stood straight with his arms stretched out, one by his head and the other straight out at a right angle as if he were dancing. He was still above the platform at this stage and he bounced gently to test the rope. Seemingly satisfied, he took a couple of steps forward. There was nothing now between him and a sheer drop, but Aldo looked directly ahead, calm and focused.

Linnell had her eyes squeezed tightly shut, as did many of the others in their group, but Thandie fixed her gaze on Aldo's skilful feet, willing them to carry him safely across to the other mountain.

The rope swayed significantly but this didn't seem to affect Aldo's balance. He progressed forwards, slowly and steadily, until he was an indistinct shape, lost in the clouds.

"I see the other side!" he called out.

No one replied. They remained silent as instructed. But in Thandie's mind, she willed him across. *Don't call out, don't look down, just keep going.*

Then the rope stopped swaying. Thandie's heart lurched. Had he stopped? Had he fallen?

Thandie put her hands to her mouth.

And then the high voice came, ringing out from the other mountain. "I am here! All in one piece! Here comes the basket!"

The rope began to shift in a new direction, the pulley system squeaking into action as Aldo pulled from the other side.

ACROSS THE RAVINE
Thandie

At the sound of Aldo's voice, a great cheer went up. A couple of girls burst into tears. Linnell jumped up and hugged Thandie.

Thandie was relieved he was safe but she didn't want to celebrate too early; the pulley system looked decidedly rickety and she wouldn't be able to relax until they had all travelled safely across.

"Do you mind if I go first?" whispered Linnell. "It brings back such awful memories and I can't face being left alone on the mountainside again."

"Of course," said Thandie. "I don't mind going last."

She pulled Linnell safely across herself, and then helped organize the others. There was no jostling, no complaining or suggesting who should go ahead of whom. They were all quiet again. Disorientated, probably, or lost in their own thoughts.

One by one, they travelled across in the basket and the rope held for them all.

When it was Thandie's turn, she lay back in the basket, looking at the cobalt sky. She remembered flying to the castle, the feeling of being on Kemi's back. This journey had been tiring, distressing, scary, but it had also been the adventure of her life.

On the other side, Thandie handed Aldo his slippers. "Thank you," she said. "We are all grateful to you."

He smiled and shrugged. "No problem, it is what I do. And I knew that my brother was behind me. He will always be there to protect me."

Thandie wondered what his story was and how he had lost his beloved brother, but now was not the time to ask. Now it was time to go home.

THE LONG WALK HOME
Thandie

There were no more ravines to cross, no more unicorns to battle. Now, all they had to do was get down this mountain. Luckily, the summer days were long and they had hours of sunlight left. None of them wanted to spend another night in the mountains.

When they had trudged downhill for two hours or more, they took a break. None of them had any food, and her few crusts of bread didn't stretch far; but they could take the weight off their tired feet for a few moments and there was a stream nearby where they could quench their thirst.

Thandie and Linnell sat by each other. They were virtual strangers but they had a connection now: they would always have a connection. And there was something about Linnell – the colour of her hair and eyes, the outer vulnerability with steely core – that made Thandie think of Hetty. "You remind me of someone," she said.

Linnell was immediately interested. She seemed to be the type of person who would be content to talk about herself. "Who?"

"A girl from home. We share a room in our foster mother's house."

Linnell tilted her head to one side. "Your foster sister?"

"Yes."

"You are lucky to have a sister. I'm all alone."

Thandie nodded, taking this in.

They sat in silence for a couple of moments and then Thandie rummaged in her bag to see if there were any supplies left from Yannick's house. She found a couple of greengages, bruised in places but acceptable. She handed one to Linnell, who bit into it.

"How did you know my song?" asked Linnell. "Did he teach you?"

Thandie narrowed her eyes. She wasn't sure who Linnell meant by "he".

"Sander. The piper," said Linnell. "He was your friend up there in the castle, wasn't he?"

Thandie nodded.

Linnell knitted her brows together. "So was he good then, in the end? He helped us?"

"I think so. But he didn't teach me the song."

"Then...?"

"I met your father. He taught us both."

Linnell's blue eyes filled with tears. "He is alive!"

"Yes. He is well. These greengages are from your tree. He

misses you."

Linnell held out the half-eaten fruit, looking at it as though she might recognize it. "He is not angry?"

Angry! How could Linnell believe that her dear, sweet father would be angry? "No. He grieves for you."

"I was so foolish."

Thandie nodded. "But you were not the only one." She gestured to the rest of the group. "Dozens of people gave their memories away."

Linnell stared at Thandie, her blue eyes wide. "But not you. You were stronger."

Thandie shook her head. "No. I nearly gave away everything, just like the rest of you. For something that I badly wanted."

More tears welled in Linnell's eyes. She seemed to Thandie like someone who would cry a lot. Unlike her, Thandie rarely cried. She patted Linnell on the back and Linnell took a deep, shuddering breath. "I am so happy of course to be rescued and to be going home to my father but…" She trailed off.

Thandie thought she understood. "It means you are going back to your old life?

"Yes. It feels as though I had my one chance to improve my life and now that has gone—"

"No. I know what you're thinking, but it's simply not true. You never run out of chances. It is not a choice between having your dreams magically granted or spending the rest of your life on your father's farm."

Linnell answered softly. "I don't see how."

Thandie held the other girl by the hands, speaking to her as if their ages were reversed.

"You can make a difference to your own life. Study hard. If you educate yourself then there will always be a chance for you. Do you understand?"

Linnell nodded. "Maybe one day, when the farm is mine, I could sell it, or join up with one of the bigger farms in Arvale…"

"Yes," cried Thandie. "You can achieve anything you want, and in the meantime you know that your father loves you an unimaginable amount. With his support, you can do anything."

There was silence for a moment. Thandie hoped that Linnell really meant these things, that life might change a little for her when she went home.

"What about you?" said Linnell. "Are you happy with your life? What do you plan to do after all this is over?"

Thandie thought for a moment. "I think … that my life was actually not as bad as I thought and maybe for a time I can be happy with things the way they are. Also, like you, I have people who love me, although it has taken me a long time to realize that."

A few of the others had begun to stand, looking ready to resume the journey. Thandie's feet were still sore and throbbing but she knew it was time to go. "Let's carry on, it can't be far now."

Linnell agreed. "But will you lead us? You're a better leader than me. I shall walk at the back and make sure that no one strays from the path."

Thandie stood. "Yes, I'll lead." She rummaged in the holder for Sander's pipe – her pipe now. "And I shall play, to keep our spirits up."

They set off again. As she put the pipe to her mouth, her fingers tingled. She was itching to play, she realized. Something had happened. Something to do with Sander giving her his pipe and then sacrificing himself for them. Was it a kind of magic? Thandie had to play. It might be two or more hours yet, but she would play until they were all safely down from the mountain.

She played the happiest tunes she knew. She played marching songs, celebration songs, the Arvale harvest song and the Essendor wintertide song. She played all of their songs. When she played Linnell's song, a little yellow bird fluttered past, and made its way along the line of people, almost as if it was looking for someone.

CHAPTER TWENTY

DOWN FROM THE MOUNTAIN
Yannick

That evening, Linnell's father splashed his evening milk over the rim of his cup. The sun was setting and the old man found it increasingly hard to see when the light was dim.

He took the warm drink out to his porch and sat, gazing at Mount Opacus and its two Sentries as he did every evening. Every evening he hoped to see a smiling girl with straw-coloured hair walk around the corner, back to him. There had been many disappointing evenings but since the visit from the strange, bold girl and her shifty-looking companion, his hope had been renewed. He was not the only one looking for his precious daughter: other people were looking for the stolen ones and one day they would succeed.

He took a few sips of his drink as he stared into the dark green mass of trees, halfway up the nearest mountain. The appearance of the trees changed according to the slant of the sun or the position of the clouds, but this evening, there was something different. Far away on the mountainside were some unfamiliar dots. He rubbed his eyes. Herds of goats and cows lived on these slopes, and he had seen them do many strange things. He had known dairy cows that walked in line and queued politely, but the creatures he was looking at now were not cows. It was hard to see that distance but, unless he was very much mistaken, the creatures were people.

He watched them for some minutes, peering and squinting until he was quite, quite sure that this was not the hopeful imaginings of an old man. Then, he heard a sound. A pretty, trilling sound that he hadn't heard for two years. A pretty bird flew past, and a flash of yellow caught his eye. "Sunbeam," he whispered, as the little canary, still singing, perched briefly on top of its old cage.

Yannick left his cup of milk on the porch, found his walking stick by the door and went directly to Madam Lavande's, still in his slippered feet. This time he wasn't going to tell any brave young men, who would insist he stay at home. He knew that Madam Lavande would understand, even though she was a good ten years younger than him.

She was sitting out on her own porch as she did every evening.

He went right up to her, touched her arm. He dispensed with any formal greeting and said, "I need to go to the mountain. They are coming back."

Madam Lavande didn't question who was coming back, or what could be important enough for her to leave the house at such an hour. Instead, she shuffled inside to get a shawl and her wooden clogs, and then offered a steady arm to Yannick to guide him to the foothills.

They moved slowly. Yannick felt every tree root beneath his feet and his hip joints protested at the distance, but he had to do this. Sunbeam fluttered along with them and then disappeared in the direction of the mountain. They reached the spot where the mountains met the woods, but a fast stream ran past, preventing them from progressing any further. They stood by the stream, watching and listening. The dots from the mountain must be drawing nearer because he could hear pipe playing – a marching song. He recognized the clear sound of that particular instrument, which, he was fairly certain, was the one that the boy had played in his kitchen. Had they succeeded, and brought his Linnell back to him?

Other people started to gather by the stream. Whether they had seen the procession of people, as Yannick had done, or whether them pipe playing had roused them from their beds, farmers and their families arrived by the side of the stream.

The first person emerged from the trees. It was not the pipe-playing boy. Instead it was the bold girl with the warm eyes and the dark hair, playing his pipe like an expert. His heart pounded in anticipation. Thandie. That was her name. She had promised him. He tried to catch her eye from across the river but she was too far away to see him. Why was she playing now, and not the suspicious-looking boy who had accompanied her? She stood to the side and continued playing, turning to face the trees from which she had just emerged. Her expression was difficult to read.

Another girl, who looked familiar to Yannick, emerged from the trees. She was about the age that Linnell had been when she was stolen away and looked tired but unhurt. A woman to Yannick's right screamed in recognition, then shouted, "Posy!

Posy my love! You've come back." She ran towards her, splashing and wading through the river, which reached up to about her knees, soaking her long skirts.

The girl – Posy – gazed around looking confused. First she glanced at Thandie and at the faces across the stream. Then she saw the woman and her hands flew to her face. "Mama! Is it you?" She ran to meet her mother and they hugged each other tightly.

But Yannick didn't watch their emotional reunion for long. He kept his eyes on the people coming into view. A boy followed, and then two more girls. Then more and more children.

The waiting people moved large stones and branches into the water so that the children could cross without getting wet. They ushered them over and welcomed them, fretting around them. Most of them, of course, did not have families to greet them, as word had not yet travelled that far, but every so often a shout would go up, indicating that one of the Arvale children was safely home.

Yannick just stood, holding on to Madam Lavande's arm and watching each new face appear. She patted his hand gently and continuously, saying nothing. Every time he saw a blonde head, his heart stopped for a moment, but he did not find the beloved face he was looking for. Was it possible that Linnell had changed beyond all recognition in the two years she had been missing? He did not believe this to be possible. Surely he would recognize her anywhere. Anyway, the children that had appeared were all younger that Linnell would be now.

The children kept coming. There were so many of them and yet Linnell wasn't there. The stream of children became a trickle and then stopped. He felt that if she didn't appear then he might give up living right there and then. But there in the shelter of the trees, he saw one last person coming down the mountainside. Was it his imagination, or did she have straw-coloured hair? And a little yellow bird fluttering alongside her?

Before he trusted his eyes, he trusted his ears. The pipe playing stopped and a single, sweet voice sang out in the stillness of the morning. A voice he thought he might never hear again.

"To me you are the mountain,
To me you are the sea,
To me you are the forest,
You're everything to me."

The old man staggered forwards, faster than he'd imagined he would ever walk again, using his stick to propel him. Madam

Lavande was left behind. A couple of the villagers helped him on to the makeshift stepping-stones and somehow he was across and stumbling towards the lower slopes of the mountain.

That was when Linnell saw him. She broke away from the mountain path, half-running, half-sliding down the green slope. He stopped, leaning on his walking stick, and she ran towards him, thudding into him with such force that it was surprising the elderly man wasn't knocked to the ground. But they were supporting each other, clasped in each other's arms with tears pouring down their faces.

WATCHING
Thandie

There was nobody at the foot of the mountain to greet Thandie. She had known there wouldn't be, but it was still hard to watch the lucky Arvale children greet their families. Especially Linnell.

Thandie had stopped playing when she heard Linnell sing. She didn't want to spoil the moment between Linnell and Yannick. Thandie sat on the rock, knees pulled up to her chest, staring at father and daughter. There was such love between them.

If she saw her mother after all these years, what would it be like? Thandie felt sure she would recognize her, but would she recognize Thandie? She had been tiny child and now she was almost an adult – taller probably than her mother had been. But Thandie felt surprisingly empty at the thought. Her mother was like a dream to her now – a dream that she would always hold but that she would no longer build her life around.

Watching Linnell hug her father, Thandie knew that there were three people – three solid, real, living people – who would greet her in that way. And after she had eaten a warm meal, had a bath and seen all the stolen ones head home, then she knew exactly where to find them.

HEADING HOME
Thandie

Thandie stayed that first night with Linnell and her father. Not in Linnell's room this time, but in the kitchen, the table pushed against the wall. The people of Arvale sent messengers on horseback to all the towns and cities in the kingdom to spread the news, but it would take a couple of days at least for them to reach Essendor, and still more time to send all the children home again. Thandie could not bear to wait any longer. Besides, Linnell and her father had a lot of talking to do and didn't need a visitor getting in the way.

Her legs were worn out. They had begun to wobble at the end of the long journey home, but now, they ached worse that she had ever known. It was agonizing to climb up or down steps, or to sit down or stand up. Still, despite feeling unable to take another step, Thandie felt it would be more painful to wait.

So, when Thandie heard Linnell get up with the sun, and leave for the cow barn, she got up herself and scribbled a farewell note which she left on the kitchen table.

She hoped that she and Linnell meet again one day but couldn't face a goodbye in person. The last few days had been far too emotional already. She pulled on her battered boots and took one last look at Linnell's view. She squinted up at the thick clouds above Mount Opacus, still surprised that there was no sign of a castle. It was as if she had dreamed the whole thing. She mentally said her own goodbyes and then trudged around the back of Linnell's cottage, towards the woods.

Thandie planned to travel east, using the low road around the mountain. She couldn't face going up; she doubted she would ever want to set foot on another mountain. She walked through the brightening meadows, then into the shadows of the forest, where it was still dark. As she had told Sander many times, Thandie wasn't scared of the dark, but she was still alert to dangers that could be lurking. She found herself reaching for the pipe, which she knew had a certain power of protection. She put it to her lips and felt safer, knowing that she could scare a wild animal away, or charm another animal to be on her side. She realized then that she probably also had the power to charm people to be on her side, as Sander had done. What a great responsibility that was.

Something moved in the bushes. It was only a small movement, but Thandie had spent enough time out in the natural environment to know that it was not a bird or a rodent; it was a larger animal than that. She stopped, listened. She could hear its breath. She held her own breath and faced the bushes. She was patient. She would make a decision on what to do when she knew exactly what she was facing.

Then, out of the bushes poked a familiar furry face. Grey and white with a long snout and distinctive yellow eyes.

"Kemi! How did you find me?"

The wolf stepped slowly out from her hiding spot and pushed her head into Thandie's hand. Thandie had not expected to see

Kemi or any of the flying wolves again. She hadn't realized that they even ventured this far down the slopes. She thought that they were animals of the mountains. And of the air, of course. Thandie looked around for the rest of the pack.

"Have you come on your own?"

Kemi stared at Thandie, her yellow eyes blinking slowly. Thandie met her gaze. Sander had told her not to stare directly at a wolf but this was not that sort of look. Kemi trusted her and had come to find her.

She realized she still had the pipe in position and began to move her fingers instinctively. She didn't think about the notes or the tune but she played the memory of meeting the wolves. She played the tumbling cubs and the first sight of the alpha pair and Sander's charming song and her own delight.

And Kemi understood. With her ears pricked up to the music, she came and stood at Thandie's side, where Thandie could feel her warm furry flank rippling with her steady breath.

When Thandie had finished playing, Kemi began to walk slowly away and Thandie thought for a moment that their time together was over. Perhaps Kemi had simply come to say goodbye. But then the she-wolf stopped some distance away and turned her head and shoulders towards Thandie.

Thandie thought she understood. "You want me to follow you, don't you?"

So Thandie followed, taking a wolf's path through the forest, which involved walking through long grass and past prickly branches. Thandie didn't have the same thick fur as Kemi and soon found that her arms and legs were covered in scratches, but she kept on, at Kemi's pace, wondering where they were heading.

When they were through the forest, out in a wide meadow, Kemi lay down with her chin on the ground and her forepaws bent as she had done in the hills of Wending. Thandie knew what this meant. Kemi was offering her a ride. She laughed and climbed carefully on to the wolf's back. They sat for a moment as she tried to remember how Sander had told the wolves where they wanted to travel. It was a bit different to travelling by coach. She couldn't just hop in and speak to the driver. Or maybe speaking to the driver was exactly what she should do.

"I need to get to Essendor. Do you know where that is?" Thandie pointed over the Grey Mountain in the direction of the capital.

Thandie didn't know if Kemi understood the words or the gesture but she really felt that the message got through. In some ways she didn't mind where Kemi took her, as long as it wasn't back to the castle in the clouds.

This time, rather than adopting her "launch" position, Kemi stood and began to run. It was a bumpy ride, but Thandie managed to hold on. Once they had reached what Thandie guessed must be top speed, Kemi unfolded her wings in a swift movement. With a couple of giant flaps, the pair flew off the ground. Last time, they had begun their journey at mountain height but this time, they had to reach that same height from ground level.

Kemi threw back her head and pointed her nose into the air so that she was in an almost vertical position. Thandie's legs were positioned behind Kemi's wings as she'd been shown, and she slid rapidly backwards towards Kemi's tail end. She threw herself forwards, close to Kemi's body, gripping the bony base of her wings.

In a few seconds, the sharp ascent was over and they were horizontal once again. Kemi panted rapidly – it had been hard work for her – and Thandie patted her back. She adjusted her position and relaxed a little now that she wasn't petrified of falling off. She was lightheaded from the sharp ascent but managed to ease the pressure in her ears by yawning. Kemi yawned too, perhaps for the same reason. They were now level with the peaks, in the light white mist of the clouds. Down below, in the foothills of the mountains above Arvale, Kemi saw a figure with a wooden pail. Linnell. Thandie waved and Linnell dropped the pail, open-mouthed. She waved back, a great big wave with both arms. Thandie was glad that she had seen her. A personal farewell would have been too painful, but the note on the table didn't seem quite enough. She hoped that Linnell would settle happily back into her old life but also that she wouldn't give up on her dreams.

Thandie was relieved to see that Kemi did not veer off towards Mount Opacus. She tried to guide Kemi, tilting her head in the direction that she wanted to travel, pressing gently with her knee in Kemi's opposite side, as she might do with a horse. She found it difficult to tell if it worked, or if Kemi had understood her earlier request, but the wolf seemed to know where to go.

They travelled towards the Grey Mountain – up and over it. Thandie grew quite cold as they flew over the peak. It was interesting to see the scenery change from green trees to grey rocks as they crossed over to the Essendor side. It was much more obvious from up in the air than from ground level. As soon as they were over the mountain, they began their descent. Kemi adopted a shallower angle for the downward flight, so Thandie didn't slide quite as much as she had done before.

Thandie kept her eyes open, and the first thing she saw when she was through the clouds was the reassuringly solid stone turrets of Essendor castle, flags fluttering in the breeze. The journey that would have taken her days took less than an hour for a flying wolf. Thandie wished that she could travel that way all the time. She would see the whole kingdom.

They landed on the mountainside across from the castle, perhaps a mile away. It was a smooth landing. Kemi dropped down on to her paws more lightly than Thandie would be able to manage if she were jumping from a stool. She folded in her wings as she did so, and Thandie leaned to her right-hand side and tumbled out on to the soft grass.

Kemi sat on the ground for a while, panting. It was a longer journey that the flight to the castle in the clouds had been. Flying wolves were not really meant to carry people, it seemed.

Thandie thought of how the wolves had devoured the grat that Sander had thrown to them outside the castle in the clouds, and she felt bad that she had nothing to offer.

"I'm sorry – I have no food," she said, and stroked Kemi's head.

Thandie played them both a recovery tune on the pipe. Then Kemi got to her feet and walked to the nearby stream, where she lapped up the water thirstily. Thandie did the same, scooping it up with her hand and drinking from there.

When they had finished, they looked at each other just as they had done in the woods earlier.

"Do you want to come and meet my people ... my pack?" Even as she asked the question, Thandie realized it was probably not a good idea. Kemi and her kind were shy creatures, who hid away in the mountains for a reason. The last thing they needed was for greedy people to come along and exploit their potential. Thandie had lived under King Zelos's rule for long enough to realize that some people would do anything for power.

By the looks of things, Kemi was not planning to stay around anyway. The rest of the pack would be missing her. She hoped that they didn't mind her absence.

Kemi came to Thandie's side and rubbed against her briefly, in what Thandie interpreted as a gesture of farewell. Then she assumed her crouching position as she had done on the cloudy mountain. And Thandie watched her leap into the air. She had only witnessed this once, because the other times she had been riding the wolf herself. It was a more graceful leap than the one she had seen Conan perform, probably because Kemi had no rider on her back to weigh her down.

Kemi soared into the air in the direction of Essendor, swooped in a low circle, then up towards the Grey Mountain. Thandie wondered if she would ever see the wolf again but she felt strongly that she would. Kemi didn't seem the type to be affectionate towards just anyone. They had a bond.

But for now, Kemi was going home.

And so was Thandie.

CHAPTER TWENTY-ONE

HOME
Thandie

Home. It was impossible to hear that word without an accompanying picture. Home, if you were lucky, was a place that meant warmth and security. A place where you could be yourself. A place where you could eat, laugh, argue, cry, think and be. Sometimes all of those things together.

For a long time, Thandie's vision of home had been quite clear. Home to her meant two people: Thandie and her mother.

Home was their little stone cottage and their fierce love. For a long time after her mother's disappearance, Thandie had clung stubbornly to that definition and refused to replace it with anything new. But since her journey, she had realized that a different place now really meant home to her. The table where she ate laughed and argued had many people squashed around it and there was often no space to think or be, let alone cry. But Madam Tilbury's was Thandie's home and as she emerged from the woods and caught a glimpse of the little house, tears sprang up in her eyes.

Behind the tears was a little panic. What if they had written her off as missing? What if they had found a replacement for her? There were plenty of needy children in Essendor and only two beds in the little room she shared with Hetty. What if they were angry with her for disappearing and decided they didn't *want* her back?

But as these questions flapped in her brain like trapped birds, she saw a figure in the boys' bedroom, looking out over the flat roof with a spyglass. It was too tall to be Tib. It must be Finch. Bird-watching, no doubt. But he hadn't yet recognized her. She waved with both hands, high above her head. After a while, he looked in her direction, training his spyglass on her. He must have seen her. He disappeared from the window.

Thandie kept on walking towards the house, still waving even though he had gone from view. Moments later, the front door swung open and three figures rushed out. Out of the house and towards her.

She was home.

FINCH, TIB AND HETTY
Thandie

All three of them ran in her direction, waving madly. The first to reach her was Finch. Good, strong, reliable Finch. He had grown even taller, she was sure, and he seemed to be growing a beard. He hugged her briefly and then stood back to gaze at her, as if he couldn't quite believe she was back.

"You did it!" he said. "We heard. Ma and Berwick have gone to find you. They've taken a coach around the road to meet you. How did you miss them?"

So the news had reached them. "I took a shortcut," said Thandie. More detailed explanations about flying wolves could wait.

"You've done a very good thing, Thandie," he said.

Hetty was next to reach her but she held back and let Tib catch up. He was running slowly and lopsidedly, one arm holding something in his jacket. He didn't embrace her, but greeted her with a wide, warm smile. "I've got a surprise for you!"

He opened the flap of his jacket and there in the crook of his arm was a yellow, fluffy duckling. "My egg hatched," he said proudly.

Thandie reached out and gently stroked the fluffy down with a single finger. "So I see."

"Guess her name," he said.

Thandie tapped her chin. "Quackles?"

"No!"

"Webster?"

"No! Her name is *Thandie*. I called her that just in case you didn't come back."

"But I did come back, didn't I?"

Tib nodded happily. "Yes, just like you promised. Maybe I'll give her a new name now."

Tib put his left hand in Thandie's and leaned up against her, still holding his duckling in his right arm.

Hetty was the last to greet her.

It was strange, but despite their arguments, Hetty was the one she had thought about most on her journey. Perhaps the one

361

she'd missed most. Like a sister.

Hetty stood back, hands in the pockets of her apron, not looking in Thandie's direction. Thandie had to go right up to her, Tib shuffling alongside. Was Hetty still angry after all this time?

When Hetty looked up, her eyes were full of tears. She looked wary of Thandie, as if she didn't know what to expect. They just looked at each other for a couple of moments and then Thandie reached out to Hetty with her free arm. Hetty returned her hug and started crying properly, on her shoulder. "I'm sorry I didn't believe in you. And I'm sorry for the way I was when you left but I felt like the whole thing was my fault – daring you to go off in the dark – and I didn't know how to stop you… I thought something had happened to you…"

Thandie squeezed all the sorries and all the love she could manage into a one-armed embrace. "No, I'm sorry. I'm sorry for the way I was before. I've missed you. I've missed having someone to play and sing with and share a room with and I've even missed our squabbles and not-speaking."

Hetty laughed in between her tears. "Me too."

Thandie grinned. "It's good to be home," she said.

BACK ON THE ROOF
Thandie

Ma Tilbury and Berwick weren't yet back, so the four of them looked after one another that day. They didn't ask Thandie too many questions, and they told no one yet that she was home. She would need to speak to the royal council, to tell them everything that she knew, but not yet.

That evening, they sat on their old favourite spot, the roof, until Tib decided he was ready for bed. They all agreed that they were just as tired, especially Thandie, who would be happy to sleep for a week.

"I want Thandie to tuck me in tonight," said Tib.

"Of course you do," said Hetty, kindly, kissing him on the head and leaving the room.

Tib jumped into bed and sat up, waiting for her to perch on the end.

"Here, this is yours," said Thandie, handing him the catapult. "It's broken, I'm afraid."

Tib inspected it. "That's OK, it looks easy to fix. Did you use it to fight the bad unicorn?"

"No."

His face fell.

363

"Not to fight the unicorn, but it did come in very useful."

Tib looked satisfied with this and stashed the catapult in the drawer of his nightstand. He lay down and Thandie tucked the blanket all around, the way that he liked. It was a much cooler night then it had been before she left.

"Can I have a story?" he asked.

Thandie smiled. She had plenty of stories to tell, about castles in the clouds, laughing lakes and flying wolves. She knew that Tib would love to hear all about her adventures but she wasn't sure if she was quite ready to tell him. Not yet.

"I can do better than a story. I bet you didn't know that I could play the pipe?"

Tib shook his head and Thandie brought out her pipe. "This is the most powerful tune I know. This song freed the stolen ones."

She put the pipe to her lips and played Linnell's song. Only now it wasn't Linnell's song any more. It belonged to her and Tib and anyone who wanted to play it. Tib snuggled right down so that just his eyes were peeping over the coverlet and listened. Thandie thought he might be falling asleep but when she had finished playing, he moved the blanket under his chin and said, "I like it. Does it have any words?"

Thandie nodded, put down the pipe and started to sing. She tried not to worry that her voice wasn't as sweet as Linnell's.

Tib wouldn't mind; he was just glad to have her home. And the words said everything she wanted them to.

"To me you are the mountain,
To me you are the sea,
To me you are the forest,
You're everything to me."

Tib yawned. "Thandie?"

"Yes?"

"Shall we take my duck to the pond tomorrow?"

"I would like that, yes. Goodnight, Tib."

THE END

EPILOGUE

Ma Tilbury and Berwick returned the next morning, delighted to have their foster daughter home. The royal council interviewed Thandie. She told them everything she knew, about the castle in the clouds, and the Greatest Unicorn.

They went there with an army, just in case. They found the castle. Deserted and crumbling away. It seemed that buildings built with magic alone did not last long. Not a soul there. Thandie checked that last part: there was no old woman lying dead in a back room? But, no. Not a soul.

Soon after, Princess Alette returned from her quest with a cure for Queen Audrey's sleeping sickness. The beloved royal family was back, the curfew was lifted and the Midnight Unicorn returned to Essendor again. Nobody knew where their protector had been but the return of the unicorn meant that life would get back to normal again.

For Finch, Hetty, Thandie and Tib, that meant swimming in the river, arguing on the roof and playing Merels inside the city walls as the sun went down.

Acknowledgements

A big thank you to Fiz Osborne, Emma Young, Pete Matthews and all at Scholastic for making this book happen.

To my lovely friends and family.

And to the Streamers for their ongoing writing support.

HAVE YOU READ
THE MIDNIGHT UNICORN?

READ ON FOR AN EXTRACT...

CHAPTER ONE

THE SNAPPED BOUGH

The city of Essendor stood on a hill, a stone castle at its summit. Small but sturdy houses were squeezed into every available space and stone steps twisted and turned down the hill. One warm day in early autumn the red swallowtail flags fluttered on the turrets of the castle. A new queen, just married, sat on the throne and there was a celebratory feel in the air. Bunting hung in the market square where some street performers had attracted a crowd.

An arched bridge led through a gap in the city's walls and across the river to the fields beyond. Two young mothers crossed the bridge with their broods. One had an infant strapped to her back and the other held a child by the hand. Five more children walked or tottered along behind. The families were off to gather the first new berries of the season. They would each make a pie at the end of the day and if any berries were left over after baking, they would box them up to sell at the market. The hedgerows were so laden with fruit that they could pick blackberries all morning and never exhaust the supply.

Some of the older children minded the younger ones; the others got to work, although the purple stains around their mouths and the lack of fruit in their baskets gave them away.

The sweet, orangey smell of wild bergamot blew on the breeze. Time passed quickly, with singing, joking and city gossip. The women wondered about the price of goat's cheese at the dairy stall, whether this warmer weather would last, and why the queen's brother had left Essendor so suddenly.

They were so engrossed in their chat that they barely noticed one of their youngest break away in search of his own entertainment. An old willow tree with an inviting Y-shaped trunk stood close by. The little one climbed up with fearless agility. He inched along a bough which hung over the river below. On another day, all may have been well, but today the wind was blowing in the wrong direction or the stars were not aligned as they should be. The brittle bough, which had held fast all summer, snapped.

The sound of a branch splintering and a piercing shriek alerted the mothers. They dropped their baskets and rushed to the source of the cry, trying to piece together what had happened.

The child had fallen six feet and now clung on to a rock protruding from the steep bank above the river. He was just two summers old.

He saw his family looking and cried out in anguish. As the mother panicked, her eldest child began to scramble down the bank to retrieve him. But the descent was slow and the little one's pink fists could not hold on. His grip loosened and he tumbled down the bank, head over heels in a sickening acrobatic display. He vanished under the water as the movement of the river turned him on to his stomach and carried him along.

The mother gasped as if winded and the elder sister screamed, "He can't swim!"

The older children raced along the river, trying to keep up with the little boy as he tumbled along in the river's current. The mothers followed, making sure that the younger ones were with them – they didn't want to lose any more of their number. For a few yards, trees and overgrowth shielded the boy from view, then a little further along, the ground level dropped and there was a gap allowing access to the river. By the looks of things, anglers – possibly poachers – had fished there in the past. The families scrambled through and looked frantically up and down the river. The boy should have reached this point by now. His mother stared into the flowing water, holding on to her friend for support. The child was nowhere to be seen.

But then, from behind them, came a cry. A powerful cry, from a healthy little boy. There he was on the bank, shivering behind a bush, wet through but unharmed. His mother rushed to him, hugged him tightly to her chest, stripped off his clothes and wrapped her shawl around him. He was mottled and red from the cold and would soon be covered in bruises, but he was still able to cry lustily. His mother's embraces and some blackberries from the basket soon soothed him.

The woman looked around for someone to thank. It was inconceivable that her son, who was unable to swim, could have made his way to the side of the rapidly flowing river and clambered up the steep bank. But there was no rescuer in sight.

"Who pulled you out?" she asked the child.

"'Orse," said the little boy. "'Orse with a 'orn." He indicated on his head where a horn might be found.

The two women looked at one another questioningly.

"A unicorn?" whispered the mother in disbelief.

The boy nodded. "One 'orn."

"Was the unicorn silver?" asked the friend, who knew a thing or two about such animals. "With a spiralling horn and a flowing mane?"

The boy shook his head. "Like midnight."

"A midnight unicorn," whispered the mother to her friend. And louder into the empty woods, "Unicorn, if you are here, thank you for saving my child!"

From that day, he was known as the Boy River. His story spread quickly across the city and he enjoyed some fame, which was soon forgotten. But the Boy River never forgot that he was the first to set eyes on the Midnight Unicorn of Essendor.